SOLITAIRE

ALICE OSEMAN

Scholastic Press / New York

Library of Congress Cataloging-in-Publication Data available

ISBN 978-1-338-86342-0

10 9 8 7 6 5 4 3 2 1   23 24 25 26 27

Printed in the U.S.A.   37
First edition, May 2023
Book design by Stephanie Yang

AUTHOR'S NOTE

This book contains references to suicide and suicide attempts, suicidal ideation, self-harm, depression, eating disorders, and obsessive-compulsive behaviors. Please read safely and responsibly, and for more detailed content warnings, visit aliceoseman.com/content-warnings.

Solitaire shares some characters with my graphic novel series, *Heartstopper*, and it takes place during the events of *Heartstopper: Volume 4*. For those readers who have discovered this book after reading *Heartstopper*, please note that this story is very different in tone. *Solitaire* was written before the creation of *Heartstopper*, and it explores much darker themes than *Heartstopper*. *Solitaire* may not be suitable for all readers who have enjoyed *Heartstopper*.

Thank you so much to everyone who has supported my stories.

—Alice Oseman

For Emily Moore,
who stuck by me from the beginning

"And *your* defect is a propensity to hate everybody."

"And *yours*," he replied with a smile, "is willfully to misunderstand them."

—JANE AUSTEN, *PRIDE AND PREJUDICE*

PART 1

ELIZABETH BENNET: Do you dance, Mr. Darcy?

MR. DARCY: Not if I can help it.

***PRIDE AND PREJUDICE* (2005)**

ONE

I am aware as I step into the common room that the majority of people here are almost dead, including me. I have been reliably informed that post-Christmas blues are entirely normal and that we should expect to feel somewhat numb after the "happiest" time of the year, but I don't feel so different now to how I felt on Christmas Eve, or on Christmas Day, or on any other day since the Christmas holidays started. I'm back now and it's another year. Nothing is going to happen.

I stand there. Becky and I look at each other.

"Tori," says Becky, "you look a little bit like you want to kill yourself."

She and the rest of Our Lot have sprawled themselves over a collection of revolving chairs around the common-room computer desks. As it's the first day back, there has been a widespread hair-and-makeup effort across the entire sixth form, and I immediately feel inadequate.

I deflate into a chair and nod philosophically. "It's funny because it's true."

She looks at me some more, but doesn't really look, and we laugh at something that wasn't funny. Becky then realizes that I am in no mood to do anything so she moves away. I lean into my arms and fall half asleep.

My name is Victoria Spring. I think you should know that I make up a lot of stuff in my head and then get sad about it. I like to sleep and I like to blog. I am going to die someday.

Rebecca Allen is probably my only real friend at the moment. She is also probably my best friend. I am as yet unsure whether these two facts are related. In any case, Becky Allen has very long purple hair. It has come to my attention that if you have purple hair, people often look at you, thus resulting in you becoming a widely recognized and outstandingly popular figure in adolescent society; the sort of figure that everyone claims to know yet probably hasn't even spoken to. She has a lot of Instagram followers.

Right now, Becky's talking to this other girl from Our Lot, Evelyn Foley. Evelyn is considered "alternative" because she has messy hair and wears cool necklaces.

"The *real* question though," says Evelyn, "is whether there's sexual tension between Harry and *Malfoy*."

I'm not sure whether Becky genuinely likes Evelyn. Sometimes I think people only pretend to like each other.

"Only in fanfiction, Evelyn," says Becky. "Please keep your fantasies between yourself and your search history."

Evelyn laughs. "I'm just saying. Malfoy helps Harry in the end, right? So why does he bully Harry for seven years? He secretly likes him." With each word, she claps her hands together. It really doesn't emphasize her point. "It's a well-established fact that people tease people they fancy. The psychology here is unarguable."

"Evelyn," says Becky. "*Firstly,* I *resent* the fangirl idea that Draco Malfoy is some kind of beautifully tortured soul who is searching for redemption and understanding. He's essentially a massive racist. Secondly, the idea that bullying means that you fancy someone is basically the foundation of domestic abuse."

Evelyn appears to be deeply offended. "It's just a book. It's not real life."

Becky sighs and turns to me, and so does Evelyn. I deduce that I am under pressure to contribute something.

"I think Harry Potter's a bit shit, to be honest," I say. "Sort of wish we could all move on from it."

Becky and Evelyn just look at me. I get the impression that I've ruined

4

this conversation, so I mumble an excuse and lift myself off my chair and hurry out of the common-room door. Sometimes I hate people. This is probably very bad for my mental health.

There are two grammar schools in our town: Harvey Greene Grammar School for Girls, or "Higgs" as it is popularly known, and Truham Grammar School for Boys. Both schools, however, accept all genders in Years 12 and 13, the two final years of school known countrywide as the sixth form. So, now that I am in Year 12, I have had to face a sudden influx of guys. Boys at Higgs are on par with mythical creatures, and having an actual *real* boyfriend puts you at the head of the social hierarchy, but personally, thinking or talking too much about "boy issues" makes me want to shoot myself in the face.

Even if I did care about that stuff, it's not like we get to show off, thanks to our stunning school uniform. Usually, sixth-formers don't have to wear school uniform; however, Higgs sixth form are forced to wear a hideous one. Gray is the theme, which is fitting for such a dull place.

I arrive at my locker to find a pink Post-it note on its door. On that, someone has drawn a left-pointing arrow, suggesting that I should, perhaps, look in that direction. Irritated, I turn my head to the left. There's another Post-it note a few lockers along. And, on the wall at the end of the corridor, another. People are walking past them, totally oblivious. I guess people aren't observant. That, or they just don't care. I can relate to that.

I pluck the Post-it from my locker and wander to the next.

Sometimes I like to fill my days with little things that other people don't care about. It makes me feel like I'm doing something important, mainly because no one else is doing it.

This is one of those times.

The Post-its start popping up all over the place.

The penultimate Post-it I find depicts an arrow pointing forwards, and is situated on the door of a closed computer room on the first floor. Black fabric covers the door window. This particular computer room, C16, was closed last year for refurbishment, but it doesn't look like anyone's bothered getting started. It sort of makes me feel sad, to tell you the truth, but I open C16's door anyway, enter, and close it behind me.

There's one long window stretching the length of the far wall, and the computers in here are bricks. Solid cubes. Apparently, I've time-traveled to the 1990s.

I find the final Post-it note on the back wall, bearing a URL for something called SOLITAIRE.

Solitaire is a card game you play by yourself. It's what I used to spend my IT lessons doing and it probably did a lot more for my intelligence than actually paying attention.

It's then that someone opens the door.

"Dear God, the age of the computers in here must be a *criminal offense*."

I turn slowly around.

A boy stands before the closed door.

"I can hear the haunting symphony of dial-up connection," he says, eyes drifting, and, after several long seconds, he finally notices that he's not the only person in the room.

He's a very ordinary-looking, not ugly but not hot, miscellaneous boy. His most noticeable feature is a pair of large, thick-framed square glasses that sort of make him look like he's wearing 3D cinema glasses. He's tall and has a side parting. In one hand, he holds a mug; in the other, a piece of paper and his school planner.

As he absorbs my face, his eyes flare up, and I swear to God they double in size. He leaps towards me like a pouncing lion, fiercely enough that I stumble backwards in fear that he might crush me completely. He leans forward so that his face is centimeters from my own. Through my reflection in his ridiculously oversized spectacles, I notice that he has one blue eye and one green eye. Heterochromia.

He grins violently.

"Victoria Spring!" he cries, raising his arms into the air.

I say and do nothing. I have a headache.

"You are Victoria Spring," he says. He holds the piece of paper up to my face. It's a photograph. Of me. Underneath, in tiny letters: *Victoria Spring, 11A*. It has been on display near the staffroom—in Year 11, I was a form leader, mostly because no one else wanted to do it so I got volunteered. All the form leaders had their pictures taken. Mine is awful. It was before I cut my hair so I sort of look like the girl from *The Ring*. It's like I don't even have a face.

I look into the blue eye. "Did you tear that right off the display?"

He steps back a little, retreating from his invasion of my personal space. He's got this intense smile on his face. "I said I'd help someone look for you." He taps his chin with his planner. "Blond guy . . . skinny trousers . . . walking around like he didn't really know where he was . . ."

I do not know *any* guys and certainly not any blond guys who wear skinny trousers.

I shrug. "How did you know I was in here?"

He shrugs too. "I didn't. I came in because of the arrow on the door. I thought it looked quite mysterious. And here you are! What a *hilarious* twist of fate!"

He takes a sip of his drink.

"I've seen you before," he says, still smiling.

I find myself squinting at his face. Surely I must have seen him at some point in the corridors. Surely I would remember those hideous glasses. "I don't think I've ever seen *you* before."

"That's not surprising," he says. "I'm in Year 13, so you wouldn't see me much. And I only joined your school last September. I did my Year 12 at Truham."

7

That explains it. Four months isn't enough time for me to commit a face to memory.

"So," he says, tapping his mug. "What's going on *here*?"

I step aside and point unenthusiastically to the Post-it on the back wall. He reaches up and peels it off.

"Solitaire. Interesting. Okay. I'd say we could boot up one of these computers and check it out, but we'd probably both expire before Internet Explorer loaded. I bet you any money they all use Windows 95."

He sits down on one of the swivel chairs and stares out of the window at the suburban landscape. Everything is lit up like it's on fire. You can see right over the town and into the countryside. He notices me looking too.

"It's like it's pulling you out, isn't it?" he says. He sighs to himself. "I saw this old man on my way in this morning. He was sitting at a bus stop with headphones on, tapping his hands on his knees, looking at the sky. How often do you see that? An old man with headphones on. I wonder what he was listening to. You'd think it would be classical, but it could have been anything. I wonder if it was sad music." He lifts up his feet and crosses them on top of a table. "I hope it wasn't."

"Sad music is okay," I say, "in moderation."

He swivels round to me and straightens his tie.

"You are definitely Victoria Spring, aren't you." This should be a question, but he says it like he's already known for a long time.

"Tori," I say, intentionally monotone. "My name is Tori."

He puts his hands in his blazer pockets. I fold my arms.

"Have you been in here before?" he asks.

"No."

He nods. "Interesting."

I widen my eyes and shake my head at him. "What?"

"What *what*?"

"What's interesting?" I don't think I could sound less interested.

"We both came looking for the same thing."

"And what is that?"

"An answer."

I raise my eyebrows. He gazes at me through his glasses.

"Aren't mysteries *fun*?" he says. "Don't you *wonder*?"

It's then that I realize that I probably don't. I realize that I could walk out of here and literally not give a crap about Solitaire or this annoying, loud-mouthed guy ever again.

But because I want him to stop being so goddamn patronizing, I swiftly remove my phone from my blazer pocket, type the URL into the internet address bar, and open up the web page.

What appears almost makes me laugh—it's an empty blog. A troll blog, I guess.

What a pointless, pointless day this is.

I thrust the phone into his face. "Mystery solved, Sherlock."

At first, he keeps on grinning, like I'm joking, but soon his eyes focus downwards onto the phone screen and, in a kind of stunned disbelief, he removes the phone from my hand.

"It's . . . an empty blog . . ." he says, not to me but to himself, and suddenly (and I don't know how this happens) I feel deeply, *deeply* sorry for him. Because he looks so bloody *sad*. He shakes his head and hands my phone back to me. I don't really know what to do. He literally looks like someone's just died.

"Well, er . . ." I shuffle my feet. "I'm going to form now."

"No, no, wait!" He jumps up so we're facing each other.

There is a significantly awkward pause.

He studies me, squinting, then studies the photograph, then back to me, then back to the photo. "You cut your hair!"

I bite my lip, holding back the sarcasm. "Yes," I say sincerely. "Yes, I cut my hair."

"It was so *long*."

"Yes, it was."

"Why did you cut it?"

I had gone shopping by myself at the end of the summer holidays because there was so much crap I needed for sixth form and Mum and Dad were busy and I just wanted it out of the way. What I'd failed to remember was that I am awful at shopping. My old schoolbag was ripped and dirty so I trailed through nice places—River Island and Zara and Urban Outfitters and Mango and Accessorize. But all the nice bags there were, like, fifty pounds, so that wasn't happening. Then I tried the cheaper places—New Look and Primark and H&M—but I couldn't find one I liked. I ended up going round all the shops selling bags a billion bloody times before having a slight breakdown on a bench by Costa Coffee in the middle of the shopping center. I thought about starting Year 12 and all the things that I needed to do and all the new people that I might have to meet and all the people I would have to talk to and I caught a reflection of myself in a Waterstones window and I realized then that most of my face was covered up and who in the name of God would want to talk to me like that and I started to feel all of this hair on my forehead and my cheeks and how it plastered my shoulders and back and I felt it creeping around me like worms, choking me to death. I began to breathe very fast, so I went straight into the nearest hairdresser's and had it all cut to my shoulders and out of my face. The hairdresser didn't want to do it, but I was very insistent. I spent my schoolbag money on a haircut.

"I just wanted it shorter," I say.

He steps closer. I shuffle backwards.

"You," he says, "do not say anything you mean, do you?"

I laugh again. It's a pathetic sort of expulsion of air, but for me that qualifies as a laugh. "Who *are* you?"

He freezes, leans back, opens out his arms as if he's the Second Coming of Christ, and announces in a deep and echoing voice: "My name is Michael Holden."

Michael Holden.

"And who are you, Victoria Spring?"

I can't think of anything to say because that is what my answer would be really. Nothing. I am a vacuum. I am a void. I am nothing.

Mr. Kent's voice blares abruptly from the tannoy. I turn round and look up at the speaker as his voice resonates down.

"All sixth-formers should make their way to the common room for a short sixth-form meeting."

When I turn back round, the room is empty. I'm glued to the carpet. I open my hand and find the SOLITAIRE Post-it inside it. I don't know at what point the Post-it made its way from Michael Holden's hand to my own, but there it is.

And this, I suppose, is it.

This is probably how it starts.

TWO

The large majority of teenagers who attend Higgs are soulless, conformist idiots. I have successfully integrated myself into a small group of girls who I consider to be "good people," but sometimes I still feel that I might be the only person with a consciousness, like a video-game protagonist, and the rest are computer-generated extras who have only a select few actions, such as "initiate meaningless conversation" and "hug."

The other thing about Higgs teenagers, and maybe most teenagers, is that they put very little effort into 90 percent of everything. I don't think that this is a bad thing because there'll be lots of time for "effort" later in our lives, and trying too hard at this point is a waste of energy that might otherwise be spent on lovely things such as sleeping and eating and illegally downloading music. I don't really try hard to do anything. Neither do many other people. Walking into the common room and being greeted by a hundred teenagers slumped over chairs, desks, and the floor is not an unusual occurrence.

Kent hasn't arrived yet. I head over to Becky and Our Lot in the computer corner; they seem to be having a conversation about whether Michael Cera is actually attractive or not.

"Tori. Tori. Tori." Becky taps me repeatedly on the arm. "You can back me up on this. You've seen *Juno*, yeah? You think he's cute, right?" She slaps her hands against her cheeks and her eyes kind of roll backwards. "Awkward boys are the hottest, aren't they?"

I place my hands on her shoulders. "Stay calm, Rebecca. Not everyone loves the Cera like you do."

She starts to babble on about *Scott Pilgrim vs. the World*, but I'm not really listening. Michael Cera is not the Michael I'm thinking about.

I somehow excuse myself from this discussion and begin to patrol the common room.

Yes. That's right. I'm looking for Michael Holden.

At this point, I'm not really sure *why* I am looking for him. As I've probably already implied, I do not get interested in very many things, particularly not people, but it irritates me when someone thinks that they can start a conversation and then just get up and *leave*.

It's *rude*, you know?

I pass all the common-room cliques. Cliques are a very *High School Musical* concept, but the reason they are so clichéd is because they really do exist. In a predominantly all-girls' school, you can pretty much expect each year to be divided into three main categories:

1. Popular girls who hang out with the cool boys from the boys' school and use fake IDs to get into clubs. They seem to want to be either very nice to you or very horrible to you and which one they go for is all down to various things that are completely out of your control. Very intimidating.

2. Girls who are perfectly happy to be as nerdy or uncool as they like, which some people interpret as being "weird," but I sort of admire because they truly do not give a shit about what people think of them, so they just enjoy their niche hobbies and get on with their lives. Good for them.

3. So-called "normal" girls. All the people who are somewhere between those two groups, I guess. Which probably means they've repressed their actual personalities to fit in and once they leave school they'll all have giant awakenings and actually become interesting people. School is hell.

I'm not saying that everyone fits into one of these groups. I love that there are exceptions because I hate that these groups exist. I mean, I don't know where *I'd* go. I suppose I'd be group 3 because that's definitely what Our Lot is. Then again, I don't feel very similar to anyone from Our Lot. I don't feel very similar to anyone at all.

I circle the room three or four times before concluding that he's not here. Whatever. Maybe I just imagined Michael Holden. It's not like I care anyway. I go back to Our Lot's corner, slump onto the floor at Becky's feet, and close my eyes.

☁·‥·

The common-room door swings open as Mr. Kent, Deputy Head, strides into the crowd, followed by his usual posse: Miss Strasser, who can only be five years older than us, maximum, and our Head Girl, Zelda (I'm not even joking—her name really is that fantastic). Kent is a sharp-angled sort of man most often noted for his startling resemblance to Alan Rickman, and is probably the only teacher in this school to hold true intelligence. He is also my English teacher, and has been for over five years, so we actually know each other fairly well. That's probably a bit weird. We do have a Headmistress, Mrs. Lemaire, who is widely rumored to be a member of the French government, explaining why she never appears to be present in her own school.

"I want some *quiet*," says Kent, standing in front of an interactive whiteboard, which hangs on the wall just below our school motto: *Confortamini in Domino et in potentia virtutis eius*. The sea of gray uniforms turns to face him. For a few moments, Kent says nothing. He does this a lot.

Becky and I grin at each other and start counting the seconds. This is a game we play. I can't remember when it started, but every single time we're in assembly or a sixth-form meeting or whatever, we count the length of his silences. Our record is seventy-nine seconds. No joke.

When we hit twelve and Kent opens his mouth to speak—

Music begins to play out of the tannoy.

It's the Darth Vader theme from *Star Wars*.

An instant uneasiness soars over the sixth form. People turn their heads wildly from side to side, whispering, wondering why Kent would play music through the tannoy, and why *Star Wars*. Perhaps he's going to start lecturing us on communicating with clarity, or persistence, or empathy and understanding, or skills of interdependence, which are what most of the sixth-form meetings are about. Perhaps he's trying to make a point about the importance of leadership. Only when the pictures begin to appear on the screen behind him do we realize what is, in fact, going on.

First, it's Kent's face photoshopped into Yoda's. Then it's Kent as Jabba the Hutt.

Then it's Princess Kent in a golden bikini.

The entire sixth form bursts into uncontrollable laughter.

The real Kent, stern-faced but keeping his cool, marches out of the room. As soon as Strasser similarly disappears, people begin to tear from group to group, reliving the look in Kent's eyes when his face appeared on Natalie Portman's, complete with white Photoshop face paint and an extravagant hairdo. I have to admit, it's kind of funny.

After Kent/Darth Maul leaves the screen, and as the orchestral masterpiece reaches its climax through the speakers above our heads, the interactive whiteboard displays the URL for SOLITAIRE.

Becky brings the site up on a computer and Our Lot clusters round to have a good look. The troll blog has one post now, uploaded two minutes ago—a photo of Kent staring in passive anger at the board.

We all start talking. Well, everyone else does. I just sit there.

"Some kids probably thought it was clever," snorts Becky.

"Well, yeah, it *is* clever," says Evelyn, her long-established superiority complex making its regular appearance. "It's sticking it to the *man*."

I shake my head, because nothing is clever about it apart from the skill of the person who managed to morph Kent's face into Yoda's. That is Photoshop Talent.

Lauren is grinning widely. Lauren Romilly is a social smoker and seems to love chaos. "I can see the Insta post already. This has probably broken my Twitter feed."

"I need a photo of this on my Insta," continues Evelyn. "I could do with a couple of thousand more followers."

"Go away, Evelyn," dismisses Lauren. "You're already internet famous."

This makes me laugh. "Just post another photo of your dog, Evelyn," I say quietly. "He already gets, like, twenty thousand likes."

Only Becky hears me. She grins at me, and I grin back, which is sort of nice because I rarely think of funny things to say.

And that's it. That's pretty much all we say about it.

Ten minutes and it's forgotten.

To tell you the truth though, this prank has made me feel kind of weird. The fact of the matter is that *Star Wars* was actually a major obsession of mine when I was a kid. I guess I haven't watched any of the films for a few years now, but hearing that music brings back something. I don't know what. Some feeling in my chest.

Ugh, I'm getting sentimental.

I bet whoever did this is really pleased with themselves. It kind of makes me hate them.

Five minutes later, I've just about dozed off, my head on the computer desk and my arms barricading my face from all forms of social interaction, when somebody pats me on the shoulder.

I jerk upwards and gaze blearily in the direction of the pat. Becky's looking at me oddly, purple strands cascading around her. She blinks.

"What?" I ask.

She points behind her, so I look.

A guy is standing there. Nervous. Face in a sort of grinning grimace. I realize what's going on, but my brain doesn't quite accept that this is possible, so I open my mouth and close it three times before coming up with:

"Jesus Christ."

The guy steps towards me.

"V-Victoria?"

Excluding my new acquaintance Michael Holden, only two people in my life have ever called me Victoria. One is Charlie. And the other is:

"Lucas Ryan," I say.

I once knew a boy named Lucas Ryan. He cried a lot, but liked Pokémon just as much as I did so I guess that made us friends. He once told me he would like to live inside a giant bubble when he grew up because you could fly everywhere and see everything, and I told him that would make a terrible house because bubbles are always empty inside. He gave me a Batman key ring for my eighth birthday, a *How to Draw Manga* book for my ninth birthday, Pokémon cards for my tenth birthday, and a T-shirt with a tiger on it for my eleventh.

I sort of have to do a double take because his face is now an entirely different shape. He'd always been smaller than me, but now he's at least a whole head taller and his voice, obviously, has broken. I start to look for things that *are* the same as eleven-year-old Lucas Ryan, but all I've got to go on is his grayish hair, skinny limbs, and awkward expression.

Also, he is the "blond guy in skinny trousers."

"Jesus Christ," I repeat. "Hi."

He smiles and laughs. I remember the laugh. It's all in the chest. A chest laugh.

"Hi!" he says, and smiles some more. A nice smile. A calm smile.

I dramatically leap to my feet and look him up and down. It's actually him.

"It's actually you," I say, and have to physically restrain myself from reaching out and patting him on the shoulders. Just to check he's really there and all.

He laughs. His eyes go all squinty. "It's actually me!"

"Wh— Ho— Why?"

He starts to look kind of embarrassed. I remember him being like that. "I left Truham at the end of last term," he says. "I knew you went here, so . . ." He fiddles with his collar. He used to do that too. "Erm . . . I thought I'd try to find you. Seeing as I don't have any friends here. So, erm, yes. Hello."

I think you should be aware that I have never been very good at making friends, and primary school was no different. I acquired only the one friend during those seven years of mortifying social rejection. Yet while my primary school days are not days that I would choose to relive, there was one good thing that probably kept me going, and that was the quiet friendship of Lucas Ryan.

"Wow." Becky, unable to keep away from potential gossip, intervenes. "How do you two know each other?"

Now I am a fairly awkward person, but Lucas really takes the biscuit. He turns to Becky and goes red again and I almost feel embarrassed *for* him.

"Primary school," I say. "We were best friends."

Becky's shaped eyebrows soar. "No *waaay*." She looks at both of us once more, before focusing on Lucas. "Well, I guess I'm your replacement. I'm Becky." She gestures around her. "Welcome to the Land of Oppression."

Lucas, in a mouse voice, manages: "I'm Lucas."

He turns back to me. "We should catch up," he says.

Is this what friendship reborn feels like?

"Yes . . ." I say. The shock is draining my vocabulary. "Yes."

People have started to give up on the sixth-form meeting as it's the start of Period 1 and no teachers have returned.

Lucas nods at me. "Erm, I don't really want to be late to my first lesson or anything—this whole day is going to be kind of embarrassing as it is—but I'll talk to you some time soon, yeah? I'll find you on Facebook."

Becky stares in relatively severe disbelief as Lucas wanders away, and grabs me firmly by the shoulder. "Tori just talked to a *boy*. No—Tori just held a conversation *by herself*. I think I'm going to cry."

"There, there." I pat her on the shoulder. "Be strong. You'll get through this."

"I'm extremely proud of you. I feel like a proud mum."

I snort. "I can hold conversations by myself. What do you call this?"

"*I* am the only exception. With everyone else, you're about as sociable as a cardboard box."

"Maybe I am a cardboard box."

We both laugh.

"It's funny . . . because it's true," I say, and I laugh again, on the outside at least. Ha ha ha.

THREE

The first thing I do when I get home from school is collapse onto my bed and turn on my laptop. This happens every single day. If I'm not at school, you can guarantee that my laptop will be somewhere within a two-meter radius of my heart. My laptop is my soulmate.

Over the past few months, I've come to realize that I'm far more of a blog than an actual person. I don't know when this blogging thing started, and I don't know when or why I signed up to this website, but I can't seem to remember what I *did* before and I don't know what I'd do if I deleted it. I severely regret starting this blog, I really do. It's pretty embarrassing. But it's the only place where I ever find people who are sort of like me. People talk about themselves here in ways that people don't in real life.

If I delete it, I think I'll probably be completely alone.

I don't blog to get more followers or whatever. I'm not Evelyn. It's just that it's not socially acceptable to say sad stuff out loud in the real world because people think that you're attention-seeking. I hate that. So what I'm saying is that it's nice to be able to say whatever I want. Even if it is only on the internet.

After waiting a hundred billion years for my internet to load, I spend a good while on my blog. There are a couple of cheesy anonymous messages—a few of my followers get all worked up about some of the pathetic stuff I post. Then I check Facebook. Two notifications—Lucas and Michael have sent friend requests. I accept both. Then I check my email. No emails.

And then I check the Solitaire blog again.

It's still got the photo of Kent looking hilariously passive, but apart from that the only addition to the blog is the title. It now reads:

Solitaire: Patience Kills.

I don't know what these Solitaire people are trying to do, but "Patience Kills" is the stupidest imitation of some James Bond film title that I have ever heard. It sounds like a betting website.

I take the SOLITAIRE Post-it out of my pocket and place it precisely in the center of the only empty wall in my room.

I think about what happened today with Lucas Ryan and, for a brief moment, I feel kind of hopeful again. I don't know. Whatever. I don't know why I bothered with this. I don't even know why I followed those Post-its into that computer room. I don't know why I do anything, for God's sake.

Eventually, I find the will to get up and plod downstairs to get a drink. Mum's in the kitchen on the computer. She's very much like me, if you think about it. She's in love with Microsoft Excel the way I'm in love with Google Chrome. She asks me how my day was, but I just shrug and say that it was fine, because I'm fairly sure that she doesn't care what my answer is.

It's because we're so similar that we stopped talking to each other so much. When we do talk, we either struggle to find things to say or we just get angry, so apparently we've reached a mutual agreement that there's really no point trying anymore. I'm not too bothered. My dad's quite chatty, even if everything he says is extraordinarily irrelevant to my life, and I've still got Charlie.

The house phone rings.

"Get that, would you?" says Mum.

I *hate* the phone. It's the worst invention in the history of the world because, if you don't talk, nothing happens. You can't get by with simply listening and nodding your head in all the right places. You *have* to talk. You have *no option*.

I pick it up anyway, because I'm not a horrible daughter.

"Hello?" I say.

"Tori. It's me." It's Becky. "Why the hell are you answering the phone?"

"I decided to rethink my attitude towards life and become an entirely different person."

"Say again?"

"Why are you calling me? You never call me."

"Dude, this is absolutely too important to text."

There's a pause. I expect her to continue, but she seems to be waiting for me to speak.

"Okay—"

"It's Jack."

Ah.

Becky has called about her almost-boyfriend, Jack.

She does this to me very often. Not call me, I mean. Ramble at me about her various almost-boyfriends.

While Becky is talking, I put "mms" and "yeahs" and "oh my Gods" where they need to be. Her voice fades a little as I drift away and picture myself as her. As a lovely, happy, hilarious girl who gets invited to at least two parties a week and can start up a conversation within two seconds. I picture myself entering a party. Throbbing music, everyone with a bottle in their hand— somehow, there's a crowd around me. I'm laughing, I'm the center of attention. Eyes light up in admiration as I tell another of my hysterically embarrassing stories, perhaps a drunk story, or an ex-boyfriend story, or simply a time that I did something remarkable, and everyone wonders how I manage to have such an eccentric, adventurous, carefree adolescence. Everyone hugs me. Everyone wants to know what I've been up to. When I dance, people dance; when I sit down, ready to tell secrets, people form a circle; when I leave, the party fades away and dies, like a forgotten dream.

"—you can guess what I'm talking about," she says.

I really can't.

"A few weeks ago—God, I should have told you this—we had *sex*."

I sort of freeze up because this takes me by surprise. Then I realize that this has been coming for a long time. This is what most people do when you get to this age. You start finding partners, kissing, having sex. I have no issues with people doing that—like, I'm sex positive, and Becky has wanted to have sex with Jack for quite a while. And I know that kissing and having sex isn't a race, and there are some people who never end up wanting to do those things anyway. But I guess it makes me feel like she's braver than me. She's putting herself out there. She's getting what she wants. And what am I doing? Nothing. I have no idea what I want.

"Well—" There is literally nothing I can say about this. "—I'm happy for you?"

There's a pause. "That's it?"

"Was it . . . good?"

She laughs. "It was both of our first times, so, no, not really. It was still fun, though."

"Oh. Okay."

"Are you judging me?"

"What? No!"

"I feel like you are."

"I'm not. I promise." I try to sound more positive. "I genuinely am happy for you."

She seems satisfied by this and starts explaining how Jack has this friend who would supposedly be "perfect" for me, while I sit there, stewing in guilt because I am a terrible friend and a terrible person who gets jealous of my best friend for being everything I wish I was. Confident. Outgoing. Happy.

Once I get off the phone, I sort of stand there in the kitchen. Mum's still clicking away at the computer and I start to feel, again, like this whole day has been pointless. An image of Michael Holden appears in my head and then an image of Lucas Ryan and then an image of the Solitaire blog. I decide that I need to talk to my brother. I pour myself some diet lemonade and leave the kitchen.

💬

My brother Charles Spring is fifteen years old and a Year 11 at Truham Grammar. In my opinion, he is the nicest person in the history of the universe, and I know that *nice* is kind of a meaningless word, but that's what makes it so powerful. It's very hard to simply be a "nice" person because there are a lot of things that can get in the way. When he was little, he refused to throw out any of his possessions because to him they were all special. Every baby book. Every outgrown T-shirt. Every useless board game. He kept them all in sky-high piles in his room because everything supposedly had some kind of meaning. When I asked about a particular item, he'd tell me how he found it at the beach, or how it was a hand-me-down from our nan, or how he bought it when he was six at London Zoo.

He got rid of a lot of that stuff as he grew up, though, and things aren't quite as happy as they were back then. Charlie's had a really difficult time over the past few months. He has an eating disorder that got pretty bad last summer, and he's had a couple of self-harm relapses too, but he spent a few weeks at a psychiatric ward, which sounded terrifying at first but ended up really helping. He's in therapy now and he's working on getting better. And he's still the same kid who has a lot of love to give.

In the living room, it is extremely unclear what Charlie, his boyfriend, Nick, and my other brother, Oliver, are doing. They've got these cardboard boxes, and I mean there's, like, *fifty* of them, piled up all over the room. Oliver, who is seven years old, appears to be directing the operation as Nick and Charlie build up the boxes to make some kind of shed-sized sculpture. The piles of boxes reach the ceiling. Oliver has to stand on the sofa to be able to oversee the entire structure.

Eventually, Charlie walks round the small cardboard building and notices me staring in from the doorway. "Victoria!"

I blink at him. "Shall I bother asking?"

He gives me this look as if I should know exactly what is going on. "We're building a tractor for Oliver."

I nod. "Of course. Yes. That's very clear."

Nick appears. At first glance, Nicholas Nelson, a Year 12 like me, looks exactly like the kind of scary lads you'd see crammed at the back of the school bus, ready to throw sandwiches at you. But in reality, Nick is actually the human embodiment of a golden retriever puppy, as well as being Truham's rugby captain and a genuinely lovely person. I can't really remember when Nick and Charlie became Nick-and-Charlie, but Nick has stuck with Charlie through all the hardest parts of his mental illness, so, in my book, he's definitely all right.

"Tori." He nods at me very seriously indeed. "Good. We need more free labor."

"Tori, can you get the Sellotape?" Oliver calls down, except he says "thellotape" instead of "Sellotape" because he recently lost a front tooth.

I pass Oliver the thellotape, then point towards the boxes and ask Charlie: "Where did you get all of these?"

Charlie just shrugs and walks away, saying, "They're Oliver's, not *mine*."

So that's how I end up building a cardboard tractor in our living room.

When we're finished, Charlie, Nick, and I sit inside it to admire our work. Oliver goes round the tractor with a marker pen, drawing on the wheels, the mud stains, and the machine guns "in case the cows join the Dark Side." It's sort of peaceful, to be honest. Every box has a big black arrow printed on it pointing upwards.

Charlie is telling me about his day. He loves telling me about his day.

"Saunders asked us who our favorite musicians were and I said Muse and *three* people asked me if I liked them because of *Twilight*. *Three*."

I snort. "To be fair, the only Muse songs I know are from *Twilight*."

Nick nods. "Same. I watched the first *Twilight* movie a lot as a kid."

Charlie raises his eyebrows. "Can't believe I'm going to have to dump you due to your terrible taste in movies."

Nick laughs and wraps his arms around Charlie's waist. "Aw, you sad you come second place to Robert Pattinson?"

Charlie laughs too, and then there's a short silence, in which I lie down and look up at the cardboard ceiling.

I start to tell them about today's prank. And that leads me to thinking about Lucas and Michael Holden.

"I met Lucas Ryan again today," I say. I don't mind telling this sort of stuff to Nick and Charlie. "He joined our school."

Nick and Charlie blink at the same time.

"Lucas Ryan . . . as in primary-school Lucas Ryan?" Charlie frowns.

"Lucas Ryan left Truham?" Nick frowns. "Crap. He was gonna help me revise for our psychology mock."

I nod to both of them. "It was nice to see him. You know. Because we can be friends again. I guess. He was always so nice to me."

They both nod back. It's a knowing sort of nod.

"I also met some guy called Michael Holden."

Nick, who had been in the middle of taking a sip of tea, chokes into his cup. Charlie grins, widely, and starts to giggle.

"What? Do you know him?"

Nick recovers enough to speak, though still coughs every few words. "Michael fucking Holden. Shit. *He'll* go down in Truham legend."

Charlie lowers his head, but keeps his eyes on me. "Watch out for him. I always found him a bit scary, to be honest."

"Do you remember when he tried to get everyone to do a flash mob for the Year 11 prank?" says Nick. "And in the end he just did it by himself on the lunch tables?"

"What about when he talked about the injustice of authority for his Year 12 prefect speech?" says Charlie. "Just because he got detention for having that argument with Mr. Yates during his mock exams!"

This confirms my suspicion that Michael Holden is not the sort of person with whom I would like to be friends. Ever.

Charlie looks up at Nick. "Is he straight? I heard he's not straight."

Nick shrugs. "That might just have been a rumor."

"Yeah, maybe." Charlie frowns. "We'd probably know if he was out."

They pause and both look at me.

"Look," says Nick, gesturing sincerely to me with one hand, "Lucas Ryan's a cool guy. But there's something up with Michael Holden. I mean, it wouldn't surprise me if he was behind that prank."

The thing is, I don't think that Nick is right. I don't have any evidence to support this. I'm not even sure why I think this. Maybe it was something about the way Michael Holden spoke—like he believed everything he said. Maybe it was how sad he was when I showed him the empty Solitaire blog. Or maybe it was something else, something that doesn't make sense, like the colors of his eyes, or his ridiculous side parting, or how he managed to get that Post-it note into my hand when I can't even remember our skin touching. Maybe it's just because he's too *wrong*.

As I'm thinking this, Oliver enters the tractor and sits down in my lap. I pat him affectionately on the head and give him what's left of my diet lemonade because Mum doesn't let him drink it.

"I don't know," I say. "To be honest, I bet it was just some twat with a blog."

FOUR

I'm late because Mum thought I said eight. I said seven thirty. How can you confuse eight with seven thirty?

"Whose birthday is it?" she asks while we're in the car.

"No one's. We're just meeting up."

"Do you have enough money? I can sub you."

"I've got fifteen pounds."

"Will Becky be there?"

"Yep."

"And Lauren and Evelyn?"

"Probably."

When I speak to my parents, I don't actually sound very grumpy. I'm usually quite cheerful-sounding when I talk. I'm good at that.

It's Tuesday. Evelyn organized some "start of term" thing at Pizza Express. I don't really want to go, but I think it's important to make the effort. Social convention and all.

I say hello to the people who notice my entrance, then sit at the end of the table. I nearly die when I realize that Lucas is here. I know, already, that I'm going to find it difficult to think of things to say to him. I successfully avoided him for the rest of yesterday and all of today for this exact reason. Obviously, Evelyn, Lauren, and Becky took the opportunity to make him the "boy" of our group. Having a boy in your social group is the equivalent of having a house with a pool, or a designer shirt with the logo on it, or a Ferrari. It just makes you more important.

A waiter hurries over to me so I order a diet lemonade and stare down the long table. All the people are chatting and laughing and smiling and it sort of makes me feel a bit sad, like I'm watching them through a dirty window.

"Yeah, but most of the girls who move to Truham only move because they want to be around boys all the time." Becky, seated next to me, is talking at Lucas, who is seated across from us. "Seems like kind of a dumb reason."

"To be fair," he says, "Truham girls are basically worshipped."

Lucas catches my eye and smiles his awkward smile. He's got this hilarious Hawaiian shirt on: the tight-fit kind with the collar done right up and the sleeves slightly rolled. He doesn't look as embarrassed as yesterday—in fact, he looks *fashionable*. I didn't think he would be that sort of guy. The sort of guy who wears Hawaiian shirts.

"Only because boys at all-boys' schools aren't used to being around girls," says Evelyn, who is next to Lucas, waving her arms around to emphasize her point. "I've said it before and I'll say it again: Single-sex schools are a terrible idea."

"It's not real life," says Lucas. "In real life, all genders hang out together."

"I am jealous of the Truham uniform, though," sighs Lauren. "Like, our uniform makes us look twelve years old."

"It's not real life," says Lucas, nodding earnestly. "In real life, there are boys and there are girls and there are kids who don't identify as either. Not just one or the other."

"But that *tie*," says Becky. "I mean, *I can't even*."

They all nod and then start talking about something else. I continue to do what I do best. Watch.

There's a boy sitting next to Lauren, talking to the girls at the opposite end of the table. His name is Ben Hope. Ben Hope is *the guy* at Higgs. And by *the guy*, I mean that one boy in the sixth form that every single girl in the entire school has a crush on. There's always one. Tall and slim-built. Skinny trousers and tight shirts. He usually straightens his dark brown hair and, I swear to God, it defies gravity because it swishes in a kind of organized vortex, but when he doesn't straighten it, it's all curly and he just looks so cute you want to die. He always appears to be serene. He skateboards.

I, personally, do not "fancy" him. I'm just trying to express his perfection.

Ben Hope notices me staring. I need to control my staring.

Lucas is talking at me. I think that he's trying to involve me in this conversation, which is kind of nice, but also irritating and unnecessary. "Tori, do *you* like Bruno Mars?"

"What?"

He hesitates, so Becky steps in. "Tori. Bruno Mars. Come on. He's fabulous, right?"

"What?"

"The. Song. That. Is. Playing. Do. You. Like. It?"

I hadn't even registered that music was playing in this restaurant. It's "Grenade" by Bruno Mars.

I quickly analyze the song.

"I think . . . it's unlikely anyone would want to catch a grenade for anyone else. Or jump in front of a train for someone else. That's very counterproductive." Then, quieter, so no one hears: "If you wanted to do either of those things, it would be for *yourself.*"

Lauren smacks her hand on the table. "Exactly what I said."

Becky laughs at me and says, "You just don't like it because it's Top 40."

Evelyn steps up. Dissing anything mainstream is her personal area of expertise. "Chart music," she says, "is filled with auto-tune and terrible dance tracks."

If I'm completely honest, I don't even like music that much. I just like individual songs. I find one song that I really love and then I listen to it about twenty billion times until I hate it and have ruined it for myself. At the moment, it's "Message in a Bottle" by the Police, and by Sunday I will never want to listen to it again. I'm an idiot.

"If it's so crap, then why does it make it onto the charts?" asks Becky.

Evelyn runs a hand through her hair. "Because we live in a commercialized world where everyone buys music just because someone else has."

It's right after she finishes saying this that I realize silence has swept over our table. I turn round and experience minor heart failure.

Michael Holden has swooped into the restaurant.

I know immediately that he is coming for me. He's grinning, eyes locked on this end of the table. All heads turn as he pulls over a chair and makes himself comfortable at the head of the table between me and Lucas.

Everyone sort of stares, then murmurs, then shrugs, and then gets on with eating, assuming that he must have been invited by someone else. Everyone except me, Becky, Lucas, Lauren, and Evelyn.

"I need to tell you something," he says to me, eyes on fire. "I absolutely need to tell you something."

Lauren speaks up. "You go to our school!"

Michael actually holds out a hand for Lauren to shake. I find myself genuinely unable to tell whether he's being sarcastic or not. "Michael Holden, Year 13. Nice to meet you . . . ?"

"Lauren Romilly. Year 12." Lauren, bemused, takes the hand and shakes it. "Er—nice to meet you too."

"No offense," says Evelyn, "but, like, why are you here?"

Michael stares at her intensely until she realizes that she needs to introduce herself.

"I'm . . . Evelyn Foley?" she says.

Michael shrugs. "Are you? You sound uncertain."

Evelyn does not like to be teased.

He winks at her. "I needed to talk to Tori."

There is a long and grating silence before Becky says, "And . . . er . . . how do you know Tori?"

"Tori and I happened to meet in the midst of our Solitaire investigations."

Her head tilts to one side. She looks at me. "You've been *investigating*?"

"Erm, *no*," I say.

"Then . . . ?"

"I just followed this trail of Post-it notes."

"What?"

"I followed a trail of Post-it notes. They led to the Solitaire blog."

"Ah . . . that's cool . . ."

Meanwhile, Michael is helping himself to our leftover starters. With his free hand, he points ambiguously towards Becky. "Are you Becky Allen?"

Becky slowly turns to Michael. "Are you psychic?"

"Just a fairly capable Facebook stalker. You're all lucky I'm not a serial killer." His finger, still flexed, gravitates towards Lucas. "And Lucas Ryan. We've met already." He smiles at him so forcefully that it comes across as patronizing. "I should thank you. You're the one who led me to this girl."

Lucas nods.

"I like your shirt," says Michael, eyes glazing slightly.

"Thanks," says Lucas, definitely not meaning it.

I start to wonder whether Lucas knew Michael at Truham. Judging by Nick and Charlie's reaction, he probably did. Maybe he doesn't really want to associate with Michael Holden. It's almost making me feel *sorry* for Michael Holden. For the *second time*.

Michael looks past Becky. "And what's your name?"

For a moment, I don't quite realize who he's talking to. Then I see Rita. She pokes her head round from Becky's other side.

"Er, Rita. Rita Sengupta." She laughs. I'm not sure why she laughs, but she does anyway. Rita is probably the only other girl with whom I am civil, besides Becky and Lauren and Evelyn. She hangs around with Lauren, but you tend not to notice her. She's the only girl I know who can pull off a pixie crop.

Michael lights up like it's Christmas morning. "Rita! That is a *fantastic* name. *Lovely Rita!*"

By the time I realize that he's referring to the Beatles song, the conversation has already moved on. It's surprising I even recognize it. I hate the Beatles.

"So, you and Tori just . . . *met*? And started talking?" asks Becky. "That seems sort of unlikely."

It's funny because it's true.

"Yes," says Michael. "Unlikely, yes. But that is what happened."

Once again, he looks into my face, casually blanking the entire group. I cannot articulate how uncomfortable I feel right now. This is worse than drama GCSE.

"Anyway, Tori, there's something I want to tell you."

I blink, sitting on my hands.

Lauren and Becky and Evelyn and Lucas and Rita are listening intently. Michael glances at each face over his large glasses.

"But . . . I, erm, can't remember what it was."

Lucas sneers. "You tracked her all the way down to this restaurant to tell her something and now you can't even remember what it is?"

This time Michael picks up on Lucas's tone. "*Excuse me* for having a memory like a sieve. I feel I deserve credit for making the effort to come here."

"Why couldn't you just send her a message on Facebook?"

"Facebook is for trivialities such as what takeaways people are having and how many 'lols' they had the night before with their 'gals.'"

Lucas shakes his head. "I just don't get why you'd actually come down here and then *forget*. You wouldn't forget if it was something important."

"On the contrary, you'd probably be more likely to forget the most important things of all."

Becky interjects: "So are you and Tori friends now?"

Michael continues to contemplate Lucas before addressing Becky. "That is a fantastic question." Then he faces me. "What do you think? Are we friends now?"

I genuinely can't think of an answer, because the answer, in my opinion, is definitely not *yes*, but it's definitely not *no* either.

"How can we be friends if you don't know anything about me?" I say.

He taps his chin thoughtfully. "Let's see. I know that your name is Victoria Spring. You're in Year 12. Your Facebook indicates that you were born on April fifth. You are an introvert with a pessimist complex. You're wearing pretty plain clothes—jumper, jeans—you don't like embellishments and fuss. You don't care about dressing up for people. You'll have ordered a margherita pizza—you're a picky eater. You rarely update your Facebook—you don't care for social activities. But you followed the Post-it trail yesterday, just like I did. You're curious." He leans in. "You like to act as if you care about nothing, and if you carry on like that, then you're going to drown in the abyss you have imagined for yourself."

He stops. His smile vanishes, leaving only its ghost.

"Jesus, mate, you are a *stalker!*" Lauren attempts a laugh, but no one else joins in.

"No," Michael says. "I just pay attention."

"It's like you're in love with her or something," says Evelyn.

Michael smiles a knowing smile. "I suppose it is a bit like that."

"You're gay though, aren't you?" says Lauren, forever unafraid to say what other people are thinking. "Like, I heard that you're gay."

"Oooh, you've *heard* about me?" He leans in. "Intriguing."

"Are you though?" asks Lucas, trying unsuccessfully to sound casual.

Michael smiles. "I guess you could say I'm not too fussy about gender." Then he grins and points a finger at Lucas. "You never know, it might be *you* I'm in love with."

Lucas immediately goes red.

"So you're pansexual?" asks Becky, and Michael shrugs as if to say, *it's a mystery.*

"I need to pee," I say, even though I don't, and I leave the table and find myself in the restaurant bathroom staring at myself in the mirror while P!nk is telling me to "raise my glass." I stay there for too long. Older ladies shoot me disapproving looks as they waddle in and out of cubicles. I don't know what I'm doing really. I just keep thinking about what Michael said.

Drowning in my abyss. I don't know. Why does that matter? Why does that bother me?

Jesus Christ, why did I bother coming out tonight?

I continue to stare at myself in this mirror and I imagine a voice reminding me to be funny and chatty and happy, like a normal person. As the voice reminds me, I start to feel a bit more positive about stuff, even though any residual enthusiasm for seeing Lucas again has drained away. I think it's because of that Hawaiian shirt. I go back into the restaurant.

FIVE

"That was one hell of a pee," says Michael as I sit down. He's still here. Part of me was hoping he wouldn't be.

"You sound impressed," I say.

"I am, actually."

Becky, Evelyn, and Lauren are now talking across the table to some other girls from our year who I don't really know. Lucas smiles briefly at me. Rita's laughing and smiling, mainly at Lauren.

"So you're not straight?" I ask.

He blinks. "Wow. This is quite a big deal to you guys."

It's not a big deal. I don't really care at all.

Michael sighs. "Everyone's attractive, to be honest, even if it's just something small, like some people have really beautiful hands. I don't know. I'm a little bit in love with everyone I meet."

"So . . . bisexual?" Nick's bisexual, but he doesn't fancy everyone he meets. He's a bit Charlie obsessed, to be honest.

Michael smiles and leans forward. "You love all these words, don't you? Gay, bisexual, pansexual—"

"No," I interrupt. "Not really."

"Then why label people?"

I tilt my head. "Because that's life. Without organization, we descend into chaos."

Staring amusedly, he stretches back again into the chair. I can't believe I just used the word *descend*.

"Well, if you care so much, what are you?" he asks.

"What?"

"What's your sexuality?"

"Er, straight?"

"And what does that *mean* for you, Tori Spring? Have you fancied many boys in your time?"

I actually haven't. Ever. Presumably this is because I have a very low opinion of most people.

I look down. "I guess I'll just go with *straight* until proven otherwise."

Michael's eyes twinkle, but he doesn't comment.

"Are you going to remember what you came to tell me?" I ask.

He strokes his sharply parted hair. "Maybe. Maybe tomorrow. We'll see."

Soon after that everyone declares that they're leaving. I accidentally spent £16, so Lucas insists on giving me the extra pound, which I guess is pretty nice of him. Once we're all standing outside the restaurant, he starts chatting earnestly with Evelyn. Most of the people here are heading to Lauren's house for a big sleepover thing or whatever. They're all going to get drunk and stuff even though it's a Tuesday. Becky explains that she didn't invite me because she knew that I definitely wouldn't want to come (it's funny because it's true), and Ben Hope overhears her and gives me this kind of pitying look. Becky smiles at him, the pair momentarily united in feeling sorry for me. I decide that I'm going to walk home. Michael decides that he's coming with me and I don't really know how to stop him so I guess this is happening.

We have been moving in silence through the high street. It's all Victorian and brown and the cobblestone road is sort of curved like we're in the bottom of a trench. A man in a suit hurries past, and he's asking someone on the phone, "Do you feel anything yet?"

I ask Michael why he's walking home with me.

"Because I live this way. The world does not revolve around you, Victoria Spring." He's being sarcastic, but I still feel kind of put out.

"*Victoria.*" I shudder.

"Huh?"

"Please don't call me *Victoria.*"

"Why's that?"

"It makes me think of Queen Victoria. The one who wore black all her life because her husband died. And 'Victoria Spring' sounds like a brand of bottled water."

Wind is picking up around us.

"I don't like my name either," he says.

I instantly think of all the people I dislike named Michael. Michael Bublé, Michael McIntyre, Michael Jackson.

"Michael means 'who resembles God,'" he says, "and I think that if God could choose to resemble any human being . . ."

He stops then, right in the street, looking at me, just looking, through the lenses of his glasses, through the blue and green, through depths and expanses, bleeding one billion incomprehensible thoughts.

". . . he wouldn't choose me."

We continue to walk.

Imagine if I had been given some Biblical name like Abigail or Charity or, I don't know, *Eve*, for God's sake. I'm not exactly a believer and it probably means that I'm going to hell, if it even exists, which, let's be honest, it probably doesn't. That doesn't bother me very much because whatever happens in hell can't be much worse than what happens here.

I realize then that I'm freezing. I'd forgotten it was the middle of winter and raining and all I've got is this shirt and jumper and thin jeans. I regret not calling Mum, but I hate bothering her because she always does this sighing thing where she's all like, "no, no, it's perfectly fine, I'm not bothered," but I can tell that she is most definitely bothered.

Silence and a faint smell of Indian takeaway continue all the way up the high street and then we take a right onto the main town road where the three-story houses are. My house is one of these.

I stop when I get to my house. It's darker than the others because the streetlamp closest to it is not working.

"This is where I live," I say, and start to walk off.

"Wait, wait, wait," he says. I turn back round. "Can I ask you something?"

I cannot resist a sarcastic comment. "You just did, but please continue."

"Can we really not be friends?"

He sounds like an eight-year-old girl trying to win back her best friend after she accidentally insulted their new school shoes and got herself disinvited from their birthday party.

He's wearing only a T-shirt and jeans too.

"How are you not freezing?" I say.

"Please, Tori. Why don't you want to be friends with me?" It's like he's desperate.

"Why do *you* want to be friends with *me*?" I shake my head. "We're not in the same year. We're not similar in any way whatsoever. I literally do not understand why you even care about—" I stop then, because I was about to say "me," but I realized midway through that that would be a truly horrific sentence.

He looks down. "I don't think that . . . I understand . . . either . . ."

I'm just standing there, staring.

"Are you high?" I ask.

He shakes his head and laughs. "I remember what I was going to tell you, you know."

"You do?"

"I remembered it the whole time. I just didn't want everyone to hear it because it's not their business."

"Then why did you come and find me at a busy restaurant? Why not just find me at school?"

For a second, he genuinely seems to be offended. "Don't you think I've *tried*?" He laughs again. "You're like a ghost!"

It takes a lot of willpower not to turn round and leave.

"I just wanted to tell you that I'd seen you before."

Jesus Christ. He already told me that.

"You told me that yesterd—"

"No, not at Higgs. I saw you when you came to look round Truham. Last year. It was me who took you round the school."

The revelation blossoms. I remember exactly now. Michael Holden had shown me attentively round Truham when I was deciding whether to go there for sixth form. He'd asked me what A levels I wanted to do, and whether I liked Higgs very much, and whether I had any hobbies, and whether I cared much about sports. In fact, everything he'd said had been utterly unremarkable.

"But . . ." It's impossible. "But you were so . . . *normal.*"

He shrugs and smiles and the raindrops on his face almost make him seem as if he's crying. "There's a time and a place for being normal. For most people, normal is their default setting. But for some, like you and me, normal is something we have to bring out, like putting on a suit for a posh dinner."

What, now he's being profound?

"Why did you need to tell me this? Why did you need to track me down? Why was it that important?"

He shrugs again. "It wasn't, I guess. But I wanted you to know. And when I want to do something I usually do it."

I stare at him. Nick and Charlie were right. He's the strangest person I've ever met.

He holds up a hand and sends me a slight wave.

"See you soon, Tori Spring."

And then he wanders away. I'm left standing under the broken streetlamp in my black jumper and the rain, wondering whether I'm feeling anything yet and realizing that it's all very funny because it's all very true.

SIX

I head inside, go into the dining room, and say hello to my family. They're still at dinner, as usual. Well, except Oliver. Since dinner's kind of a two-to-three-hour job in our house, Oliver's always allowed to leave the table once he's done. I can hear him playing *Mario Kart* in the living room and I decide to join him. If I could swap bodies with someone for a day, I would choose Oliver.

"Toriiii!" As soon as I enter, he rolls over on the futon and stretches his arm towards me like a zombie rising out of the grave. He must have got yogurt all down his school jumper today. And he has paint on his face. "I can't win on Rainbow Road! Help me!"

I sigh, sit down on the futon next to him, and pick up the spare Wii remote. "This track is impossible, bro."

"No!" he whines. "Nothing's impossible. I think the game's cheating."

"The game can't cheat."

"It is. It's cheating on purpose."

"It's not cheating you, Ollie."

"*Charlie* can win. It just doesn't like me."

I produce a large and exaggerated gasp, springing up from the futon. "Are you suggesting that Charlie is *better* at *Mario Kart* than *moi*?" I start to shake my head. "Nope. Nuh-uh. I'm the *Mario Kart* Empress."

Oliver laughs, his fluffy hair waving around atop his head. I fall back onto the futon, lift him up, and sit him on my lap.

"All right," I say. "Rainbow Road is going down."

I don't keep track of how long we're playing for, but it must be quite a while because when Mum comes in, she's pretty irritated. And that's extreme, for her. She's a very emotionless person.

"Tori," says Mum. "Oliver should have been in bed an hour ago."

Oliver doesn't seem to hear her. I glance up from the race.

"That's not really my job," I say.

Mum looks at me, expressionless.

"Oliver, it's bedtime," she says, still looking at me.

Oliver quits the game and trots off, high-fiving me on the way. Even when he's gone, Mum doesn't stop looking at me.

"Do you have something to say?" I ask.

Apparently, she doesn't. She turns and leaves. I get in a quick round of Luigi Circuit before heading to my own room. I don't think my mum likes me very much. That doesn't matter, because I don't really like her either.

I put the radio on and blog until the early hours. The radio is playing all this dubstep crap, but I've got it on quietly so I don't care too much. I can't be bothered to leave my bed except to make at least five trips downstairs for more diet lemonade. I check the Solitaire blog, but there's nothing new. So I spend ages scrolling down all my favorite blogs, reblogging screencaps of *Donnie Darko* and *Submarine* and *The Simpsons* taken out of context. I write a couple of whiny posts about I don't even know what and I almost change my display picture, but can't find anything where I look normal, so I fiddle around with my blog theme's HTML for a bit to see if I can remove the gaps between each post. I stalk Michael's Facebook, but he seems to use it even less than I do. I watch a bit of *QI*, but I don't really find it interesting or funny anymore, so instead I watch *Little Miss Sunshine*, which I didn't finish yesterday. I never seem to be able to finish watching a film on the same day I start it because I can't bear the thought of the film ending.

After a while, I put my laptop by my side and lie down. I think about all the other people who were at the restaurant who are probably now drunk and getting off with each other on Lauren's parents' sofas. At some point I fall asleep, but I can hear all these creaky noises coming from outside and something in my brain decides that there is definitely some kind of giant and/or demon stomping around in the road so I get up and close the window just to make sure that whatever it is cannot get inside.

When I get back into bed, every single thing that you could possibly think about in one day decides to come to me all at once and suddenly there's a small lightning storm inside my head. I think about Solitaire, and then I think about Michael Holden and why he said we should be friends and what he was really like when he was at Truham. Then I remember Lucas and how embarrassed he was, and I wonder why he made all that effort trying to find me. Then I remember his Hawaiian shirt, which still enormously irritates me because I hate to think that he's become some indie-band wannabe. So I open my eyes and wander around the internet to take my mind off it all, and, once I feel relatively okay again, I fall asleep with the glare of my blog home page warming my face and the hum of my laptop soothing my mind like crickets at a campsite.

SEVEN

We didn't expect anything more from Solitaire. We thought the one prank would be the end of it.

We were quite a way off.

On Wednesday, all the clocks magically vanished and were replaced by pieces of paper reading *Tempus Fugit*. It was funny at first, but after a few hours when you're midway through a lesson and you can't check your phone and you have no way of finding out what the time is—well, it pretty much makes you want to scratch out your eyeballs.

On the same day, there was hysteria in school assembly when the tannoy started playing Justin Timberlake's "SexyBack," the most well-received song of the Year 8 Higgs-Truham disco, as Kent walked up the hall stage stairs and the word *SWAG* appeared on the projector screen.

On Thursday, we turned up to find that two cats had been let loose within the school. Apparently, the caretakers managed to get one of them out, but the other cat—an underfed ginger thing with massive eyes— evaded capture all day, strolling in and out of lessons and through corridors. I quite like cats, and I saw it for the first time at lunch in the cafeteria. I almost felt like I'd made a new friend, the way it hopped onto a chair and sat with Our Lot as if it wanted to join in our gossip and offer its views about celebrity Twitter rows and the current political climate. I noted to myself that I should probably start collecting cats, seeing as they are very likely to be my sole companions in ten years' time.

"My future pet will definitely be a cat," said Becky.

Lauren nodded. "Cats are Britain's national animal."

"My boyfriend has a cat called Steve," said Evelyn. "Isn't that an excellent name for a cat? *Steve.*"

Becky rolled her eyes. "Evelyn. Dude. When are you going to tell us who your boyfriend is?"

But Evelyn just smiled and pretended to be embarrassed.

I peered into the dark eyes of the cat. It met my gaze thoughtfully. "Do you remember when some lady got caught on camera dumping a cat into a brown bin and it made national news?"

Every single prank so far has been photographed and displayed on the Solitaire blog.

Anyway.

Today is Friday. People are beginning to find it less funny as Madonna's "Material Girl" has been stuck on repeat all morning over the tannoy. I used to have a small obsession with this song, and I am coming extremely close to hurling myself from a window and it's only 10:45 a.m. I'm still not quite sure how Solitaire is managing to do all this as Zelda and her prefects have been patrolling the school ever since Wednesday's clocks fiasco.

I'm sitting at a table playing chess on my phone during a free period, blasting some Radiohead song into my ears to block out the vomit-inducing music. The common room has only a scattering of people, mostly Year 13s revising for January retakes. Miss Strasser is overseeing the room because, during lesson times, the common room is reserved for people revising and silence is mandatory. This is why I like this room. Except today. Strasser's hung a spare school jumper over the tannoy speaker, but it's not doing much.

In the corner of the common room, Becky and Ben are sitting together. They are not doing any work, and they are both smiling. Becky keeps tucking her hair behind her ears. Ben takes Becky's hand and starts to draw on it. I look away. So long, Jack.

Someone taps me on the shoulder, so suddenly that I have a miniature spasm. I take my headphones out of my ears and swivel round.

Lucas stands before me. Every time we passed in the corridors this week, he gave me these weird little scrunched-up smiles. Anyway, right now he has his bag slung over one shoulder and in his other arm he has a pile of at least seven books.

"Hi," he says, just above a whisper.

"Hi," I say. There's a short pause, before I follow up with: "Er, do you want to sit here?"

Embarrassment pours over his face, but he quickly replies, "Yeah, thanks." He pulls out the chair next to me, dumps his bag and books on the desk, and sits down.

I've still got my phone in my hand and I'm just kind of staring at him.

He sticks a hand into his bag and withdraws a Sprite can. He places it in front of me, like a cat would place a half-chewed mouse in front of its owner.

"I was at the shop at break," he says, without looking me in the eye. "Is lemonade still your favorite?"

"Er . . ." I look down at the Sprite can, not quite sure what to make of it. I do not point out that Sprite is not real lemonade or diet. "Erm, yeah, it is. Thanks, that's, er, really nice of you."

Lucas nods and turns away. I open the Sprite, take a sip, replace my headphones, and return to my game. After only three more moves, I have to remove my headphones again.

"You're playing chess?" he asks. I hate questions that need not be asked.

"Erm, yes."

"Do you remember chess club?"

Lucas and I were members of our primary-school chess club. We played each other every time and not once could I beat him. I always threw a tantrum whenever I lost. God, I used to be a twat.

"No," I say. I lie a lot for no reason. "No, I don't."

He pauses and for a moment I think he sees through me, but he's too embarrassed to push it.

"You have a lot of books," I say. As if he wasn't aware of this.

He nods, smiling awkwardly. "I like to read. And I've just been in the library."

I recognize all the titles, but of course I haven't read any of them. T. S. Eliot's *The Waste Land*, Thomas Hardy's *Tess of the d'Urbervilles*, Ernest Hemingway's *The Old Man and the Sea*, F. Scott Fitzgerald's *The Great Gatsby*, D. H. Lawrence's *Sons and Lovers*, John Fowles's *The Collector*, and Jane Austen's *Emma*.

"So what are you reading now?" I ask. The books at least provide a topic of conversation.

"*The Great Gatsby*," he says. "F. Scott Fitzgerald."

"What's that about?"

"It's about . . ." He pauses to think. "It's about someone who's in love with a dream."

I nod as if I understand. I don't. I don't know a single thing about literature, despite studying it for A level.

I pick up *Emma*. "Does this mean you actually like Jane Austen?" We're still studying *Pride and Prejudice* in class. It's soul-destroying, and not in a good way. Do not read it.

He tilts his head as if it's a deeply serious question. "You sound surprised."

"I am. *Pride and Prejudice* is dreadful. I can barely get past the first chapter."

"Why's that?"

"It's the literary equivalent of a poorly cast rom-com."

Someone gets up and tries to walk past us, so we both have to tuck in our chairs a little.

Lucas is looking at me very carefully. I don't like it.

"You're so different," he says, shaking his head and squinting at me.

"I may have grown a few centimeters since I was eleven."

"No, it's—" He stops himself.

I put down my phone. "What? It's what?"

"You're more serious."

I don't ever remember not being serious. As far as I'm concerned, I came out of the womb spouting cynicism and wishing for rain.

I'm not really sure how to reply. "Well, I guess I'm not exactly a comedian."

"No, but you were always dreaming up all these imaginary games. Like our Pokémon battles. Or the secret base you made out of the sectioned-off corner of the playground."

"Would you like to have a Pokémon battle?" I fold my arms. "Or am I too unimaginative for that?"

"*No.*" He's digging himself into a hole and it's actually quite funny to watch. "I . . . oh, I don't know."

I raise my eyebrows. "Quit while you're ahead. I'm boring now. I'm a lost cause."

I instantly wish I'd just shut up. I always do this thing where I accidentally say self-deprecating stuff that makes other people feel really awkward, especially when it's true. I start to wish I'd never offered to let him sit with me. He quickly returns to the work he got out of his bag.

"Material Girl" is still playing over and over. Apparently, the caretakers are trying to fix it, but at the moment the only solution appears to be cutting the electrics of the entire school, which, according to Kent, would classify as "giving in." He's got that World War II attitude, old Mr. Kent. I take a quick glance out of the windows behind the computers. I know I should be doing some homework too, but I'd much rather play chess and admire the windy grayness outside. That's my major problem with school. I really don't do anything unless I actually want to. And most of the time I don't want to do anything at all.

"You've had quite a good first week," I say, my eyes still focused on the sky.

"Best week of my entire life," he says. Seems like an exaggeration to me, but to each their own.

Lucas is such an innocent guy. Awkward and innocent. In fact, he's so awkward that it's almost as if he's putting it on. I know he's probably not, but that's still the way it comes across. I mean, awkward is very in fashion at the moment. It's frustrating. I have experienced my fair share of awkward, and awkward is *not* cute, awkward does *not* make you more attractive, and awkward *certainly* should not be fashionable. It just makes you look like an idiot.

"Why did we stop being friends?" he asks, not looking at me.

I pause. "People grow up and move on. That's life."

I regret saying this, however true it might be. I see a kind of sadness fizzle into his eyes, but it quickly disappears.

"Well," he says, and turns to me, "we're not grown-up yet."

He takes out his phone and starts to read something on it. I watch as his face melts into something confusing. The pips that signal the end of break somehow manage to sound over the music and he puts the phone away and starts to gather his stuff.

"Got a lesson?" I ask, and then realize that this is one of those pointless questions that I hate.

"History. I'll see you later."

He walks several paces before turning as if he has something else to say. But he just stands there. I give him a strange sort of smile, which he returns and then walks away. I watch as he meets a boy with a large quiff at the door and they start up a conversation as they exit the common room.

Finally at peace, I return to my music. I get to wondering where Michael Holden might be. I haven't seen him since Tuesday. I don't have his phone number or anything. Even if I did, it's not like I would text him. I don't text anyone.

I don't really do much for the next hour. To tell you the truth, I'm not even sure if I'm supposed to be in a lesson, but I really can't find the will to move. I briefly wonder again who Solitaire might be, but I conclude for the billionth time that I just don't care. I set an alarm on my phone to remind me to take Charlie to therapy tonight because Nick is busy, and then I sit very still with my head on one arm and doze off.

I wake up just before the pips go again. I swear to God I'm a freak. I mean it. One day I'm going to forget how to wake up.

EIGHT

I'm sprawled on the computer desks in the common room at 8:21 a.m. on Monday with Becky raving on about how cute Ben Hope was at Lauren's (that was six days ago, for God's sake) when someone bellows with extreme resonance from the door: "HAS ANYONE SEEN TORI SPRING?!"

I wake from the dead. "Oh Christ."

Becky roars my location across the air and before I have time to hide under the desk, Head Girl Zelda Okoro is standing in front of me. I flatten my hair, hoping it will make me invisible. Zelda is an excellent head girl and genuinely a nice, fun person, but I have always refused to get involved with any of her schemes, which seem to require lots of effort and enthusiasm, two things of which I have very little.

"Tori. I'm nominating you for Operation Inconspicuous."

It takes several seconds for this information to register.

"No, you are not," I say. "No. *No*."

"Yes. You haven't got a say. The Deputy Heads voted on who they wanted in Year 12."

"What?" I slump back onto the desk. "What for?"

Zelda puts her hands on her hips and tilts her head. "We're facing a crisis, Tori." She speaks way too fast and in extremely short sentences. I don't like it. "Higgs is facing a crisis. A team of eight prefects just isn't going to cover it. We're upping the stakeout ops team to fifteen. Operation Inconspicuous is a go. Tomorrow. 0700."

"I'm sorry—*what* did you just say?"

"We've come to the conclusion that most of the sabotage must be happening during the early hours. So we're staking out tomorrow morning. 0700. You'd better be there."

"I hate you," I say.

"Don't blame me," she says. "Blame Solitaire." She strides away.

Becky, Evelyn, Lauren, and Rita are all around me. Lucas too. I think he's one of Our Lot now.

"Well, you're obviously in the teachers' good books," says Becky. "Next thing you know, they'll be making you an actual prefect."

I shoot her a look of severe distress.

"Yeah, but if you were a prefect, you could skip the lunch queue," says Lauren. "Fast food, man. And you could give Year 7s detentions whenever they're being too cheerful."

"What did you even do to make the teachers like you?" asks Becky. "You don't exactly do much."

I shrug at her. She's right. I don't do much at all.

Later in the day, I pass Michael in the corridor. I say "pass," but what actually happens is he shouts "TORI" so loudly that I manage to drop my English folder on the floor. He lets out this deafening laugh, his eyes scrunching up behind his glasses, and he actually stops and stands still in the middle of the corridor, causing three Year 8s to bump into him. I look at him, pick up my folder, and walk right past.

I'm in English now. Reading *Pride and Prejudice*. Now that I've reached Chapter 6, I have established that I hate this book with a profound passion. It's boring and clichéd, and I constantly feel the urge to hold it over a lit match. The women only care about the men and the men don't seem to care about anything at all. Except Darcy maybe. He's not so bad. Lucas is the only person I can see who is reading the book properly, with his calm and quiet expression, but every so often he checks his phone. I scroll through a few blogs on my own phone under the desk, but there really isn't anything interesting on there.

Becky is in the seat next to me and she's talking to Ben Hope. Unfortunately, I can't avoid them without moving to a different seat or leaving the class or dying. They are playing Dots and Boxes in Ben's school planner. Becky keeps losing.

"You're *cheating!*" she exclaims, and attempts to grab Ben's pen. Ben laughs a very attractive laugh. They have a small wrestling match over the pen. I try not to throw up or dive under the table from sheer cringe.

In the common room at lunch, Becky tells Evelyn all about Ben. At some point, I interrupt their conversation.

"What happened to Jack?" I ask her.

She gives me a long look. "You want to know now?"

I'm confused. "Uh . . . yeah?"

"You just didn't seem that bothered when I called you about him. I thought I was annoying you."

There's a pause. I have no idea what to say. She hadn't annoyed me when she'd called me, she'd just inadvertently reminded me that I hate myself, like many things do.

I guess I was the one annoying her. Because I'd sounded like I didn't care.

"It didn't work out. We broke up a few days after that," Becky concludes, her face expressionless, and then she turns back to Evelyn.

NINE

Dad gets me to school at 6:55 a.m. the next day. I am in a trance. In the car, he says: "Maybe if you catch them in the act, you'll get a community award."

I don't know what a community award is, but I feel that I'm probably the least likely person in the world to get one.

Zelda, her prefects, the nominated helpers, and even old Kent are in the hall and I'm the only one there who came in school uniform. It's basically nighttime outside. The school heating hasn't started up yet. I praise myself for putting on two pairs of tights this morning.

Zelda, in leggings and running shoes and an oversized Superdry hoodie, takes charge.

"Okay, Team Ops. Today's the day we're catching them, yeah? Everyone's got a separate area of the school. Patrol that area and call me if you find anything. Nothing's been done to the school since Friday so there's a chance they won't turn up today. But we're going to do this until we feel that the school is safe, whether we end up catching anyone or not. Meet back in the hall at eight."

Why did I even come here?

The prefects begin to chat among themselves, and Zelda speaks to each person individually before sending them off into the unlit, unheated depths of the school.

When she gets to me, she presents me with a piece of paper and says, "Tori, you're patrolling the IT suites. Here's my number."

I nod at her and go to walk off.

"Er, Tori?"

"Yeah?"

"You look a bit . . ." She doesn't finish her sentence.

It's 7 a.m. She can piss off.

I walk away, throwing the piece of paper in a bin as I pass it. I come to a halt upon finding Kent standing ominously by the hall entrance.

"Why me?" I ask him, but he just raises his eyebrows and smiles at me, so I roll my eyes and walk away.

Wandering around the school like this is peculiar. Everything's so still. Serene. No air circulation. I'm walking through a freeze-frame.

The IT suite is in C Block, on the first floor. There are six computer rooms: C11, C12, C13, C14, C15, and C16. The usual whir of the suite is absent. The computers are all dead. I open up C11, switch on the lights, and repeat this for C12, C13, and C14 before giving up and taking a seat on a swivel chair inside C14. What does Kent even think he's doing involving me in this? As if I'm going to do any kind of "patrolling." I kick the floor and spin. The world hurricanes around me.

I don't know how long I do this, but when I stop to read the time, the clock wavers in front of my eyes. When it calms down, it reads 7:16 a.m. I wonder for at least the sixteenth time what I am doing here.

It is then that I hear a distant sound of the Windows booting-up jingle.

I get off my chair and step into the corridor. I look one way. I look the other. The corridor dissolves into darkness both ways, but out of the open door of C13 glares a hazy blue glow. I creep down the corridor and go inside.

The interactive whiteboard is on, the projector whirring happily, the Windows desktop on display. I stand before the board, staring into it. The desktop wallpaper is a sloped green field beneath a blue sky. The harder I stare, the wider the board seems to spread, wider and wider, until the fake pixelated world invades my own. The computer that is linked to the screen hums.

The door to the room shuts by itself, like I'm in *Scooby-Doo*. I run and grab the handle, but it's locked. For a second I just stare at myself in the door window.

Someone's locked me in an IT room, for God's sake.

Stepping backwards, I see the board change in the blank monitors' reflections. I spin on the spot. The green field has gone. In its place is a blank page of Microsoft Word with the cursor flashing on and off. I try smashing at the keyboard of the computer that's hooked up to the board and wildly swishing the mouse across the table. Nothing happens.

I'm starting to sweat. My brain isn't accepting this situation. I come up with two possibilities.

One: This is a sick joke by someone I know.

Two: Solitaire.

And that's when text rolls across the white screenscape.

Attention **Team Ops**,
Please refrain from panic and alarm.

Pause.
What?

SOLITAIRE is a friendly neighborhood watch organization, dedicated to aiding the adolescent population by targeting the most common cause of teenage anxiety. We are on your side. You should not be afraid of any action we will/will not take.
We hope that you will support SOLITAIRE's future actions and come to feel that school need not be a place of solemnity, stress, and isolation.

Someone is deliberately trying to freak the prefects out. As I'm not a prefect, I am choosing not to freak out. I don't know what I feel about this, but it definitely isn't freaked out.

We leave you with a video that we hope will enlighten your morning.

SOLITAIRE

Patience Kills

The page of text remains on screen for several seconds before Windows Media Player pops up in front of it. The cursor zooms to the play button and the video begins.

The footage is kind of blurry, but you can make out two figures on a stage, one at a piano, one with a violin in her hands. The violinist holds her instrument up to her chin, raises her bow, and together the two begin to play.

Only after the first eight bars, and after the camera has zoomed in, do I realize that the musicians can be no more than eight years old.

I don't know what the piece of music is. It doesn't matter. Because sometimes I hear a piece of music and I can't do anything but sit there. Sometimes in the morning, the radio turns on and a song is playing and it's so beautiful that I just have to lie there until it's over. Sometimes I'm watching a film, and it's not even a sad scene, but the music is so sad that I can't help but cry.

This is one of those times.

Eventually, the video ends and I just stand there.

I guess Solitaire thinks they're being intellectual and deep. Making us watch that video and writing with such eloquence, like people who think that they're hilarious for using the word *thus* in school essays. It half makes me laugh and half makes me want to shoot them.

The fact remains that C13's door is still locked and I'm still trapped here. I want to cry out, but I don't. I don't know what to do.

I threw away Zelda's number, like the idiot I am. I don't know anyone else here.

I can't call Becky. She wouldn't come. Dad's at work. Mum's in her PJs. Charlie won't get to school for another forty-five minutes.

There is only one person who would help me.

There is only one person who is going to believe me.

I pull my phone out of my blazer pocket.

"Hello?"

"Before I say anything else, I have a question."

"Tori?! Oh my God, you *actually* called me!"

"Are you a real person?"

I've been considering the possibility that Michael Holden is a figment of my imagination. This is probably because I fail to understand how someone with a personality like his could survive in this shitty world and also because I fail to understand why someone with a personality like his would take any interest in a misanthropic, pessimistic asshole like myself.

I found his number posted in my locker yesterday lunchtime. It was written on one of those Solitaire pink Post-its with an arrow drawn on it, except now he'd added his phone number and a smiley face. I *knew* that it was Michael. Who else would it be?

There's a long pause before he says, "I promise—I *swear*—that I am a completely real person. Here. On the earth. Living and breathing."

He waits for me to say something and, when I don't, he continues, "And I can understand why you would ask me that so I'm not offended or anything."

"Okay. Thanks for . . . erm . . . clearing that up."

I proceed to explain in the most nonchalant way I can muster that I am locked in an IT classroom.

"Lucky for you that I decided to turn up to help today," he says. "I knew something like this would happen. This is why I had to give you my number. You're totally a danger to yourself."

And then he appears, strolling casually past, phone pressed to his ear, not even aware that I'm only meters from him.

I pound my hand repeatedly on the door window. Michael reverses several steps, uncharacteristically frowning, and peers at me. Then he grins, hangs up the phone, and waves wildly.

"Tori! Hey!"

"Get me out," I say, laying my hand flat against the window.

"Are you sure it's locked?"

"No, I just *forgot* how to open a door."

"I'll open it if you do something for me first."

I bash the window several more times, as if he's some kind of animal and I'm trying to scare him into action. "I quite literally do not have time for this—"

"Just one thing."

I stare at him, hoping that it's strong enough to paralyze, if not kill him.

He shrugs at me, though I don't know why. "Smile."

I slowly shake my head. "What is wrong with you? You don't understand what just happened to me."

"If you prove to me you have the capacity to smile, I will believe that you are a human being and I will let you out." He's completely serious.

My hand drops. I could not be smiling any less than I am now. "I hate you."

"No, you don't."

"Just let me out."

"You asked me if I was a real person." He adjusts his glasses and his voice suddenly quiets. It's unnerving. "Did it occur to you that I might not believe that *you* are a real person?"

So I smile. I don't know what it ends up looking like, but I move my cheek muscles and wrench the sides of my mouth up a little to make the crescent-moon shape with my lips. Michael's reaction reveals that he had not, in fact, expected me to do it. I immediately regret giving in. His eyes stretch wide and his own smile drops and is gone.

"Holy crap," he says. "That was actually really difficult for you."

I let it go. "All right. We're both real. Turn the lock."

And he does.

We look at each other, and then I start to barge past him, but he steps in front of me, placing his hands on each side of the doorframe.

"*What?*" I'm going to have a breakdown. This guy. Jesus Christ.

"Why were you locked in an IT room?" he asks. His eyes are so wide. Is he . . . is he *concerned*? "What happened in there?"

I glance to one side. I don't really want to look him in the eyes. "Solitaire hacked the whiteboard. Sent round a message to the prefects. And a video."

Michael gasps like a cartoon. He removes his hands from the doorframe and places them on my shoulders. I cower backwards.

"What did it say?" he asks, half-amazed, half-terrified. "What was the video?"

In any other situation, I don't think I'd bother telling him. I mean, who cares, right?

"Go look for yourself," I mutter.

I step back into the room and he skips round me towards the projector computer.

"It's just something stupid," I say, collapsing onto a swivel chair next to him. "And actually you won't be able to do anything on that computer anyw—"

But Michael is moving the mouse totally normally, flying the cursor back towards the Word document.

He reads the entire message aloud.

"Patience kills," he mumbles. "*Patience kills.*"

He then insists that we watch the video, which I agree to mostly because I thought it was so lovely the first time. When it finishes, he says, "You thought that was 'just something stupid'?"

There's a pause.

"I can play the violin," I say.

"Seriously?"

"Er, yeah. Well, not anymore. I stopped practicing a few years ago."

Michael gives me this weird look. But then it's gone and suddenly he's impressed. "You know, I bet they've hacked the whole school. That is absolutely outstanding."

Before I have a chance to disagree, he's opened up a browser and typed in the URL for Solitaire.

The Solitaire blog pops up. With a new text post at the top of the screen. Michael breathes so loudly I can hear him.

00:30 January 11th

Solitairians.

The first Solitaire meetup will take place on Saturday, January 22nd, 8 p.m. onwards, at the third house from the river bridge.

All are welcome.

When I look up at Michael, he is carefully taking a photograph of the post on his phone.

"This is gold," he says. "This is the best discovery I've made all day."

"It's only half past seven," I say.

"It's important to make lots of discoveries every day." He stands back up. "That's what makes one day different from the next."

If that statement is true, that explains a lot of things about my life.

"You look so freaked out." Michael sits down in the chair next to me and leans forward so that his face is parallel to my own. "We made progress. Be excited!"

"Progress? Progress with what?"

He frowns. "The Solitaire investigation. We have made a significant leap forward here."

"Oh."

"You still don't sound excited."

"Can you imagine me being excited about anything?"

"Yes, I can actually."

I glare at his stupid, smug face. He starts tapping his fingers together.

"Anyway," he says, "we're going to their meetup."

I hadn't thought about that. "Er, we are?"

"*Er*, yeah. It's next Saturday. I will drag you there if I have to."

"Why do you want to go? What is the point of this?"

He opens his eyes very wide. "You aren't curious?"

He's delusional. He's more delusional than I am, and that's saying something.

"Um, look," I say. "It's perfectly okay to hang out, like, if you want. But I don't care about Solitaire and, to be totally honest, I don't really want to get involved. So, er, yeah. Sorry."

He gives me a long look. "Interesting."

I say nothing.

"They locked you in this room," he says, "and you still don't care. Why not consider it this way: They're the evil criminal organization and you're Sherlock Holmes. I'll be John Watson. But we've got to be the Benedict Cumberbatch and Martin Freeman Sherlock and Watson because the BBC *Sherlock* is infinitely greater than all other adaptations."

I stare at him.

"It's the only adaptation that gets the bromance *right*."

"Jesus Christ," I whisper.

Eventually, we get up and leave. Or at least I do. And he follows, shutting the door behind him. For the first time, I realize that he's wearing just his shirt, tie, and trousers, no jumper or blazer.

"Aren't you cold?" I say.

He blinks at me. His glasses are enormous. His hair is so neat that it's almost made of stone. "Why, are you?"

We head down the corridor and, after we've almost reached the end, I notice that Michael is no longer at my heels. I turn round. He has stopped directly in front of C16 and opened it up.

He frowns. It looks a little odd on his face.

"What?" I ask.

It takes him longer than it should to answer. "Nothing," he says. "I thought there would be something here, but there's nothing."

Before I have a chance to question what the bloody hell he's talking about, someone behind me cries, "Tori!"

I spin back round. Zelda is striding towards me with the energy of someone who wakes up at 6:00 a.m. on Sundays to go jogging. "Tori! Have you found anything?"

I think about whether to lie or not.

"No, we didn't find anything. Sorry."

"What do you mean 'we'?"

I turn back to Michael. Or the space where Michael had been standing. But he's not there. Only then do I wonder what it really was that made him decide to turn up at school at half past seven in the morning.

TEN

I spend the rest of the day thinking about what Michael had said in front of C16. Later on, I go back to have a look myself, but he was right—there's nothing.

I guess getting locked in an IT room kind of shook me up.

I don't tell Becky about any of the Solitaire stuff. She's very busy spreading the word about her costume birthday party, which is to be held on Friday, and I don't think she'd really care much.

At lunch, Lucas finds me in the common room. I'm trying to read another chapter of *Pride and Prejudice*, but I think I'm just going to watch the film version because this book is brain-melting. The common room is pretty empty—everyone's probably walked up to Asda because the food in our school is prison food.

"All right?" Lucas says, seating himself at my table. I hate that. *All right.* I mean, is it a greeting or a question? Do you respond with "good, thanks" or "hello"?

"Not too bad," I say, sitting up a little. "You?"

"I'm good, thanks."

I can physically feel him searching for something to say. After a stupidly long pause, he reaches towards me and taps the book I'm holding. "You hate reading, right? Why don't you just watch the film?"

I blink at him and say, "Er, I don't know."

After another stupidly long pause, he asks, "You going to Becky's on Friday?"

What a dumb question.

"Er, yeah," I say. "I assume you are too."

"Yes, yeah. Who are you dressing up as?"

"I don't know yet."

He nods as if what I've said actually means something.

"Well, I'm sure you'll look good," he says, and then quickly adds, "because, you know, when we were little, you were really into dressing up and stuff."

I don't remember ever dressing up as anything except a Jedi. I shrug at Lucas. "I'll find something."

And then he just turns bright red, like he does, and sits there watching me attempt to read for some time. So awkward. Jesus Christ. Eventually, he gets out his phone and starts texting and, when he goes off to talk to Evelyn, I get to wondering why he is always hovering around like some ghost who doesn't want to be forgotten. I don't want to talk to him really. I mean, I thought that it'd be nice to try and rekindle this friendship, but it's too hard. I don't want to talk to anyone.

Of course, I tell Charlie everything when we get home. He doesn't know what to say about Solitaire's mysterious message. Instead, he tells me I should stop talking to Michael so much. I am not sure what I think about that.

At dinner, Dad asks, "How'd it go this morning?"

"We didn't find anything," I say. Another lie. I must be borderline pathological.

Dad starts talking about another book that he's going to lend me. He's always lending me books. Dad went to university when he was thirty-two and did an English literature degree. He now works in IT. Nevertheless, he's always hoping that I'll turn out to be some philosophical thinker who has read a lot of Chekhov and James Joyce.

Anyway, this time it's *Metamorphosis* by Franz Kafka. I nod and smile and try to sound a little interested, but it probably isn't at all convincing.

Charlie quickly changes the subject by telling us about some film he and Nick watched over the weekend, *An Education*, which from Charlie's description sounds like a total mockery and patronization of teenage girls worldwide. Oliver then tells us about his new toy tractor and why it's so much more majestic than all his other toy tractors. To Mum and Dad's delight, we finish dinner within one hour, which must be a new record.

"Well done, Charlie! Great job!" says Dad, slapping him on the back, but Charlie just winces away from him. Mum nods and smiles, which is about as expressive as she gets. It's like Charlie's won the Nobel Prize. He escapes the kitchen without saying a word and comes to watch *The Big Bang Theory* with me. It's not a very funny program, but I still seem to watch at least one episode every single day.

"Who would I be," I ask at one point, "if I were any of the *Big Bang Theory* characters?"

"Sheldon," says Charlie without hesitation. "But, like, not as loud about your views."

I turn my head towards him. "Wow. I'm offended."

Charlie snorts. "He's the only reason this show is any good, Victoria."

I think about this and then nod. "That's probably true."

Charlie lies still on the sofa, and I watch him for a minute. His eyes are sort of glazed, like he's not really watching the TV, and he's fiddling with his shirtsleeves.

"Who would I be?" he asks.

I stroke my chin thoughtfully, before declaring, "Howard. Definitely. Because you're always chatting up the ladies . . ."

Charlie chucks a cushion at me from the other sofa. I scream and cower in the corner, before hurling a barrage of cushions back at him.

Tonight I watch the Keira Knightley *Pride & Prejudice* and find it to be almost as dreadful as the book. The only tolerable character is Mr. Darcy. I don't see why Elizabeth finds him proud at the beginning because it's quite clearly obvious that he's just shy. Any normal human being should be able to identify that as shyness and feel sorry for the poor guy because he's dreadful at parties and social gatherings. It's not really his fault. It's just the way he is.

I blog some more and lie awake listening to the rain and forget what the time is and forget to change into my pyjamas. I add *Metamorphosis* to my pile of unread books. I put *The Breakfast Club* on, but I'm not really watching so I skip to the best part, the part where they're all sitting in a circle and they reveal those deep and personal things and they cry and all that. I watch that scene three times and then turn it off. I listen for the giant/demon, but it's more of a rumbling tonight, a deep growling rumble like a drum. In the swirly wallpaper of my room, stooped yellow figures creep back and forth and back and forth until I'm hypnotized. In my bed, someone has placed an enormous glass cage on top of me and the air is slowly stewing sour. In my dreams, I'm running around in circles atop a cliff, but there's a boy in a red hat catching me every time I try to jump off.

ELEVEN

"I'm not joking, Tori. This is an extremely serious decision."

I look Becky squarely in the eye. "Oh, I know. This could determine the whole future of human existence."

We are in her bedroom. It's 4:12 p.m., Friday. I'm sitting cross-legged on her double bed. Everything in here is pink and black; if this room were a person, it would be a Kardashian on a moderate income. There's a poster of Edward Cullen and Bella Swan on the wall. Every time I see it I want to put it through a shredder.

"No, seriously though, I'm not even joking." She holds up each of the costumes again, one in each hand. "Tinker Bell or an angel?"

I stare at each. They're not very different, except one is green and one is white.

"Tinker Bell," I say. "At least Tinker Bell is from a movie. 'Angel' has to be one of the most generic fancy dress costumes ever."

She nods and chucks the angel outfit onto a steadily growing mountain of clothes. "That's what I thought." She starts changing. "Who are you going as again?"

I shrug. "I wasn't going to dress up. I thought I could wear my invisibility cloak."

Becky, in just her bra and knickers, puts her hands on her hips. I know I shouldn't feel awkward because I've been her best friend for over five years. I still do though. Since when did nudity become so normal?

"Tori. You are dressing up. It's my fancy-dress party and I say so."

"Fine." I think hard, weighing up my options. "I could go as . . . Snow White?"

Becky pauses as if waiting for the punchline.

I frown. "What?"

"Nothing. I didn't say anything."

"You don't think I could go as Snow White."

"No, no, you could be Snow White. If you want."

I look at my hands. "All right. I'll . . . er . . . think about it." I twirl my thumbs. "I could . . . make my hair . . . all wavy . . ."

She seems satisfied and puts on the tiny green dress with fairy wings.

"Are you going to try and talk to people tonight?" she asks.

"Is that an actual question or an order?"

"An order."

"I make no promises."

Becky laughs and pats me on my cheek. I hate that. "Don't worry. I'll look after you. I always do, don't I?"

💬

At home, I put on a white shirt and a black skater skirt I bought once for some job interview I never showed up to. Then I locate my favorite black jumper and black tights. My hair is just about long enough to style into tiny plaits and I draw on more eyeliner than usual.

Wednesday Addams. I was sort of kidding with Snow White. I despise Disney anyway.

I leave the house around seven. Nick, Charlie, and Oliver are just sitting down to dinner. Mum and Dad are going to see a play and then staying at a hotel tonight. To be honest, it was Charlie and me who insisted that they stay overnight rather than make the two-hour drive home. I guess they were kind of worried about not being there for Charlie. I almost decided to stay home and not go to Becky's party, but Charlie assured everyone that he would be fine, which I'm sure he will be, because Nick's staying round this evening. And I'm not even going to be out for very long.

💬

It's a dark party. The lights are dimmed and teenagers are spilling out of the house. I pass the smokers and the social smokers who gather in rings outside. Smoking is so pointless. The only reason I can think of for smoking is if you want to die. I don't know. Maybe they all want to die. I recognize most people from school and from Truham, and there are Year 11s through to Year 13s here and I know for a fact that Becky doesn't know them all personally.

A selection of Our Lot is squeezed into the conservatory, along with a few other people I don't know. Evelyn, scrunched into the corner of a sofa, spots me first.

"Tori!" She waves so I wander over. Eyeing me thoughtfully, she says, "Who are you?"

"Wednesday Addams," I say.

"Who?"

"Have you seen *The Addams Family*?"

"No."

I shuffle my feet. "Oh." Her own outfit is rather spectacular: straightened hair put up in a classy bun, insect sunglasses, and a fifties dress. "You're Audrey Hepburn."

Evelyn throws her arms into the air. "THANK YOU! *Someone* at this party has some bloody *culture!*"

Lucas is here too, sitting next to a girl and a boy who have basically merged into one being. He's wearing a beret and a rolled-sleeve stripy T-shirt with these skin-tight, ankle-length black jeans and he has an actual string of garlic bulbs hung around his neck. Somehow, he looks both very fashionable and very ridiculous. He waves shyly at me with his beer can. "Tori! *Bonjour!*"

I wave back and then practically run away.

First, I go to the kitchen. There are a lot of Year 11s in here, mostly girls dressed as a variety of Disney princesses, and three boys dressed as Superman. They're chatting excitedly about Solitaire's pranks, apparently finding them hilarious. One girl even claims she took part in them.

Everyone seems to be talking about the Solitaire meetup blog post—the one that Michael and I found after he broke me out of that IT classroom. Apparently, the entire town is planning to attend.

I find myself standing next to a lonely-looking girl, possibly a Year 11 but I'm not too sure, who is dressed as a very accurate David Tennant from *Doctor Who*. I immediately feel a kind of connection with her because she looks so alone.

She looks at me and as it's too late to pretend I haven't been staring I say, "Your costume is, er, really good."

"Thank you," she says, and I nod and walk off.

Ignoring the beers and WKDs and Bacardi Breezers, I raid Becky's fridge for some diet lemonade. With my plastic cup in hand, I amble into the garden.

It's a truly magnificent garden: slightly sloped with a pond at the bottom, enclosed by clusters of bare willow trees. Groups are huddled all over the wooden decking and the grass, even though it's about 0 degrees Celsius. Somehow, Becky has got her hands on an actual floodlight. It's as bright as the sun and the groups of teenagers spill swaying shadows over the grass. I spot Becky/Tinker Bell with a different group of Year 12s. I go up to her.

"Hey," I say, sliding into the circle.

"Toriiiiiiiii!" She's got a bottle of Baileys Irish Cream in her hand with one of those curly plastic straws in it. "Dude! Guess what! I've got something so amazing to tell you! It's just so amazing! You're going to die, it's so so so amazing! You are going to die!"

I smile at her even though she's shaking me by the shoulders and spilling Baileys on me.

"You. Are going. To DIE."

"Yes, yes, I'm going to die—"

"You know Ben Hope?"

Yes, I know Ben Hope, and I also know exactly what she's about to say.

"Ben Hope asked me out," she splutters.

"Oh," I say, "my God!"

"I know! I, like, did not expect a *thing*! We were chatting earlier and he admitted he liked me; oh my God, he was so cute and *awkward!*" And then she talks for quite a while about Ben Hope while sipping on her Baileys, and I'm smiling and nodding and definitely feeling really pleased for her.

After a while, Becky starts repeating the whole story to some girl dressed as Minnie Mouse and I feel myself getting a bit bored so I check my blog on my phone. There's a little (1) symbol, signifying I have a message:

Anonymous: *Thought for the day: Why do cars always part for ambulances?*

I read the message several times. It could be from anyone, I guess, though no one I know in real life knows about my blog. Stupid anons. Why do cars always part for ambulances? Because the world is not filled with assholes. That's why.

Because the world is not filled with assholes.

As soon as I make that deduction, Lucas finds me. He's a little bit drunk.

"I can't work out who you are," he says, always so *embarrassed*.

"I'm Wednesday Addams."

"Aah, so cute, so cute." He nods knowingly, but I can tell that he has no idea who Wednesday Addams is.

I look past him, out into the floodlit garden. All the people are just blurred darkness. I feel a bit sick and this diet lemonade is giving me a nasty taste in my mouth. I want to go and pour it down the sink, but I think I'll feel even more lost if I don't have something to hold on to.

"Tori?"

I look at him. The garlic was a bad move. It doesn't smell great. "Mm?"

"I asked if you were all right. You look like you're having a midlife crisis."

"It's not a midlife crisis. It's just a life crisis."

"Pardon? I can't hear you."

"I'm fine. Just bored."

He smiles at me like I'm joking, but I'm not joking. All parties are boring.

"You can go and talk to other people, you know," I say. "I really don't have anything interesting to say."

"You always have interesting things to say," he says. "You just don't say them."

I lie and say I need another drink even though my cup is more than half-full and I feel really sick. I get out of the garden. I'm out of breath and so angry for no reason. I barge through the crowds of stupid, drunk teenagers and lock myself in the downstairs bathroom. Someone's been sick in here—I can smell it. I look at myself in the mirror. My eyeliner has smudged so I sort it out. Then I tear up and ruin it again and try not to start crying. I wash my hands three times and take the plaits out of my hair because they look idiotic.

Someone's banging on the door of the bathroom. I've been in here for ages just staring at myself in the mirror, watching my eyes tear up and dry and tear up and dry. I open the door ready to punch them in the face and find myself directly opposite Michael goddamn Holden.

"Oh, thank Christ." He races inside and, without bothering to let me leave or shut the door, he lifts the toilet seat and starts to pee. "Thank. Christ. I thought I was going to have to piss in the flower bed, for Christ's sake."

"All right, just pee with a lady present," I say.

He waves his hand casually.

I get out of there.

As I exit through the front door, Michael catches up to me. He's dressed as Sherlock Holmes. Even the hat.

"Where are you going?" he asks.

I shrug. "It's too hot in there."

"It's too cold out here."

"Since when did you acquire a body temperature?"

"Will you ever be able to talk to me without making a sarcastic comment?"

I turn and start walking farther away, but he's still in pursuit.

"Why are you following me?"

"Because I don't know anyone else here."

"Don't you have any Year 13 friends?"

"I—er . . ."

I stop on the pavement outside Becky's drive.

"I think I'm going home," I say.

"Why?" he asks. "Becky's your friend. It's her birthday."

"She won't mind," I say. She won't notice.

"What are you going to do at home?" he asks.

Blog. Sleep. Blog. "Nothing."

"Why don't we crash in a room upstairs and watch a film?"

Coming from any other person's mouth, it would sound like he's asking me to go into a room and have sex with him, but because it's Michael who says this, I know that he's being completely serious.

I notice that the diet lemonade in my cup has gone. I can't remember when I drank it. I want to go home, but I don't because I know I won't sleep. I'll just lie there in my room. Michael's hat looks really stupid. He probably borrowed that tweed jacket from a dead body.

"Fine," I say.

TWELVE

There is a line that you cross when forming relationships with people. Crossing this line occurs when you transfer from knowing someone to knowing *about* someone, and Michael and I cross that line at Becky's seventeenth-birthday party.

We go upstairs into Becky's room. He, of course, begins to investigate, while I drop and roll onto the bed. He passes the poster of Edward Cullen and Bella No-Expression Swan, raising a skeptical eyebrow at it. He trails along the shelf of dancing-show photographs and medals and the shelf of preteen books that have lain untouched for years, and he steps over the piles and piles of crumpled dresses and shorts and T-shirts and knickers and bras and schoolbooks and bags and miscellaneous pieces of paper until, finally, he opens a wardrobe, bypasses the shelves of folded-up clothes, and locates a small row of DVDs.

He pulls out *Moulin Rouge*, but, seeing the look on my face, quickly replaces it. A similar thing happens when he retrieves *It's a Boy Girl Thing*. After a moment more, he gasps and grabs a third DVD, leaps across the room to the flat-screen, and switches it on.

"We're watching *Beauty and the Beast*," he says.

"No, we are not," I say.

"I think you'll find that we are," he says.

"Please," I say. "No. What about *The Matrix*? *Lost in Translation*? *Lord of the Rings*?" I don't know why I'm saying this. Becky owns none of these films.

"I'm doing this for your own good." He inserts the DVD. "I believe that your psychological development has substantially suffered due to lack of Disney charm."

I don't bother asking what he's talking about. He clambers onto the bed next to me and props himself up on the headboard with a pillow. The Disney logo appears on screen. Already I can feel my eyes bleeding.

"Have you ever even watched a Disney film?" he asks.

"Er, yeah."

"Why do you hate Disney?"

"I don't hate Disney."

"Then why don't you want to watch *Beauty and the Beast*?"

I turn my head. He's not watching the film, even though it's started. "I don't like films that are fake," I say. "Where the characters and the story are really . . . perfect. Things don't happen like that in real life."

He smiles, but it's a sad smile. "Isn't that the point of films?"

I wonder why I'm here. I wonder why he's here. The pathetic dubstep beat downstairs is the only thing I can hear. There are some cartoons on the screen, but really they're just moving shapes. He starts talking to me.

"Did you know," he says, "that, in the original story, Belle has two sisters? But in this film she's an only child. I wonder why. It's not that fun being an only child."

"Are you an only child?"

"Yep."

This is mildly interesting. "I've got two brothers," I say.

"Are they like you?"

"No. They're really not."

The Beauty is being courted by a heavily muscled man. He is not attractive, but I sympathize with his dislike of literature.

"She really likes to read," I say, shaking my head at the girl in blue. "That's got to be unhealthy."

"Don't you do English lit A level?"

"Yes, because I can bullshit my way through it, but I don't approve of it. I hate books."

"I probably should have done English. I would have been good at it."

"Why didn't you?"

He looks at me and smiles. "I think it's better to just read and not study books."

The Beauty has sacrificed her freedom to save her father. It's very sentimental. And now she's crying about it.

"Tell me something interesting about you," says Michael.

I think for a moment. "Did you know that I was born on the day that Kurt Cobain supposedly killed himself?"

"Actually, yes. He was only twenty-seven, the poor guy. Twenty-seven. Maybe we'll die when we're twenty-seven."

"There's nothing romantic about death. I hate it when people use Kurt Cobain's suicide as an excuse to worship him for being such a tormented soul."

Michael pauses and stares at me, before saying, "Yeah. I guess so."

Beauty has gone on a hunger strike. That is until the cutlery and crockery of the house put on a singing and dancing performance for her. Now she's being chased by wolves. I am struggling to keep up with the plotline.

"Tell me something interesting about you," I say.

"Erm," he says, "I'm, like, ridiculously unintelligent?"

I frown at him. This is obviously untrue.

He reads my mind. "Seriously. I haven't got above a C grade in any subject since Year 8."

"What? Why?"

"I just . . ."

It seems almost impossible for someone like Michael to be unintelligent. People like Michael—people who get stuff done—they're always smart. Always.

"When it comes to the exams . . . I generally don't write what they want me to write. I'm not very good at, er, sorting out all the stuff in my head. Like, I take biology A level and I completely understand what polypeptide synthesis is, but I can't write it down. I just don't know what the examiners want to hear. I don't know whether I just forget things, or maybe I don't know how I'm supposed to explain it. I just *don't know*. And it's fucking *horrible*."

Throughout this, he makes swirly gestures with his hands. I imagine all of the pieces of information flying around in strands inside his brain, unable to form themselves into comprehensible words. It seems to make sense.

"It's so unfair," he continues. "School literally doesn't care about you unless you're good at writing stuff down or you're good at memorizing or you can solve bloody equations. What about the other important things in life? Like being a decent human being?"

"I hate school," I say.

"You hate everything."

"It's funny because it's true."

He turns to me again. We look at each other. On screen, a petal falls from the rose, which I'm pretty sure is symbolic of something.

"Your eyes are different colors," I say.

"Did I not tell you that I'm a magical anime girl?"

"Seriously, why though?"

"My blue eye conceals the power of my past life, and I use it to summon my guardian angels to assist me in my struggle against the forces of darkness."

"Are you drunk?"

"I'm a poet."

"Well, control yourself, Lord Tennyson."

He grins. *"The stream will cease to flow."* He's quoting a poem obviously, but one I've never heard. *"The wind will cease to blow, the clouds will*

78

cease to fleet, the heart will cease to beat; for all things must die."

I chuck a pillow at him. He leans over to avoid it, but my aim is spectacular.

"All right, all right," he laughs. "It's not as romantic as it looks. Someone threw a rock at my eye when I was two, so, basically, I'm pretty much half-blind."

On screen, they're dancing. It's a little odd. An old woman is singing. I find myself singing along—apparently, I've heard this song before. Michael joins me. We sing alternate lines.

And then we are silent for a long time, watching the colors on the screen. I don't know how long the silence lasts, but at some point I hear Michael sniff and I see him move his hand up to his face. When I look round, I see that he's crying, actually crying. I am momentarily confused. I study the screen. The Beast has just died. And Beauty is holding him, crying herself, and oh, wait, a tear falls onto his fur, and then all kinds of trippy magic happens and, yep, there you go, he has miraculously returned from the dead. Oh, and he's become handsome as well. Isn't that fantastic? This is the kind of crap I hate. Unrealistic. Sentimental.

But Michael is crying. I don't really know what to do. He's got one hand on his face, and his eyes and nose are scrunched up. It's like he's trying to hold the tears inside.

I decide to pat his other hand, which is resting on the bed. I hope this comes across as comforting, not sarcastic. I think it turns out okay because he grabs my hand in return and squeezes it with extreme force.

The film ends shortly after that. He turns it off with the remote and we sit in silence looking at the black screen.

"I knew your brother," Michael says, after a very long time.

"Charlie?"

"From Truham . . ."

I turn my head, not really finding anything to say.

Michael continues. "I never spoke to him. He always seemed sort of quiet. But kind."

It's then that I decide to tell him. I don't know why this happens. But I get this urge. My brain gives up. I can't hold on to it.

I tell him about Charlie.

Everything.

About his eating disorder. His obsessive compulsions. The self-harm.

To be honest, I shouldn't have brought it up. He spent a few weeks at a psych ward and he's in therapy now. And he's got Nick. I mean, he's still recovering, but he's gonna be fine. It's all gonna be fine.

I don't know when I fall asleep, but I do. Not fully asleep. I stop being able to tell whether I'm awake or whether I'm dreaming. It's probably weird to fall asleep in this sort of situation, but I'm starting to not really care about stuff like that anymore. What surprises me the most is how suddenly it happens. Normally, it takes forever. Normally, when I'm trying to sleep, I do all these silly things like I roll over and imagine that I'm sleeping next to someone and I reach out and caress their hair. Or I clasp my hands together and after a little while I start thinking it's somebody else's hand I'm holding, not my own. I swear to God there's something wrong with me. I really do.

But this time I feel myself roll over slightly so I'm resting on his chest, under his arm. He smells vaguely of bonfires. At some point, I think someone opens the door and sees us lying there half asleep together. Whoever it is looks at us for a moment before quietly shutting the door again. The shouting downstairs begins to ease even though the music is still pumping. I half listen for any demonic creatures outside the window, but it's a silent night. Nothing traps me. It's nice. I feel the air in the room and it's like there is none.

My phone rings.

"Hello?"

"Tori, are you coming home yet?"

"Oliver? Why aren't you in bed?"

"I was watching *Doctor Who*."

"You didn't watch the Weeping Angels episode, did you?"

". . ."

"Ollie? Are you all right? Why did you call me?"

". . ."

"Oliver? Are you there?"

"Something's wrong with Charlie."

My face must then do something very unusual because Michael gives me this look. This funny, terrified look.

"What . . . has happened?"

". . ."

"What's happened, Oliver? What's Charlie done? Where is he?"

"I can't get in the kitchen. Charlie shut the door and I can't open it. I can hear him."

". . ."

"When are you coming home, Tori?"

"I'm coming home right now."

I hang up.

Michael is awake. I am cross-legged in the middle of the bed. He is cross-legged opposite me.

"Shit," I say. "Shit shit shit shit shit shit fucking fuck."

Michael doesn't even ask. He just says, "I'll take you home."

We're running. Out the door and down the stairs and through the people. Some still partying, some piled on the floor, some making out, some crying. I'm almost at the front door when Becky catches me. She is fucked.

"I'm *fucked*." She grabs my arm really tight.

"I'm going now, Becky."

"You're so *cute*, Tori. I miss you. I love you so much. You are so *beautiful* and cute."

"Becky—"

She flops onto my shoulder, knees buckling. "Don't be sad. Promise me, Tori. Promise me. Promise you won't be sad anymore."

"I promise. I have to—"

"I ha-hate Jack. He is such a . . . such . . . such a . . . bitch. I deserve a . . . someone like Ben. He is so *beautiful*. Like you. You hate everything, but you're still beautiful. You're like . . . you're a ghost. I love you so much . . . so much. Don't be . . . don't . . . sad anymore."

I don't really want to leave her because she is beyond wasted, but I need to get home. Michael actually pushes me forward, and we abandon Becky, whose legs look too spindly now, her makeup too thick, her hair too backcombed.

Michael is running and so am I. He gets on his bike. It's a real bicycle. Do people even ride these anymore?

"Get on the back," he says.

"You are joking," I say.

"It's that or walk."

I get on the back.

And with that, Sherlock Holmes and Wednesday Addams fly into the night. He's cycling so fast that the houses we pass blur into gray and brown wavy lines, and I'm clinging on to his waist so tight that my fingers have lost all feeling. I realize that I'm happy even though I shouldn't be, and the conflicting emotion only makes the moment more insane, more radiant, more immeasurable. The air tears at my face and makes my eyes water and I lose track of where we are, even though I know this town inside out, and all I can think of is that this might have been what that boy who flew away with E.T. felt like. Like I could die right now and it wouldn't matter.

We're at my house within fifteen minutes. Michael doesn't come inside. He has manners, I'll give him that. He sits up on the bike as I look back at him.

"I hope he's all right," he says.

I nod.

He nods. And cycles away. I unlock the door and enter my house.

THIRTEEN

Oliver trots sleepily down the stairs. *Thomas the Tank Engine* pyjamas. Teddy in his arm. I'm glad that he's never understood what's wrong with Charlie.

"You all right, Oliver?"

"Mmmyeah."

"You gonna go to bed?"

"What about Charlie?"

"He'll be fine. Leave it all to me."

Oliver nods and ambles back up the stairs, rubbing his eyes. I rush towards the kitchen door, which is closed.

I feel sick. I'm not even fully awake.

"Charlie." I knock on the door.

Total silence. I attempt to get in, but he's blocked it with something.

"Open the door, Charles. I'm not joking. I'll break the door."

"No, you won't." His voice is dead. Empty. But I'm relieved, because he's alive.

I turn the handle down and push with my whole body.

"Don't come in!" He sounds panicked, which makes me panicked because Charlie is never panicked and that is what makes him Charlie. "Don't come in here! Please!" There's a clattering of things being frantically moved around.

I keep heaving my body onto the door and whatever is blocking it begins to move away. I make a gap large enough for me to slip inside, and I do.

"No, go away! Leave me alone!"

I look at him.

"Get out!"

He's been crying. His eyes are dark red and purple and the darkness of the room drowns him in a haze. There's a plate of lasagna on the kitchen table, cold, untouched. All of our food has been removed from the cupboards and the fridge and the freezer and set out in order of size and color in various piles around the room. There are a couple of tissues in his hands.

He's not

better.

"I'm sorry," he croaks, slumped in the chair, head rolled backwards, eyes vacant. "I'm sorry. I'm sorry. I didn't mean to. I'm sorry."

I can't do anything. It's hard not to throw up.

"I'm sorry," he keeps saying. "I'm so sorry."

"Where's Nick?" I say. "Why is he not with you?"

He goes deep red and then mumbles something inaudible.

"What?"

"We argued. He left."

I start shaking my head. It goes from left to right to left to right in an uncontrollable act of defiance. "That bastard. That stupid bastard."

"No, Victoria, it was my fault."

My phone is in my hand and I'm punching in Nick's number. He picks up after two rings.

"Hello?"

"Do you understand the severity of what you have done, you absolute prick?"

"Tori? What are you—"

"If Oliver hadn't called me, Charlie might have . . ." I can't even say it. "This is entirely your fault."

"I'm not— Wait, what the hell's happened?"

"What the hell do you *think* has happened? He's fucking relapsed. You upset him and he's fucking relapsed. Fuck you."

"I didn't—"

"I trusted you. You were supposed to look after him and now I've walked into the kitchen and he's . . . I shouldn't have gone out. I should have been here. We're—I'm the person who is supposed to *be there* when this happens."

"Wait, wh—"

I'm holding the phone so tight, I'm shaking. Charlie is looking at me, silent tears falling from his eyes. He is so old now. He's not a little kid. In a couple of months, he'll be sixteen, like me. He looks older than me, for God's sake. He could pass for eighteen, easy.

I drop the phone, draw up a chair next to my brother, and put my arms round him.

Nick gets here and hugs Charlie immediately, the two of them mumbling apologies to each other for whatever argument they'd had. Then we clear up the kitchen. Charlie keeps wincing and clutching his head as I upset all his precious piles of tins and packets, but I do it anyway, and soon he starts to help too.

I get rid of the lasagna. I find the first-aid kit and put plasters on Charlie's arm, and by that point, he's kind of calmed down, and sounds more frustrated at himself than anything else. We knew that there'd be good days and bad days and sometimes there'd be particularly bad days like these, but he only self-harms when he's at his absolute worst. It'd been nearly three months since that last happened. I thought therapy had been helping. I thought he was doing better. I thought—

"I was doing so well," he says, and then he lets out a sad little laugh.

"This is just a blip," I tell him, and God, I hope I'm right. Just a blip. Just a relapse. He'll be fine. Everything will be fine.

Eventually, Nick and I escort him to bed.

"I'm sorry," says Charlie, lying in bed with his arm across his forehead.

I'm standing at the doorway. Nick is on the floor in Charlie's spare pyjamas, which are much too small for him, with a spare duvet and pillow. He is staring at Charlie with an expression somehow simultaneously encompassing fear and love. I haven't forgiven him yet, but I know that he will redeem himself. I know that he cares about Charlie. A lot.

"I know," I say. "But I'm going to have to tell Mum and Dad."

"I know."

"I'll come back and check on you in a bit."

"Okay."

I stand there. After a while, he says, "Are . . . you okay?"

An odd question, in my opinion. He's the one who just . . . "I'm completely fine."

I turn out the light and go downstairs and call Dad. He stays calm. Too calm. I don't like it. I want him to freak out and shout and panic, but he doesn't. He tells me that they'll come home right away. I put the phone down, pour a glass of diet lemonade, and sit in the living room for a while. It's the middle of the night. The curtains are all open.

You do not find many people like Charlie Spring in the world. I suppose I have implied this already. You especially do not find many people like Charlie Spring at all-boys' schools. If you want my opinion, all-boys' schools sound like hell. Maybe it's because I don't know many boys. Maybe it's because I get a pretty bad impression of the guys I see coming out of the Truham gates, pouring Lucozade into each other's hair, calling each other gay, and bullying gingers. I don't know.

I don't know anything about Charlie's life at that school.

I head back upstairs and peer into Charlie's room. He and Nick are now both fast asleep in Charlie's bed, Charlie curled into Nick's chest. I shut the door.

I go to my room. I start shaking again and I look at myself in the mirror for a long time and begin to wonder if I really am Wednesday Addams. I think back to the last time Charlie relapsed. October. That was worse.

It's very dark in my room, but my blog home page, open on my laptop screen, acts as a dim blue lamp. I pace around in circles, around and around until my feet hurt. I put on some Bon Iver and then some Muse and then some Noah and the Whale—you know, really dumb, angsty stuff. I cry and then I don't. There's a text on my phone, but I don't read it. I listen to the dark. They're all coming to get you. Your heartbeats are footsteps. Your brother is psychotic. You don't have any friends. Nobody feels bad for you. *Beauty and the Beast* isn't real. It's funny because it's true. Don't be sad anymore. Don't be sad anymore.

FOURTEEN

Michael Holden **Calling**

"Hello?"

"I didn't wake you up, did I?"

"Michael? No."

"Good. Sleep is important."

"How did you get my number?"

"You called me, remember? Back in the IT room? I saved your number."

"That's very sneaky of you."

"I'd call it resourceful."

"Did you call about Charlie?"

"I called about you."

". . ."

"Is Charlie okay?"

"He just had a bad night. He's at therapy with our parents right now."

"Where are you?"

"In bed."

"At two in the afternoon?"

"Yeah."

"Could I . . ."

"What?"

"Could I come over?"

"Why?"

"I don't like the thought of you there on your own. You remind me of an old person who lives alone, like, with cats and daytime television."

"Oh, really?"

"And I am a friendly young chap who would like to pop over so you can reminisce about the war and share some tea and biscuits."

"I don't like tea."

"But you like biscuits. Everyone likes biscuits."

"I'm not in a biscuit mood today."

"Well, I'm still coming over, Tori."

"You don't have to come over. I'm completely fine."

"Don't *lie*."

He's coming over. I don't bother changing out of my pyjamas or brushing my hair or seeing if my face actually looks human. I don't care. I don't get out of bed, even though I'm hungry, accepting the fact that my unwillingness to get up will probably result in my death from starvation. Then I realize that I can't possibly let my parents have *two* children who knowingly starve themselves. Oh God, dilemma. Even lying in bed is stressful.

The doorbell rings and makes my decision for me.

I stand in the porch with one hand on the open door. He stands on the top step looking much too preppy and much too tall with his hair side-parted and his glasses stupidly large. His bike is chained to our fence. I hadn't noticed last night that it actually has a basket on it. It's minus a billion degrees, but he's in a T-shirt and jeans again.

He looks me up and down. "Oh dear."

I go to shut the door on him, but he holds it open with one hand. I can't stop him after that. He just grabs me. His arms wrap round me. His chin rests on my head. My arms are trapped at my sides and my cheek is sort of squashed into his chest. The wind twirls around us, but I'm not cold.

90

He makes me a cup of tea. I hate tea, for God's sake. We drink out of faded mugs at the kitchen table.

He asks me: "What do you normally do on Saturdays? Do you go out?"

"Not if I can help it," I say. "What do you do?"

"I don't really know."

I take a sip of the dirty water. "You don't know?"

He leans back. "Time passes. I do stuff. Some of it matters. Some of it doesn't."

"I thought you were an optimist."

He grins. "Just because something doesn't matter doesn't mean it's not worth doing." The light in our kitchen is off. It's very dark. "So where shall we go today?"

I shake my head. "I can't go out. Oliver's here."

He blinks at me. "Oliver?"

I wait for him to remember, but he doesn't. "My seven-year-old brother. I did tell you I had two brothers."

He blinks again. "Oh, yeah. Yeah. You did." He's really quite excited. "Is he like you? Can I meet him?"

"Um, sure . . ."

I call Oliver and he comes downstairs after a minute or so with a tractor in one hand, still with his pyjamas and dressing gown on. The dressing gown has tiger ears on the hood. He stands on the stairs, leans over the banister, and stares into the kitchen.

Michael introduces himself of course, with a wave and a blinding smile. "Hello! I'm Michael!"

Oliver introduces himself too, with equal vigor. "My name's Oliver Jonathan Spring!" he says, waving his tractor around. "And this is Tractor Tom." He holds Tractor Tom to his ear and listens before continuing. "Tractor Tom doesn't think that you're dangerous, so you're allowed to go into the living-room tractor if you want."

"I would be absolutely delighted to visit the living-room tractor," says

Michael. I think he's a little surprised. Oliver is nothing like me whatsoever.

Oliver studies him with judging eyes. After a moment's contemplation, he holds a hand up to his mouth and whispers loudly to me: "Is he your *boyfriend*?"

This actually makes me laugh. Out loud. A real laugh. Michael laughs too, and then stops and looks at me while I continue smiling. I don't think he's seen me laugh before. Has he seen me smile properly before? He doesn't say anything. He just looks.

And that is how the rest of my Saturday comes to be spent with Michael Holden.

I didn't bother changing. Michael invades our kitchen cupboards and teaches me how to make chocolate cake, and then we eat chocolate cake for the rest of the day. Michael cuts the cake into cubes, not slices, and, when I query him on this, he simply replies, "I don't like to conform to typical cake-cutting convention."

Oliver keeps running up and downstairs showing Michael his large and varied collection of tractors, in which Michael takes a politely enthusiastic interest. I have a nap in my room between 4 p.m. and 5 p.m. while Michael lies on the floor and reads *Metamorphosis*. When I wake up, he tells me why the main character isn't really the main character or something like that, and also how he didn't like the ending because the supposed main character dies. Then he apologizes for spoiling the ending for me. I remind him I don't read.

After that, the three of us clamber inside the living-room tractor and play this old board game called the Game of Life that Michael found under my bed. You receive all this money, sort of like Monopoly, and then the object of the game appears to be to have the most successful life—the best job, the highest income, the biggest house, the most insurance. It's a very odd game. Anyway, that takes up about two hours and, after another round of cake, we play *Sonic Heroes* on the PS2. Oliver triumphantly beats us both, and I have to give him a piggyback for the rest of the evening as a result. Once I put him to bed, I make Michael watch *The Royal Tenenbaums* with me. We both cry when Luke Wilson and Gwyneth Paltrow decide they have to keep their love a secret.

It is ten o'clock when Mum, Dad, and Charlie get home. Charlie goes straight upstairs to bed without saying anything to me. Michael and I are on the sofa in the living room and he's playing me some music on my laptop. He's got it hooked up to the stereo. Piano music. Or something. It's making us both doze off, and I'm leaning on him, but not in a romantic way or anything. Mum and Dad sort of stop in the doorway and just stay there, blinking, paralyzed.

"Hello," says Michael. He jumps up and holds out a hand to Dad. "I'm Michael Holden. I'm Tori's new friend."

Dad shakes it. "Michael Holden. Right. Nice to meet you, Michael."

Michael shakes Mum's hand as well, which I think is a bit weird. I don't know. I'm no expert on social etiquette.

"Right," says Mum. "Of course. Tori's friend."

"I hope it's all right that I came round," says Michael. "I met Tori a couple of weeks ago. I thought she might be a bit lonely."

"Not at all," says Dad, nodding. "That's very kind of you, Michael."

This conversation is so boring and clichéd that I'm almost tempted to fall asleep. But I don't.

Michael turns back to Dad. "I read *Metamorphosis* while I was here. Tori told me you lent it to her. I thought it was brilliant."

"You did?" The light of literature dawns in Dad's eyes. "What did you make of it?"

They carry on talking about literature while I'm lying on the sofa. I see my mum stealing glances at me, as if trying to stare the truth out of me. *No,* I telepathically tell her. No, Michael is not my boyfriend. He cries at *Beauty and the Beast.* He taught me how to make chocolate cake. He stalked me when I went to a restaurant and pretended to forget why.

FIFTEEN

When I wake up, I can't remember who I am because I'd been having some crazy dream. Soon, however, I wake up properly to find that Sunday is here. I'm still on the sofa. My phone is in my dressing-gown pocket and I look at it to check the time. 7:42 a.m.

I immediately head upstairs and peer into Charlie's room. He's still asleep, obviously, and he looks so peaceful. It would be nice if he always looked like that.

Yesterday, Michael Holden told me a lot of things, and one of those things was where he lives. Therefore—and I'm still not quite sure how or why this happens—something on this desolate Sunday makes me get up off the sofa and journey to his house on the Dying Sun.

The Dying Sun is a clifftop overlooking the river. It's the only cliff in the county. I don't know why there's a cliff over a river because there are never normally cliffs over rivers except in films and abstract documentaries about places you will never go to. But the Dying Sun is so dramatically named because, if you stand facing out on the farthest point of the cliff, you are exactly opposite the sun as it sets. A couple of years back, I decided to take a walk around our town and I still remember the long brown house that sat mere meters away from the cliff edge, like it was ready to take a leap.

Maybe it's the fact that I can actually remember all this that causes me to wander up the long country lane and halt outside the brown house on the Dying Sun at nine o'clock in the morning.

Michael's house has a wooden gate and a wooden door and a sign on its front wall reading *Jane's Cottage*. It's somewhere you'd expect either a farmer or a lonely old person to live. I stand there, just outside the gate. Coming here was a mistake. An utter mistake. It's like nine in the morning. No one is up at nine in the morning on a Sunday. I can't just knock at someone's house. That's what you did in primary school, for God's sake.

I head back down the lane.

I've taken twenty steps when I hear the sound of his front door opening.

"*Tori?*"

I stop in the road. I shouldn't have come here. I should not have come here.

"Tori? That is you, isn't it?"

Very slowly, I turn round. Michael has shut the gate and is jogging down the road towards me. He stops before me and grins his dazzling grin.

For a moment, I don't actually believe it's him. He is positively disheveled. His hair, usually gelled into a side parting, flies around in wavy tufts, and he's wearing a truly admirable amount of clothes, including a woolly jumper and woolly socks. His glasses are slipping off his nose. He doesn't look awake and his voice, normally so wispy, is a little hoarse.

"Tori!" he says, and clears his throat. "It's Tori Spring!"

Why did I come here? What was I thinking? Why am I an idiot?

"You came to my house," he says, shaking his head back and forth in what can only be described as pure amazement. "I mean, I thought you might, but I didn't at the same time . . . you know?"

I glance to one side. "Sorry."

"No, no, I'm really glad that you did. Really."

"I can go home. I didn't mean to—"

"*No.*"

He laughs, and it's a nice laugh. He runs a hand through his hair. I've never seen him do that before.

I find myself smiling back. I'm not quite sure how that happens either.

A car rolls up behind us and we quickly move to the side of the road to let it pass. The sky is still a little orange and, in every other direction except the town, all you can see are fields, many abandoned and wild, their long grass flowing like sea waves. I start to feel like I'm actually in the *Pride and Prejudice* film, you know, that bit at the end where they go out to that field in the mist and the sun is rising.

"Would you like to . . . go out?" I say. Then quickly add: "Today?"

He is literally awestruck. Why. Am I. An idiot?

"Y-yes. Definitely. Wow, yes. *Yes.*"

Why.

I look back to the house.

"You have a nice house," I say. I wonder what it's like inside. I wonder who his parents are. I wonder how he's decorated his bedroom. Posters? Lights? Maybe he painted something. Maybe he has old board games stacked up on shelves. Maybe he has a beanbag. Maybe he has figurines. Maybe he has Aztec-patterned bedsheets and black walls, and teddies in a box, and a diary under his pillow.

He looks at the house, his expression suddenly downcast.

"Yeah," he says, "I guess." Then he turns back to me. "But we should go out somewhere."

He quickly runs back to the gate and locks it. His hair is just hilarious. But kind of nice. I can't stop looking at it. He walks back and passes me, and then turns and holds out his hand. His jumper, much too big for him, flutters around his body.

"Coming?"

I step towards him. And then I do something, like, really pathetic.

"Your hair," I say, lifting my hand and taking hold of a dark strand that covers his blue eye. "It's . . . *free.*" I move the strand to one side.

I then realize what I'm doing, jump backwards, and cringe.

For what feels like an ice age, he doesn't stop looking at me with this frozen expression, and after that I swear he goes a little red. He's still holding out his hand so I take it, but that almost makes *him* jump.

"Your hand is so cold," he says. "Do you *have* any blood?"

"No," I say. "I'm a ghost. Remember?"

SIXTEEN

Something is different in the air as we stroll down the road. We are hand in hand, but definitely not in a romantic way. Michael's face spins round and round in my mind and I come to the conclusion that I do not know the boy walking next to me. I do not know him at all.

Michael takes me to a café in town named Café Rivière. It's next to the river, hence the unoriginal name, and I have been here many times before. We are the only people there apart from the elderly French owner sweeping the floor, and we sit at a table with a gingham tablecloth and a vase of flowers by a window. Michael drinks tea. I eat a croissant.

Dying, though I don't know why, to make conversation, I start with, "So why'd you change schools?"

The immediate look on his face tells me that this was not the casual question that I had intended it to be.

I cringe. "Oh, sorry. Sorry. That was nosy. You don't have to answer."

For several long moments, he continues to drink his tea. Then he puts down the cup and stares into the flowers between us.

"No, it's fine. It's not too important." He chuckles to himself, as if remembering something. "I, er, didn't get on too well with the people there. Not teachers, not students . . . I thought a change of scene might do me some good. I thought maybe I'd get along better with girls or something stupid like that." He shrugs and laughs, but it's not a funny laugh, it's a different sort of laugh. "Nope. Obviously, my personality is far too fantastic for both girls and boys to handle."

I don't know why, but I start to feel quite sad. It's not my normal type of sad, you know, the unnecessary and self-inflicted pity party sort of sad, but it's a sad that's kind of projected outwards.

"You should be on *Waterloo Road* or *Skins* or something," I say.

He laughs again. "Why's that?"

"Because you're . . ." I finish my sentence with a shrug. He replies with a smile.

We are silent for several moments more. I eat. He drinks.

"What are you doing next year?" I ask. It's a bit like I'm giving him an interview, but for once I've got this odd feeling. Like I'm *interested*. "University?"

He absently fondles his cup. "No. Yeah. No, I don't know. It's too late now anyway—the UCAS deadline was yesterday. How am I supposed to decide on a university course? Most of the time at school I can't even decide which *pen* to use."

"I thought our school, like, *makes* you apply to uni in Year 13. Or at least apprenticeships and stuff. Even if you don't accept the place in the end."

He raises his eyebrows. "You know, school can't really *make* you do anything."

The truth of this statement is like a punch in the face.

"But . . . why didn't you apply to a few unis anyway? Just in case you decide you want to go?"

"Because I *hate* school!" This is quite loud. He starts to shake his head. "The idea of having to sit in a chair for three years and learn about stuff that isn't going to help me in life *literally* disgusts me. I've always been crap at exams and I always will be, and I *hate* that everyone thinks that you *have* to go to university to have a decent life!"

I sit there, dumbstruck.

We say nothing for a minute or so before he finally meets my eyes.

"I'll probably just stick with sports," he says, calm again, with a sheepish grin.

"Oh, right. What do you play?"

"Huh?"

"What sport do you play?"

"I'm a speed skater."

"Wait, what?"

"I'm a speed skater."

"Like racing? On ice?"

"Yup."

I shake my head. "It's like you just picked the most random sport."

He nods in agreement. "I guess it is."

"Are you any good?"

There's a pause.

"I'm okay," he says.

It has started to rain. The drops fall on the river, water meeting water, and trickle down the window like the glass is crying.

"Being a skater would be pretty cool," he says. "But, you know, it's hard. Things like that are hard."

I eat a bit more croissant.

"It's raining." He leans on his hand. "If the sun came back out, there'd be a rainbow. It'd be beautiful."

I look out of the window. The sky is gray. "There doesn't need to be a rainbow for it to be beautiful."

The café owner mumbles something. An old woman hobbles inside and sits near us by a window. I notice that the flowers on our table are fake.

"What shall we do next?" asks Michael.

I take a moment to think.

"They're playing *The Empire Strikes Back* at the cinema this afternoon," I say.

"You're a *Star Wars* fan?"

I fold my arms. "Is that surprising?"

He looks at me. "You're very surprising. In general."

Then his expression changes.

"You're a *Star Wars* fan," he says.

I frown. "Er, yeah."

"And you can play the violin."

"Erm . . . yeah."

"Do you like cats?"

I start to laugh. "What in the name of fuck are you talking about?"

"Humor me for a minute."

"Fine. Fine, yeah, cats are pretty fabulous."

"And what's your opinion about Madonna? And Justin Timberlake?"

Michael is a very strange person, but this conversation is advancing more and more towards the insanity line.

"Er, yeah. Some of their songs are good. But please tell me what you're talking about. I'm starting to worry for your mental health."

"*Solitaire.*"

We both freeze, staring at each other. The *Star Wars* prank. The violin video. The cats, "Material Girl," Justin Timberlake's "SexyBack"—

"Are you suggesting what I think you're suggesting?"

"What do you think I'm suggesting?" Michael asks innocently.

"I think you're suggesting that Solitaire has something to do with *me*."

"And what do you say to that?"

"I say that's the most hilarious thing I've heard all year." I stand up and start to put on my coat. "I'm literally the dullest person on the face of the earth."

"That's what *you* think."

Instead of arguing further, I ask, "Why are you so interested in them?"

He pauses and leans back again. "I don't know. I just get curious about this stuff, you know? I want to know who's doing it. And why." He chuckles. "I have a pretty sad life as it is."

It takes a few seconds for the full impact of his final line to reach me.

It's the first time I've heard Michael Holden say something like that.

Like something I would say.

"Hey," I say. I nod at him earnestly. "So do I."

💬

Before we leave the café, Michael buys the old woman a pot of tea. Then he takes me to the ice rink to show me how fast he can skate. It turns out he's BFFs with every single staff member. He high-fives them all on the way in, and they insist on high-fiving me as well, which is kind of weird, but also makes me feel sort of cool.

Michael is an insane skater. He doesn't skate past me, he *flies*, and everything slows and I watch his face turn towards me and this smile, his smile, stretches outwards and then he just vanishes, leaving only dragon breath. I, in comparison, fall over seven times.

After I've been wobbling around on the ice for quite some time, he decides to take pity and skate with me. I clutch his hands, trying not to fall flat on my face, as he skates backwards, pulling me along and laughing so hard at my concentration-face that tiny tears emerge out of the corners of his eyes. Once I get the hang of things, we figure skate round the rink to "Radio People" by Zapp, an underrated eighties gem and coincidentally my favorite song from *Ferris Bueller's Day Off.* On the way out, after an hour or so, he shows me the picture of him on the Skating Club board, aged ten, holding a trophy high above his head.

There's no one in town apart from a few oldies. Sleepy Sunday. We visit all the antique shops. I play on a secondhand violin and I manage to remember a surprisingly large number of pieces. Michael joins in on a piano, and we jam until the shop owners decide we're too annoying and chuck us out. In another shop, we find this amazing kaleidoscope. It's wooden and slides outwards like a telescope and we take it in turns gazing at the patterns until Michael decides to buy it. It's expensive too. I ask him why he bought it. He says because he didn't like the thought of no one ever looking into it.

We walk along the river and throw stones in and play Pooh Sticks on the bridge. We go back to Café Rivière for a late lunch and more tea for

Michael. We go to the cinema to see *Star Wars: The Empire Strikes Back*, which, of course, is excellent, and then we hang around to watch *Dirty Dancing* because apparently it's "Back to the Eighties" day. *Dirty Dancing* is a very stupid film.

Midway through the film, I get another message on my blog.

Anonymous: *Thought for the day: Why do people leave newspapers on trains?*

I show this one to Michael.

"What a *fantastic* question," he says.

I fail to see how it's a fantastic question, so I delete it, just like I did the other one.

I don't know what the time is, but it's getting dark now. We go back to the Dying Sun. A little farther along the cliff is Michael's house, glowing against the sky. This clifftop really is the best place in the world. The best end of the universe.

We balance on the edge, letting the wind flow past our ears. I dangle my legs off and, after some persuasion, so does he.

"The sun's setting," he says.

"The sun also rises," I say, before I can stop myself.

His head turns like a robot. "Say that again."

"What?"

"Say that again."

"Say what?"

"What you just said."

I sigh. "*The Sun Also Rises.*"

"And who, might I ask, wrote that?"

I sigh again. "Ernest Hemingway."

He starts shaking his head. "You hate literature. You hate it. You can't even bring yourself to read *Pride and Prejudice*."

". . ."

"Name three other Hemingway novels."

"Really? You're really going to ask me to do that?"

He smiles.

I roll my eyes. *"For Whom the Bell Tolls. The Old Man and the Sea. A Farewell to Arms."*

His mouth opens in astonishment.

"It's not like I've read any of them."

"Now I'm going to have to test you."

"Jesus."

"Who wrote *The Bell Jar*?"

". . ."

"Don't pretend you don't know it, Spring."

That's the first time he's called me by my surname only. I'm not sure what this says about our relationship.

"Fine. Sylvia Plath."

"Who wrote *The Catcher in the Rye*?"

"J. D. Salinger. You're giving me really easy ones."

"Okay, then. Who wrote *Endgame*?"

"Samuel Beckett."

"A Room of One's Own?"

"Virginia Woolf."

He gives me a long look. *"The Beautiful and Damned."*

I want to stop myself from saying the answers, but I can't. I can't lie to him.

"F. Scott Fitzgerald."

He shakes his head. "You know all the names of books, but you haven't read a single one. It's like it's raining money, but you refuse to catch a single coin."

I know that if I persisted past the first few pages, I would probably enjoy some books, but I don't. I can't read books because I know that none of it is real. Yeah, I'm a hypocrite. Films aren't real, but I love them. But books—they're different. When you watch a film, you're sort of an outsider looking in. With a book—you're right there. You are inside. You are the main character.

A minute later, he asks, "Have you ever had a boyfriend, Tori?"

I snort. "Clearly not."

"Don't say that. You're a sexy beast. You could easily have had a boyfriend."

I am not a sexy beast in any way whatsoever.

I sigh. "I don't need a man. I'm single and thriving."

This actually makes Michael laugh so hard that he has to roll over and hide his face in his hands, which makes me laugh too. We continue laughing hysterically until the sun is almost completely gone.

Once we calm down, Michael lies back in the grass.

"I hope you don't mind me saying, but Becky doesn't really seem to hang around you much at school. I mean, if you didn't know, you wouldn't guess that you were best friends." He looks at me. "You don't really talk to each other very much."

I cross my legs. Another sudden topic change. "Yeah . . . she . . . I don't know. Maybe that's why we are best friends. Because we don't need to talk much anymore." I look back at him stretched out. His arm is laid over his forehead, his hair is splayed out in the dark, and the remaining light swirls in kaleidoscope shapes in his blue eye. I look away. "She has a lot more friends than me, I guess. But that's all right. I don't mind. It's understandable. I'm quite boring. I mean, she'd have a really boring life if she just hung around with me all the time."

"You're not boring. You're the epitome of not-boring."

Pause.

"I think you're a really good friend," he says. I turn again. He smiles at me and it reminds me of his expression on the day we met—wild, shining, something not quite reachable about it. "Becky is really lucky to have someone like you."

I would be nothing without Becky, I think. Even though things are different now. Sometimes it makes me tear up thinking about how much I love her.

"It's the other way round," I say.

The clouds have mostly cleared now. The sky is orange at the horizon, leading up to a dark blue above our heads. It looks like a portal. I start thinking about the *Star Wars* film we watched earlier. I wanted to be a Jedi so badly when I was a kid. My lightsaber would have been green.

"I should go home," I say eventually. "I didn't tell my parents I was going out."

"Ah. Right." We both stand up. "I'll walk home with you."

"You really don't have to."

But he does anyway.

SEVENTEEN

When we arrive outside my house, the sky is black and there are no stars.

Michael turns and puts his arms round me. It takes me by surprise so I don't have time to react. My arms are once again trapped at my sides.

"I had a really good day," he says, holding me.

"So did I."

He lets go. "Do you think we're friends now?"

I hesitate. I can't think why. I hesitate for no reason.

I regret what I say next almost as soon as I say it.

"It's like," I say, "you really . . . you really want to be friends with me."

He looks slightly embarrassed, almost apologetic.

"It's like you're doing it for yourself," I say.

"All friendships are selfish. Maybe if we were all selfless, we would leave each other alone."

"Sometimes that's better."

This hurts him. I shouldn't have said it. I'm pushing his temporary happiness out. "Is it?"

I don't know why I can't just say that we're friends and be done with it.

"What is this? This whole thing. I met you, like, two weeks ago. None of this makes any sense. I don't understand why you want to be friends with me."

"That's what you said last time."

"Last time?"

"Why are you making this so complicated? We're not six years old."

I say, "I'm just awful at—I'm—I don't know."

His mouth turns down.

"I don't know what to say," I say.

"It's all right." He takes off his glasses to wipe them with his jumper sleeve. I've never seen him without his glasses on. "It's fine." And then, as he replaces his glasses, all the sadness disintegrates, and what's left underneath is the real Michael, the fire, the boy who skates, the boy who followed me to a restaurant to tell me something he couldn't remember, the boy who has nothing better to do than force me to get out of the house and live.

"Is it time for me to give up?" he asks, and then answers, "No, it's not."

"You sound like you're in love with me," I say. "For God's sake."

"There is no reason why I couldn't be in love with you."

"Are you in love with me?"

He winks. *"It's a mystery."*

"I'm going to take that as a no."

"Of course you are. Of course you're going to take that as a no. You didn't even need to ask me that question, did you?"

He's annoying me now. A lot. "Jesus fucking Christ! I know I'm a stupid, twattish pessimist, but stop acting like I'm some kind of manically depressed psychopath!"

And then suddenly—like a wind change or a bump in the road or the moment that makes you scream in a horror film—suddenly he's an entirely different person. His smile dies and the blue and green of his eyes darken. He clenches his fist and he snarls, he actually *snarls* at me.

"Maybe you *are* a *manically depressed psychopath.*"

I freeze, stunned, wanting to be sick.

"Fine."

I turn round

and go into the house

and shut the door.

Charlie is at Nick's for once. I go to his room and lie down. He has a world map next to his bed with certain places circled. Prague. Kyoto. Seattle. There are also several pictures of him with Nick. Nick and Charlie on the London Eye. Nick and Charlie at a rugby match. Nick and Charlie at the beach. His bedroom is so tidy. Obsessively tidy. It smells of cleaning spray.

In his bedside table is a drawer that used to have all these snacks stacked and ordered inside, but Mum found them and threw them away while he was staying at the psych ward. Now there are lots of books in the drawer. A lot that Dad's obviously given to him. I shut the drawer.

I go get my laptop and bring it into Charlie's room and scroll through some blogs.

I've ruined it, haven't I?

I'm angry that Michael said that stuff. I hate that he said that stuff. But I said stupid stuff too. I sit and I wonder whether Michael is going to talk to me tomorrow. This is probably my fault. Everything is my fault.

I wonder how much Becky will talk about Ben tomorrow. A lot. I think about who else I could hang around with. There isn't anyone. I think about how I do not want to leave this house ever again. I think about whether I had any homework to do this weekend. I think about what a dreadful person I am.

I put on *Amélie*, which is the best foreign film in the history of cinema. I tell you, this is one of the *original* indie films. It gets romance *right*. You can tell that it's *genuine*. It's not just like "she's pretty, he's handsome, they both hate each other, then they realize there's another side to both of them, they start to like each other, love declaration, the end." Amélie's romance is meaningful. It's not fake, it's believable. It's *real*.

I go downstairs. Mum is on the computer. I tell her goodnight, but it takes her at least twenty seconds to hear me, so I just head back upstairs with a glass of diet lemonade.

EIGHTEEN

Becky is with Ben Hope at school. They are together now. They're together in the common room and they're smiling a lot. After I've been sitting nearby on a swivel chair for several minutes, Becky finally notices that I'm here.

"Hey!" She beams at me, but the greeting sounds forced.

"Morning." Becky and Ben are also sitting, Becky's legs up on Ben's lap.

"I don't think I've spoken to you before," says Ben. He is so attractive that I feel extra awkward. I hate that. "What's your name?"

"Tori Spring," I say. "I'm in your maths class. And English."

"Oh, right, yeah, I thought I'd seen you!" I don't think he's seen me. "Yeah. I'm Ben."

"Yeah."

We sit there for a bit, him expecting me to continue the conversation. He clearly does not know me well.

"Wait. Tori *Spring*?" He squints at me. "Are . . . are you *Charlie* Spring's sister?"

"Yeah."

"Charlie Spring . . . who goes out with Nick Nelson?"

"Yeah."

Instantly, all traces of smarminess drop from his face, leaving only a kind of strangled anxiety. For a moment, it's almost as if he's searching for some reaction from me. But then it's gone. "Cool. Yeah, I saw him around at Truham."

I nod. "Cool."

"You knew Charlie Spring?" asks Becky.

Ben fiddles with his shirt buttons. "Not closely. Just saw him around, you know. Small world, innit!"

"Yeah," I say.

Becky is staring at me with a strange expression. I stare back at her, trying to telepathically tell her that I don't want to be here.

"Tori," says Becky, "did you do the sociology homework?"

"Yeah. Did you?"

She grins sheepishly and glances sideways at Ben. They exchange a cheeky look.

"We were busy," she giggles.

I try not to think about the connotations of the word *busy*.

Evelyn has been here the whole time, facing away from us, chatting to some other Year 12s who I don't talk to. At this point, she spins round on her chair, rolls her eyes at Ben and Becky, and says, "Ugh, why are you guys so *adorable?*"

I rummage around in my bag, find my homework, and give it to Becky.

"Just give it back in sociology," I say.

"*Aw.*" She takes the piece of paper. "You are *fabulous*. Thanks, hun."

Becky has never called me "hun" in my entire life. She has called me "man." She has called me "mate." She has called me "dude" a hundred billion times. But she has never, ever called me "hun."

The pips go and I leave without saying bye.

Lucas comes up to me at break while I'm sorting out my books at my locker. He tries to start a conversation and, to be fair, just because I feel sorry for him most of the time, I try really hard to talk to him. By "try really hard" I mean that I don't just ignore him. I feel like his hair has grown since Friday.

We get talking about Becky's party.

"Yeah, I went home kind of early," he says. "You sort of disappeared half-way through."

I wonder if he saw me with Michael.

"Yeah," I say, looking briefly at him with one hand on my locker door. "Er, I went home too."

He nods at me and puts his hands in his trouser pockets. But I can tell. I can tell that he knows I didn't go home. There's a short silence before he quickly moves on.

"I don't know if she liked my present," he says with a shrug. Then he looks at me. "I was always really good at buying presents for *you*."

I nod. This is true. "Yeah, you were."

"April fifth, yeah?"

He remembers my birthday.

I turn away, taking longer than I need to retrieve my maths textbook. "Well remembered."

Another awkward pause.

"Mine's October," he says. He's already seventeen, then. "I thought you might not remember."

"I'm not very good at remembering stuff."

"Yeah. No, it's fine."

He laughs. I start to feel a little dazed. When the pips finally go for Period 3, the relief almost makes me pass out.

By fourth period, Solitaire has struck again.

The only website that the school computers are now able to access is the Solitaire blog, which is currently displaying a large photo of a topless Jake Gyllenhaal, beneath the following words:

Solitairians.

We have reached 2,000 followers. Your reward is the destruction of all of

today's IT lessons at Higgs, à la Gyllenhaal. For those of you who do not attend Higgs, we are sure you will appreciate the Gyllenhaal regardless.
Patience Kills

The teachers are practically hurling people out of the computer rooms and all IT lessons are canceled until further notice. I applaud Solitaire for their efforts.

Kent has decided to take things up a notch, and I don't blame him. At the start of lunch, I find myself walking into the sixth-form office for a "student interview," which is teacher lingo for "interrogation." Kent's there at his computer and Strasser's there too, blinking enthusiastically. I slump into a chair. On the wall opposite, there is a poster that reads *TALK HELPS*. This is very, very pointless.

"We won't keep you long," says Strasser. "This is a safe space. Anything you say in this room will remain anonymous."

Kent gives Strasser this look.

"We just want to know if you've seen or heard anything that might be of any help," he says.

"No," I say, even though there's the messages, and the C13 hack, and the meetup. "Sorry. Nothing."

I know that this is a lie. And I do not know why I lied. I just feel that if I say something about what I've seen and heard, that will make me *involved*. And I do not like being *involved*.

"Fine," says Kent. "Just be on the lookout. I know you're not a prefect, but . . . you know."

I nod and get up to leave.

"Tori," says Kent. I turn round. He gives me a look. A different look.

But then it's gone.

"Be alert," he says. "We can't have things getting any worse."

$\left(\cdots \right)$

I'm scrolling through a blog in the common room at the end of lunch when Our Lot enters and sits at a table, having just come back from the cafeteria. Today, that's Becky and Lauren and Rita. No Lucas or Evelyn. I forgot to make myself lunch and I don't have any money, but to be honest the thought of food is making me feel slightly ill. Becky sees me at the computers and comes over. I exit the blog and put up an English essay I haven't finished.

"Why are you here by yourself?"

"I haven't done that English essay."

"What English essay? I thought we had that other homework?"

"The mini-essay. The heroes in *Pride and Prejudice*. It's due tomorrow."

"Oh. Yeah, that's so not happening. I've started to realize that I'd much rather live my life than do work."

I nod as if I understand. "Fair enough."

"You saw my Facebook update, yeah?"

"Yeah."

She sighs and puts her hands on her cheeks. "I'm just so happy! I can't even believe it! He's like the nicest guy I have ever met."

I nod and smile. "I'm so happy for you!" I keep on nodding and smiling. I'm like that Churchill Insurance bulldog. *Oh, yes.*

"Like, on Saturday, I texted him, like, did you mean all the things you said at my party, or was it just the drink talking, and he was like, no, I meant everything, I really like you."

"That's cute!"

"I really like him as well."

"Good!"

She takes out her phone and scrolls through it and then waves it around and laughs. "I haven't been this happy in ages!"

I hold my hands together in my lap. "I'm really glad for you, Becky!"

But I can see she thinks I'm lying. She thinks I don't care.

"Thanks," she says, and I wish I could tell her that I am happy for her, but everything she does makes me feel like a failure at life.

We don't say anything for a few seconds. We just smile.

"What did you do this weekend?" she asks, out of obligation.

I run my hand through my hair. A strand had been flicked over the wrong side. "Nothing. You know me."

She keeps eye contact. "I think you could be a lot more outgoing than you are. You just, like, don't try. If you tried, you could get a boyfriend really easily."

"I don't really need a boyfriend," I say.

After a little while, the pips go for form. I've finished and printed that essay. Everyone goes off to their form groups except me. I start walking to my form room, but when I turn right, Michael walks past me and seeing him makes me want to start kicking and punching things. He stops and asks, "Where are you going?" but I just walk out of the school gate and keep on walking. There is barely anyone in our dying town and it's literally Arctic temperatures, but I left my coat at school and when I finally get home I am totally alone so I get into bed and sleep until Mum wakes me for dinner, not having any idea that I ran away from school.

That evening, Charlie has an appointment with his psychiatrist at the eating disorder clinic, and we all decide to go—Mum, Dad and me—so we leave Oliver at home with Nick babysitting. Mum and Dad go in for a meeting first, leaving Charlie and me in the waiting room. This is the first time I've been to the clinic since Charlie stayed here last year, and it's still just as creepily optimistic. On the wall, there's a big painting of a rainbow and the sun with a smiley face.

This ward only cares for teenagers. Currently with us in the room is a girl, maybe my age, reading a book and a younger boy, perhaps thirteen, watching *Shrek*. I internally applaud his good movie taste.

Charlie has not talked to me since Friday. But I haven't talked to him either. After several minutes, he breaks our silence.

"Why haven't we been talking?" He's wearing a loose-fitting checked shirt and jeans. His eyes are dark and dead.

"I don't know" is all I can say.

"You're angry at me."

"I'm definitely not."

"You should be."

I fold my legs up on the sofa. "It's not like it's your fault."

"Then whose fault is it?" He leans on one hand. "Who is responsible for this?"

"*No one*," I snap. "Shit happens. Shit happens to the wrong people. You know that."

He looks at me for a long time, head slightly lowered.

"What have you been up to?" he asks.

I pause before telling him. "I was with Michael Holden all weekend."

He raises his eyebrows.

"Not like that," I say.

"I didn't say anything."

"But you were thinking it."

"Why were you with him all weekend? Are you friends now?" His eyes glimmer. "I didn't think you did that."

I frown. "He told me I was a 'manically depressed psychopath.' I don't think he . . ."

The water machine bubbles. The windows are open a crack and the breeze is rattling the 1980s blinds. Charlie looks at me.

"What else is happening?" he asks. "We haven't talked properly in ages."

I list the things. "Becky is going out with Ben Hope. She talks about him all the time. I haven't talked to Mum and Dad properly since Saturday. I haven't been sleeping a lot. And . . . Michael."

Charlie nods. "That's a lot of things."

"I know. A real array of first world problems."

"Hang on," he says, "Becky is going out with *Ben Hope*?"

"Yeah."

"Ben Hope who used to go to Truham?"

"What, do you know him?"

The question almost appears to startle him. After a short pause, he says, "Yeah, we used to be friends. Not really anymore though."

"Okay."

"I'm staying off school tomorrow as well."

"Yeah?"

"Yeah. Mum and Dad are making me. They're blowing this kind of out of proportion."

I snort. "You had a self-harm relapse, idiot."

He leans back. "Well, aren't I a drama queen?"

"Do you want me to get the bus with you on Wednesday?" Usually, I walk to school, and Charlie gets the bus. I hate the bus.

Charlie's expression softens and he smiles. "Yeah. Thanks." He adjusts himself on the sofa, so that his body is facing me. "I think you should give Michael a chance."

A chance?

"I know Nick and I said he's weird—and he *is* weird—and I know you think that it's easier to be by yourself, but every minute you spend thinking about what you're not doing, that's another minute forgetting about how to be around other people."

"I don't—"

"Michael's okay. He's proven that. I don't understand why you can't accept things like this. If you can't accept things you don't understand, then you'll spend your life questioning everything. Then you'll have to live out your life in your own head."

We're interrupted by a nurse, who enters the room and asks Charlie to join Mum and Dad in the meeting. Charlie stands up, but doesn't walk off. He looks down at me.

"Is that a bad thing?" I ask.

"Victoria, that is how you end up in a place like this."

NINETEEN

The fire alarm goes off in Period 5 the next day. I had just settled into a seat in the common room, playing "Fix You" by Coldplay over and over on repeat (pathetic, I know), when the siren began to wail. Now we're all here in the freezing wasteland of the school field, lined up in our form groups.

I hear at least three people say something about a fire in Kent's office, but, having been at an all-girls' school for over five years, I've learned not to trust anything communicated by word of mouth.

No one I really know is in my form, so I shiver and look around. I see Michael in a form a few lines away, sort of out of place among the Year 13s. He looks sort of out of place everywhere.

I start to wonder whether my outburst on Sunday is the reason why he hasn't called me or looked for me at school. I wonder whether he'll still want to be friends. Maybe I should listen to Charlie. If he thinks that Michael is okay, then he probably is, and I should give him a chance. Not that that matters, because I declined his offer anyway. It's not like he's going to give me another chance. That's okay. That's fine. I don't want to go to that Solitaire meetup this Saturday so I've at least got out of that.

I keep looking at him because there's something not quite right.

With half-shut eyes, he's staring blankly into a book, and his face is so frozen that it makes *me* tense up. In fact, I almost think he's about to cry. I can't quite see what the book is called, but it's very thick and he's nearly at the end. Also, his tie isn't tied—he's wrapped it round his neck like a scarf—and his side parting is much too far over. I wish I knew what he was reading. I know I don't like books, but you can always tell what someone is thinking by what they're reading.

A little way off Lucas wanders onto the field with Evelyn and an anonymous boy with large hair, part of the last group to arrive. Lucas looks equally sad. I begin to feel that everyone is sad. Everything is sad. All sad.

I wonder whether Lucas is Evelyn's secret boyfriend. It's possible.

I don't want to think about Lucas or Michael anymore. I withdraw my phone and load up the Solitaire blog. I wait for it to load, expecting Jake Gyllenhaal to still be at the top.

But there's a new post that's overtaken Jake. It's a blurry photo of a hand, forefinger outstretched, just about to break the glass of a school fire alarm button. Underneath, the text reads:

DO I DARE

DISTURB THE UNIVERSE?

I stare at the photo for a long time and I start to feel a bit claustrophobic. That question, those two lines of poetry, keep spinning around my head like it's been asked of me. I get to wondering how I even *know* that those two lines came from a poem because I don't think I've even glanced at a poem that hasn't been part of schoolwork. I then wonder whether I could ask Michael because he would probably know what poem it was from, but then I remember that he thinks I'm a manically depressed psychopath. So that is the end of that.

TWENTY

I get home. Everything normal happens. I say hello to Nick and Charlie. I turn on my laptop. I put a film on. And then I do something weird.

I call Michael.

16:49 p.m.

Outgoing Call

M: Hello?

T: Hi. It's Tori.

M: Tori? Really? You called me *again*? That's twice in a fortnight. You do not strike me as one who enjoys making phone calls.

T: Believe me. I'm not.

M:

T: I overreacted. I'm the one who has to say sorry. I called to say sorry.

M:

T:

M: I'm sorry too. I don't think you're a psychopath.

T: Don't you? It's a valid assumption.

M: I don't even know why we need to apologize to each other. I can't even remember what we're arguing about. I don't even think we *did* argue.

T: Are you in denial?

M: Are you?

T: What does that mean?

M: I don't know.

T: I'm just sorry I snapped at you.

M:

T: I do want to be friends with you. Can . . . can we . . .

M: We're already friends, Tori. You don't need to ask. We're already friends.

T:

M: Is Charlie all right?

T: He's all right.

M: Are you all right?

T: I'm fine.

M:

T:

M: I see Becky and Ben are pretty snug together.

T: Oh, yeah, they're practically conjoined. She's really happy.

M: Are you happy?

T: What?

M: Are you happy?

T: Yeah, I'm happy for her. She's my best friend. I'm really happy for her.

M: That's not what I asked.

T: I don't get it.

M:

T:

M: Will you still come to the Solitaire meetup with me on Saturday?

T:

M: I don't want to go alone.

T: Yeah.

M: You'll come?

T: Yes.

M:

T: Why can I hear wind? Where *are* you?

M: I'm at the rink.

T: The *ice* rink?

M: Do you know any *other* rinks?

T: You're on the phone and skating at the same time.

M: Men can multitask too, you know. Where are you?

T: Obviously at home.

M: Such a loser.

T: What's that music that's playing?

M:

T: That's film music, isn't it?

M: Is it?

T: It's from *Gladiator*. It's called "Now We Are Free."

M:

T:

M: Your film knowledge is simply magical.

T: Magical?

M: You're magical, Tori.

T: You're the one who can ice-skate. That's the closest thing to flying a human can do without a vehicle.

M:

T: You can fly, Michael.

M:

T: What?

M: I can fly.

T: You can fly.

M: No one's ever . . .

T:

M: I'd better meet you at Hogwarts then.

T: Or Neverland.

M: Or both.

T: Or both.

TWENTY-ONE

Sitting next to Charlie on the Wednesday morning bus journey calms me. I have a lot of unread messages on my blog, but I don't want to read them. It's much, much too sunny today. We meet Nick outside Truham. Nick gives Charlie a quick kiss, and they start talking to each other, laughing. I watch him and Charlie walk in, and then head up the road to Higgs.

I'm feeling sort of all right because Michael and I are okay now. I don't know why I made all that fuss the other day. No, that's a lie. I do know why. It's because I'm an idiot.

Mr. Compton, my unintelligible imbecile of a maths teacher, decides, for one lesson only, that we need to work in pairs with people we do not usually sit with. This is how I end up sitting next to Ben Hope in Wednesday's maths lesson. We exchange pleasantries, and then sit in silence while Compton begins to explain the trapezium rule in the most complicated way imaginable. Ben doesn't have a pencil case. He carries a pen and a small ruler in his breast pocket. He has also forgotten his C2 textbook. I feel that this may have been deliberate.

Halfway through, Compton leaves to photocopy some sheets and does not return for some time. To my dismay, Ben decides that he needs to talk to me.

"Hey," he says. "How's Charlie doing?"

I turn my head slowly to the left. Surprisingly, he looks genuinely concerned.

"Um . . ." Truth? Lie? "Not too bad."

Ben nods. "Yeah. Okay."

"Charlie said you used to be friends or something."

His eyes open very wide. "Erm, yeah. I guess. But you know. Like, yeah. Everyone knows Charlie. You know?"

Yeah. Everyone knows. You don't stay off school for two months without everyone finding out why.

"Yeah."

The silence between us returns. The rest of our class is chattering and it's nearly the end of the lesson. Has Compton been eaten by the photocopier?

I suddenly find myself talking. Talking *first*. This is pretty rare.

"Everyone loves Charlie at Truham," I say, "don't they?"

Ben begins to tap his pen on the table. A weirdly nervous grin spreads across his face.

"Well, I wouldn't say *everyone* exactly," he scoffs. I frown at him, and he quickly covers himself with, "No, I mean, like, people can't be liked by *everyone*, right?"

I clear my throat. "I guess not."

"I don't know him anymore really," he says.

"Yeah. Okay."

TWENTY-TWO

Lunch. Common room. I am staring into my reflection in a smudgy blank computer screen with my head in my hands. Not because I'm particularly stressed or anything—this is just a very comfortable sitting position.

"Hello," says Lucas, smiling and sitting in the chair next to me. I look up at him. He doesn't look so embarrassed today, which is colossal progress.

"Why so cheerful?" I ask.

He shrugs. "Why not?"

I roll my eyes, faking sarcasm. "I don't like your attitude."

He stares at me for a minute or so. I take out my phone and scroll through my blog feed.

Then he says, "Hey, erm, what are you up to on Saturday?"

"Er, nothing, I guess."

"Do you . . . we should do something."

". . . we should?"

"Yeah." *Now* he's embarrassed. "I mean, if you want."

"Like what?"

He shakes his head. "I don't know. Just . . . chill somewhere."

I force myself to think very carefully about this. I could try. For once. I could try to be a legitimately nice human being. "Oh, er, I said I'd go to this thing in the evening. But I'm free during the day."

He lights up. "Great! What do you want to do?"

"I don't know. It was your idea."

"Oh, yeah . . . well, you could come round mine if you want? Just watch movies . . ."

"Is Evelyn all right with that?"

Yep. I went there.

"Um . . ." He sort of laughs, like I'm joking. "What?"

"Evelyn." My voice starts to fail. "Are you not . . . you and Evelyn . . . ?"

"Er . . . we're . . . no . . ."

"Okay. Right. Cool. Just checking."

"What are you guys talking about?" Becky calls over to us. We both spin round in our chairs. "You look like you're talking about something interesting. I want gossip. *Spill*."

I put my legs up on Lucas's lap because I just can't be arsed to be reserved right now. "Obviously, we're flirting. God, Becky."

For a second, Becky thinks I'm serious. It is a truly triumphant moment.

Later, I pass Michael in the corridor. He stops and points directly at me.

"You," he says.

"Me," I say.

We speedily transfer our conversation to a stairwell.

"Are you free on Saturday?" he asks. He's got one of his stupid mugs of tea again. He's actually spilled some on his white shirt.

I'm about to say yes, but then I remember. "Er, no. I said me and Lucas would do something. Sorry."

"Ah. Don't worry." He sips his tea. "You're not allowed to ditch the Solitaire meetup though."

"Oh."

"Did you forget?"

"No. Everyone's been talking about it."

"I guess they have."

We look at each other.

"Do I *have* to go?" I say. "You are aware that I literally don't give a single fuck about Solitaire."

"I am aware," he says, which means yes, I do have to go.

The horde of lower-school girls thundering up the stairs behind us is slowly thinning. I need to get to English.

"Anyway," he says. "Yes. Get to mine Saturday evening. When you and Lucas are finished . . . canoodling." He moves his eyebrows up and down.

I slowly shake my head. "I don't think I have ever heard anyone use that word in real life."

"Well, then," he says. "I'm glad I've made your day that bit more special."

TWENTY-THREE

In my younger years, every day after school, I used to walk down the road and meet Charlie outside Truham. We'd then either ride the bus home or we would walk. Despite it only being a ten-minute bus journey, I had to put my music on my headphones near full volume. I knew that I would be deaf by the time I was twenty, but, if I had to listen to those kids every single day, I didn't think I'd make it to twenty. I didn't think I'd make it to seventeen.

I started getting the bus again on Wednesday to keep Charlie company, and it hasn't been too bad so far. We've had a good chance to talk about stuff. I don't mind talking with Charlie.

Anyway, it's Friday today, and Michael has decided that he's coming home with me.

Which is sort of nice, to tell you the truth.

Nick is waiting for me outside Truham. Nick always looks particularly dashing in his tie and blazer. The *RUGBY* patch above his school crest reflects a little sunlight. He is wearing sunglasses. Ray-Bans. He sees Michael and me approach.

"All right?" Nick nods, hands in pockets, Adidas bag strapped across his chest.

"All right," I say.

Nick studies Michael. "Michael Holden," he says.

Michael has his hands held behind his back. "You're Nick Nelson."

I see Nick's initial uncertainty ease at Michael's uncharacteristically normal reaction. "Yup. Yeah, I remember you. From Truham. You're infamous, mate."

"Yes, yeah. I'm awesome."

"Cool."

Michael smiles. "*Nicholas Nelson.* You have a really excellent name."

Nick laughs in that warm way of his, almost as if he and Michael have been friends for years. "I know, right?"

Flocks of Truham boys soar past us, running for inexplicable reasons, while the traffic on the road is unmoving. A group of Year 10 Higgs girls cozy up to a group of Year 10 Truham boys against the gate several meters away from us. There are at least three couples within the group. God.

I scratch my forehead, feeling agitated. "Where's Charlie?"

Nick raises his eyebrows and turns back towards Truham. "He's the only guy in his class who cares about classics, so he's probably been dragged into a long conversation with Rogers about, like, Greek proverbs or something—"

"Toriiiiii!"

I twirl round. Becky is dodging traffic and skipping my way, her purple locks flailing behind her.

When she arrives, she says, "Ben said he had to go to Truham and get something from last year, coursework or something, so I'm just going to wait with you guys. I don't want to stand by myself like a Larry."

I smile. It's starting to become really difficult to do that sometimes around Becky, but I make the effort and force it.

Michael and Nick are both staring at her with empty expressions that I can't read.

"What are you all doing here?" she asks.

"We're waiting for Charlie," I say.

"Oh, yeah."

"Shall we just go in and find him?" Nick suggests.

But none of us move.

"It's like we're in *Waiting for Godot*," murmurs Michael. I've heard of the play, but I haven't got any idea what Michael is talking about.

And, just to make things even more awkward, Lucas appears out of nowhere.

Nick raises his arms. "Lucas! Mate!" They embrace in a manly sort of hug, but Lucas just looks silly. They proceed to exchange pleasantries and each of them uses the words *mate* and *man* far too many times, resulting in Michael snorting, "Oh my *God*" much too loudly. Fortunately, Lucas and Nick appear not to hear. I chuckle faintly.

"What are you all doing here?" asks Lucas, deliberately pretending not to see Michael.

"Waiting for Charlie," says Nick.

"Waiting for Ben," says Becky.

"Why don't you just go look for them? I've got to go inside too, to pick up my art GCSE coursework."

"That's what Ben's doing," says Becky.

At the repeated mention of Ben, Nick seems to frown at Becky. But I might just be imagining it.

"Well, let's go, then," he says, and pushes his sunglasses farther up his nose.

"We can't," whispers Michael, oozing sarcasm, so quiet that only I hear. "*Why not?* We're waiting for Charlie. *Ah.*" He might be quoting, but I haven't read or seen *Waiting for Godot* so it's lost on me.

Nick turns on the spot and walks into the school. Becky follows immediately. Then the rest of us.

I remember instantly why I chose not to go to this school for sixth form. The boys that pass us are more than strangers. I feel trapped. As we enter the main building, the walls seem to creep higher and higher and the lights are dim and flashing, and I experience a brief flashback of the back of Michael's head, leading me towards the Truham A-level maths taster session last year. Every so often we pass these rusty old radiators, none of which appear to be emitting any heat. I start to shiver.

Michael is on my left. "I'd forgotten what it's like here. It's as if they built it out of misery."

We wind through corridors that seem to materialize in front of our feet. Michael starts whistling. Truham boys give us a lot of funny looks, particularly Michael. One group of older boys shouts, "Oi—Michael Holden—*wanker!*" and Michael spins on the spot and produces a strong double thumbs-up in their direction. We pass through a set of double doors and find ourselves in a large maze of lockers, not unlike our own Higgs locker room. It seems empty at first. Until we hear a voice.

"What the *fuck* did you say to them?"

All five of us freeze.

The voice continues. "Because I don't remember saying that you could spread *lies* about me to your retard sister."

Whoever else is there murmurs something inaudible. I already know who it is. I think everyone already knows who it is.

I spot Becky's face. I haven't seen that expression on her for a very long time.

"Do *not* make me *laugh*. I bet you couldn't wait to run and tell someone. Everyone knows you're just an attention-seeking prick. Everyone knows you're doing it for the attention. And you're telling your sister lies about us so she can spread shit around? You think you're so much better than everyone because you don't eat, and now you're back at school and, even though you haven't even *looked* at me since you hooked up with Nick Nelson, you think you can spread shit about me that isn't even fucking true."

"I don't know what you think you've heard," says Charlie, louder now, "but I literally haven't told *anyone*. Anyway, I seriously can't believe you're still *terrified* of people finding out."

There's a sharp smack and a crash. I start running towards the voices before I realize what I'm doing and I turn the corner of a locker row and Charlie is crumpled on the floor. Nick tackles Ben in his side and the pair topple down the row and into the wall at the end, and I'm kneeling down by

Charlie and I'm holding my hands up by his face, terrified that he's hurt again, really hurt, and I think I'm shaking and everything seems a bit I don't know and Nick shouts, "FUCK YOU!" and then Michael and Lucas are dragging Nick away and I'm still just sort of sitting there with my little brother with my shaking hands, wishing that I hadn't woken up this morning, I hadn't woken up yesterday, I hadn't ever woken up—

"That dick deserves it!" Ben shouts, panting. "He's a fucking liar!"

"He didn't even say anything to me," I say, calm at first. Then I'm screaming it. "HE DIDN'T EVEN SAY ANYTHING TO ME!"

Everyone is silent. Ben is breathing heavily. What I thought was attractive about him has now died and been cremated.

Michael kneels down with me, leaving Nick in the care of Lucas. Charlie's eyes are open, but he looks slightly disoriented, as you would expect of someone who's just been punched in the face.

"Do you know my name?" asks Michael, not Michael anymore, someone entirely different, someone serious, someone all-knowing.

After a pause, Charlie croaks: "Michael Holden." Then he grins. "Well . . . I've never been punched in the face before. That's a first."

Something changes in Nick and in one swift movement he's down on the floor with us. He takes Charlie into his arms. "Do we need to take him to hospital? What hurts?"

Charlie lifts his hand, waves a finger at his face, then drops it. "I think . . . I'm fine."

"Maybe he's concussed," says Nick.

"I don't want to go to hospital," says Charlie firmly.

I look around. Becky appears to have vanished and Ben is struggling to his feet and Lucas doesn't seem to know what to do with himself.

Charlie stands up surprisingly quickly. I wonder if he'll have a bruise. He looks at Ben. Ben looks back. And that's when I see it in Ben's eyes.

Fear.

"I'm not going to tell," says Charlie, "because I'm *not* a dick like you." Ben scoffs, and Charlie ignores it. "But I just feel bad that you're such a cliché."

"Get away from me," Ben snarls, but his voice wobbles, sort of like he's on the verge of tears. "Just fuck off with your boyfriend, for fuck's sake."

Nick very nearly lunges for the second time, but I see him fight to stop himself.

Ben catches my eye as we leave. I stare at him and his expression changes from hatred to what I hope might be regret. I doubt it. I want to be sick. I try to think of something to say to him, but nothing summarizes it. I hope I'm making him want to die.

Someone places a hand round my arm and I turn my head.

"Come on, Tori," says Lucas.

So I do.

On our way out, Lucas with a hand on my back, Nick and Michael walking on either side of Charlie, we pass Becky, who has for some reason pushed herself to the end of another locker row. We lock eyes. I know she's going to break up with Ben. She has to break up with Ben. She must have heard everything. She's my best friend. Charlie is my brother.

I don't understand what has happened.

"Should we feel sorry for Ben?" someone asks, maybe Michael.

"Why are there no happy people?" someone else asks, maybe me.

TWENTY-FOUR

Someone calls me on my mobile at 9:04 a.m., but I'm in bed and my phone is more than an arm's length away so I just let it ring on. At 9:15 a.m., someone rings the house phone and Charlie comes into my room, but I keep my eyes closed and pretend I'm still asleep and Charlie goes away. My bed whispers at me to stay. My curtains block out daytime.

At 2:34 p.m., Dad throws my door open and huffs and mutters and I suddenly feel sick so after another five minutes I go downstairs and sit on the sofa in the living room.

Mum comes in to get some ironing.

"Are you going to get dressed?" she asks.

"No, Mum. I'm never going to get dressed ever again. I'm going to live in my pyjamas until my death."

She doesn't say anything else. She leaves.

Dad comes into the living room. "Alive, then?"

I say nothing because I do not feel alive.

Dad sits next to me. "Are you going to tell me what's wrong?"

No, I am not.

"You know, if you want to be happier, you have to *try*. You have to put in the effort. Your problem is that you don't try."

I do try. I have tried. I have tried for sixteen years.

"Where's Charlie?" I ask.

"Round Nick's." Dad shakes his head. "Still can't believe Charlie got himself hit in the face with a cricket bat. That kid really does attract misfortune."

I do not say anything.

"Are you going to go out today?"

"No."

"Why not? What about Michael? You could spend the day with him again."

I don't really reply and Dad looks at me.

"What about Becky? I haven't seen her round here for quite a while."

I don't reply again.

He sighs and rolls his eyes. *"Teenagers,"* he says, as if the mere state of being a teenager explains every single thing about me.

And then he leaves, huffing and puffing and sighing.

I sit in my duvet on my bed, a diet lemonade in one hand and my phone in the other. I find Michael's number in my contacts and press the green button. I don't know why I'm calling him. I think it might be Dad's fault.

It goes straight to voicemail.

I drop the phone on the bed and roll over so I am completely under the covers.

Of course I can't expect him to just show up any old time. He has a life after all. He has a family and coursework and stuff. His entire existence doesn't revolve around mine.

I am a narcissist.

I rummage around the sheets and eventually locate my laptop. I flip it up. If ever in doubt about anything, my first port of call is always Google.

And I am certainly in doubt. About everything.

I type *Michael Holden* into the search bar and press Enter.

Michael Holden isn't an overly uncommon name. Lots of other Michael Holdens show up, particularly Myspace pages. Since when is Myspace still a thing? Lots of Twitter profiles show up, but I can't find my Michael Holden's Twitter. He doesn't seem to be the sort of guy who would have Twitter. I sigh and close my laptop. At least I tried.

And then, as if I'd summoned him with the closing of my laptop, my phone begins to ring. I pick it up. Michael Holden's name glares on the screen. With a kind of enthusiasm entirely unknown to me, I press the green button.

"Hello?"

"Tori! What is up?"

It seems to take me longer than necessary to say something in reply.

"Erm . . . er, not a lot."

Behind Michael's voice, the low chatter of a crowd can be heard.

"Where are you?" I ask. "What's happening?"

This time he's the one who pauses. "Oh, yeah, I didn't tell you, did I? I'm at the rink."

"Oh. Do you have practice or something?"

"Er, no. It's, erm . . . I've got a sort of competition today."

"A competition?"

"Yeah!"

"What competition?"

He pauses again. "It's, er, it's kind of . . . it's the National Youth Speed Skating Semifinals."

My stomach gives up.

"Look, I've got to go. I promise I'll call you when it's finished, yeah? And then I'll see you tonight!"

". . . yeah."

"Okay, talk later!"

He hangs up the phone. I remove it from my ear and stare at it.

National Youth Speed Skating Semifinals.

That's not just some stupid local competition.

That's—

That's *important*.

That's what he was going to invite me to today, but I'd said no, I'd said I was hanging out with *Lucas*. And then I decided to avoid Lucas anyway.

Without any further hesitation, I leap out of bed.

💬

I park Charlie's bike outside the rink. It's 4:32 p.m. and dark. I've probably missed it. I don't know why I even tried, but I did. How long are speed-skate races?

Why didn't Michael tell me about this before?

I run—yes, actually run—through the empty foyer and the double doors into the stadium. A scattering of supporters dot the stadium seating around the rink and, to my right, psyched-up skaters sit on benches. Some of them could be sixteen, some could be twenty-five. I am not good at judging boy ages.

I walk closer to the plastic casing of the rink and make my way around until I find the gate where the casing isn't so high. I stare over.

There's a race going on. For a moment, I don't know where I'm looking or who I'm looking for because they all look exactly the same in these ridiculous suits that are like catsuits and rounded helmets. Eight guys blast past me and the rush of air tears at my face and my hair that I definitely forgot to sort out before I left the house, and they lean round the corners of the rink, so close to the ice, brushing it with their fingertips. I don't understand how they don't just fall over.

When they pass me the second time, that's when I see him; he turns his head, showing me his bulbous eyes behind large goggles and a ridiculously concrete expression. The eyes find me and his body turns, his hair swept backwards, and his face, beyond surprised, stays parallel to mine. I know instantly that something has changed.

He stares. At me maybe. His whole face expands, it illuminates, and all else seems to fade into fog and I place a hand against the plastic casing and everything inside me rushes to my feet.

I'm not sure if he really sees me. I don't cheer. I just stand there.

He pulls out in front. The crowd screams, but then some other blur of a boy flies from the group, and he's reached Michael, and he's passed Michael, and I realize that the race is over and Michael has come second.

I back away from the rink and shelter myself slightly behind the stands as the skaters make their way to the gate. Older men in tracksuits greet the boys, and one of them pats Michael on the back, but something is wrong, something is very wrong, something about Michael is wrong.

He's not "Michael Holden."

He's removed his skates and goggles. He takes off his helmet and gloves and drops them onto the floor.

His face contorts into a kind of scrunched-up snarl, his fists curl so his skin drains of color, and he storms past the man and tramps over to the benches. He reaches a row of lockers and looks into them, blankly, chest visibly expanding and contracting. With an almost terrifying malice, he throws a crazed punch at the lockers, wailing a subdued howl of rage. Turning, he hurls a kick at a pile of racing helmets, scattering them about the floor. He clutches his hair, as if trying to pull it out.

I've never seen Michael like this.

I know I shouldn't be so surprised. I haven't even known Michael for three weeks. But my perceptions of people rarely change and, when they do, it's never this drastic. It's weird how you see someone who smiles all the time and you assume that they're happy all the time. It's weird how someone is nice to you and you assume that they're a wholly "good person." I did not think Michael could be so serious about something, or so angry. It's like watching your dad cry.

What scares me the most, though, is that absolutely nobody in this entire swarm of human beings seems to notice.

So I barge my way towards him. I'm furious. I hate all these people for not caring. I'm hurling them out of the way as I walk, Michael Holden never leaving my eyesight. I reach him, breaking out of the crowd, and watch as he begins to manically attack some piece of paper that he had in his pocket. For several seconds, I don't really know what to do about it. But I then find myself saying:

"Yes, Michael Holden. Tear that fucking paper."

He drops everything, spins round, and points directly at me.

The anger softens into sadness.

"Tori," he says, but I don't hear it, I only see his mouth form the words.

He's wearing a catsuit and he's quite red and his hair is slick with sweat and his eyes are spinning in an electrified fury, but it's *him*.

Neither of us really knows what to say.

"You came second," I blurt eventually, pointlessly. "That's amazing."

His expression, passive, sad, so odd, doesn't change. He retrieves his glasses from his pocket and puts them on.

"I didn't win," he says. "I didn't qualify."

He looks away. I think he's welling up a little.

"I didn't think you were actually here," he says. "I thought I'd imagined you." A pause. "That's the first time you've called me Michael Holden."

His chest is still moving quickly up and down. He looks older, somehow, in the spandex suit, and taller. The suit is mostly red, with some orange and black areas. He has a whole life that I don't know about in this suit—hundreds of hours on the ice, training, entering competitions, testing his stamina, trying to eat right. I don't know about any of that. I *want* to know.

I open my mouth and close it several times.

"Do you get angry a lot?" I say.

"I'm always angry," he says.

Pause.

"Usually, other things override it, but I'm always angry. And sometimes . . ." His eyes drift vaguely to the right. "Sometimes . . ."

The crowd buzzes and I hate them even more.

"What happened to you and Lucas?" he asks.

I think about the phone calls that I'd been "asleep" for. "Oh. Yeah. No. That's not . . . no. I didn't feel very well."

"Oh," he says.

"You know . . . I don't actually *like* Lucas . . . like *that*," I say.

"Okay," he says.

We are silent for several long moments. Something in his face changes. It looks a bit like hope, but I can't really tell.

"Aren't you going to criticize me?" he asks. "Tell me that it's just a skating competition? That it doesn't mean anything?"

I ponder this. "No. It means something."

He smiles. I would say that he looks like the original Michael again, but he doesn't. There's something new in the smile.

"Happiness," he says, "is the price of profound thought."

"Who's that a quote from?" I ask.

He winks. "Me."

And I'm alone again in this crowd and I feel an odd feeling. It's not happiness. I know that it's brilliant that he came second in a national qualifier, but all I can think about is how Michael is just as good at lying as I am.

TWENTY-FIVE

We fail to find out whose house it is, but "the third house from the river bridge" really is right on the river. The broad garden slopes into the water, which laps persistently at the dirt. There's an old rowing boat tied to a tree that hasn't been used for probably centuries and over the river you can see right across the flat countryside. The fields, darkened under the night, blend into the horizon, as if unsure themselves quite where the earth stops and the sky begins.

This "meetup" is not a meetup.

It's a house party.

What had I been expecting? I had been expecting chairs. Nibbles. A speaker. Perhaps a PowerPoint presentation.

The evening is cold and it keeps trying to snow. I desperately want to be in my bed and my stomach is all tight and tense. I hate parties. I always have. I always will. It's not even for the right reasons; I hate them and I hate the people who go to them. I have no justification. I'm just ridiculous.

We walk past the smokers and through the open door.

It's about 10 p.m. Music pounds. Clearly, no one lives in this house—it's entirely bare of furniture save for a couple of deck chairs set up in the living room and on the garden patio, and I'm aware of a kind of neutral color scheme. The only thing giving the house any life at all is the impressive collection of artwork on the walls. There isn't any food, but there are bottles and colorful shot glasses everywhere. People are milling around in corridors and rooms, lots of them smoking cigarettes, lots of them smoking weed, very few of them sitting.

Many of the girls I recognize from Higgs, though Michael does not suspect that any of these casual partygoers are the masterminds behind Solitaire. There are older kids I don't recognize. Some must be twenty, if not older. It makes me feel sort of nervous, to tell you the truth.

I don't know why I'm here. I actually see the Year 11 girl from Becky's party, the one who had come as the Doctor. She's by herself, like last time, and she looks a little lost. She's walking very slowly along the corridor, without a drink, peering sadly at this painting of a wet cobbled street with red umbrellas and warm café windows. I wonder what she's thinking. I imagine that it's somewhat similar to what I'm thinking. She doesn't see me.

The first people we find are Becky and Lauren. I should have guessed that they would come, seeing as they attend all the parties in this town, and I really should have guessed I'd find them smashed. Becky points at us with the hand that's not clasping a bottle.

"Oh my God, it's Tori and Michael, you guys!" She whacks Lauren repeatedly on the arm. "Lauren! Lauren! Lauren! It's *Sprolden!*"

Lauren frowns. "Mate! I thought we'd agreed on Mori! Or Tichael!" She sighs. "Man, your names just aren't good enough, like, they don't work, they don't work like Klaine or Romione or Destiel or Merthur . . ." They both giggle uncontrollably.

I start to feel even more nervous. "I didn't think you guys would be interested in Solitaire."

Becky waves the bottle, shrugging and rolling her eyes around. "Hey, a party's a party's a party . . . I dunno . . . some guy . . . but, like, it's *Solitaire,* we've, like, infiltrated *Solitaire* . . ." She brings her finger up to her mouth. "*Shhhhhhhh.*" She drinks from the bottle. "Listen, listen, do you know what song this is? We, like, cannot work it out."

"It's 'Smells Like Teen Spirit.' Nirvana."

"Oh, right, yeah, oh my God, I thought it was that. It, like, it does not say the song title in the lyrics."

I look at Lauren, who's gazing around her in awed wonder.

"You all right, Lauren?" I ask.

She comes back to earth and cackles at me. "Isn't this party sick?" She raises her arms in an "I don't know" gesture. "It's snowing hot guys and the drinks are free!"

"That's great for you," I say, the will to be a nice person slowly drifting away.

She pretends not to hear me and they walk off, laughing at nothing.

Michael and I circle the party.

It's not like in films, or Channel 4 teen dramas, where everything turns slo-mo, lights flashing, people jumping up and down with pointing hands raised. Nothing's like that in real life. People are just standing around.

Michael talks to a lot of people. He asks everyone about Solitaire. We run into Rita, hanging quietly with a group of girls from my year. She sees me and waves, which means that I have to say hello to her.

"Hey," she says as I walk over to her. "How's Charlie? Heard there was a fight or something. Ben Hope, wasn't it?" Not much stays private in a town like this, so it's hardly surprising that everyone knows.

"It wasn't a fight," I say very quickly, and then clear my throat. "Er, yeah, he's all right. Bruised but all right."

Rita nods understandingly. "Ah, okay. Well, I'm glad he's not hurt too badly."

After that, Michael and I end up caught inside a circle of Year 13s in the kitchen. Michael claims that he's never spoken to any of them.

"No one knows, like, no one knows who made it," one girl says. "There are rumors it's some dealer from the estate or, like, a teacher who got sacked and wants revenge."

146

"Stick around," interrupts a guy wearing a snapback bearing the word *JOCK*. "Like, keep checking the blog, innit. I've heard things are gonna get well good when they put up the next post later."

There's a pause. I look down at the newspapered floor. There's a headline reading *27 DEAD* and a picture of a burning building.

"Why?" says Michael. "Why's that?"

But the guy just blinks, then asks, "Why aren't you drinking?"

I decide to be a normal person and find something proper to drink. Michael disappears for a long time so I pick up this big old bottle from somewhere and sit alone outside on a deck chair, feeling like a middle-aged, alcoholic husband. It's gone eleven and everyone's drunk. Whoever's DJ'ing relocates to the garden, and after a while it's unclear whether I'm in some small-town garden or at Reading Festival. I spot Nick and Charlie through the living-room window, kissing in a corner like it's their last day on earth, despite Charlie's bruised face. I guess they look romantic. Like they really are in love.

I get up and go inside to look for Michael, but whatever this stuff is that's in the bottle, it's kind of strong, so next thing I know I've lost all sense of time, space, and reality, and I have no idea what I'm doing. I find myself in the hallway again, in front of that painting of the wet cobbled street with red umbrellas and warm café windows. I can't stop looking at it. I force myself to turn round and spot Lucas at the other end of the corridor. I'm not sure whether he sees me or not, but he quickly disappears into another room. I wander away and get lost in the house. Red umbrellas. Warm café windows.

Michael grabs me out of nowhere. He pulls me away from wherever the hell I was—the kitchen maybe, lost in a sea of Boy London hats and chinos— and we start to walk through the house. I don't know where we're going. But I don't try to stop him. I'm not sure why.

As we're walking, I keep looking at his hand wrapped round my wrist. Maybe it's because I've had stuff to drink, or maybe it's because I'm really cold, or maybe it's because I'd sort of *missed* him while he'd been gone, but whatever it is—I keep thinking how nice it feels to have his hand round my wrist. Not in some weird, perverted way. His hand is just so big compared to mine, and so warm, and the way his fingers are curled round my wrist, it's like they were always supposed to do that, like they're matching pieces in a jigsaw. I don't know. What am I talking about?

Eventually, when we're outside and in the crowd of manic dancers, he slows and does a spin in the mud. It's sort of weird when he gazes at me. Again, I blame the drink. But it's different. He looks so nice standing there. His hair kind of swishing in the wrong direction and the firelight reflecting in his glasses.

I think he can tell I've had a bit to drink.

"Will you dance with me?" he shouts over the screams.

I inexplicably start to cough. He rolls his eyes at me and chuckles. I start thinking about proms and weddings and, for a few seconds, I actually forget that we're just in some garden where the ground looks like shit and the people are all dressed in near-identical outfits.

He removes his hand from my wrist and uses it to flatten his hair, and then he stares at me for what feels like a whole year. I wonder what he sees. Without warning, he grabs both of my wrists and literally kneels at my feet.

"Please dance with me," he says. "I know that dancing is awkward and out-dated, and I know that you don't like doing stuff like that and, if I'm honest, neither do I, and I know that the night isn't going to last very long and soon everyone will just go home back to their laptops and their empty beds, and we'll probably be alone tomorrow, and we all have to go to school on Monday—but I just think that if you tried it, you know, *dancing*, you might feel for a few minutes that all of this, all of these *people* . . . none of it is really too bad."

I look down and meet his eyes.

I start to laugh before kneeling down too.

And then I do something really weird.

Once I'm on my knees—I really can't help it—I kind of fall forward into him and fling my arms round him.

"Yes," I say into his ear.

So he puts his arms round my waist, lifts us both to our feet, and resumes pulling me through the adolescent expanses.

We reach the center of the crowd clustered round the DJ.

He puts his hands on my shoulders. Our faces are centimeters apart. It's so loud he has to scream.

"*Yes*, Tori! They're playing the Smiths! They're playing the beautiful Smiths, Tori!"

The Smiths are the band of the internet—more specifically, and unfortunately, a band that many people listen to simply because Morrissey has that vintage, self-deprecating coolness that everyone seems to crave. If the internet were an actual country, "There Is a Light That Never Goes Out" would be its national anthem.

I feel myself step slightly backwards.

"Do you . . . do you have . . . a *blog*?"

For a second, he's confused, but then he just smiles and shakes his head. "Jesus, Tori! Do I have to have a blog to like the Smiths? Is that the rule now?"

And this is the moment, I guess, when I decide that I couldn't care less about anything else tonight, I couldn't care less about blogs or the internet or films or what people are wearing, and yes, yes, I am going to have fun, I am going to have a good time, I am going to be with my one and only friend, Michael Holden, and we are going to dance until we can't even breathe and we have to go home and face our empty beds. So when we start jumping up and down, smiling so ridiculously, looking at each other and at the sky and not really at anything, Morrissey singing something about shyness, I really don't think things can be so bad after all.

TWENTY-SIX

At 12:16 a.m., I go inside because if I don't pee I think my bladder will erupt. Everyone is waiting for Solitaire's blog post, which, according to recent rumor, will be published at 12:30 a.m. People are sitting, phones in their hands. I find the bathroom and, when I leave it, I see Lucas alone in a corner, texting. He sees me staring and jumps up, but rather than walking towards me, he quickly exits. Like he's trying to avoid me.

I follow him into the living room, intending to apologize for forgetting about hanging out with him today, but he doesn't see me. I watch as he wanders up to Evelyn. She is wearing these hooped earrings, chunky heels, leggings with upside-down crosses on them, and a faux-fur coat. Her messy hair is piled up on the top of her head. Lucas, similarly, is in tonight's hipster getup—a loose Joy Division T-shirt with the sleeves rolled, too-tight jeans, and desert boots. Lucas says something to her and she nods back at him. That's it, I've decided. Despite what Lucas said, they are definitely a couple.

I go back outside. It has finally started to snow. Properly. The music's over, but everyone's skipping around, screaming, trying to catch flakes in their mouths. I look out at the scene. The flakes float on the water and dissolve, joining with the river as it sails past me towards the sea. I love snow. Snow can make anything beautiful.

It's then that I see Becky again.

She's with a guy up against a tree and I know she's definitely still drunk because they're not even kissing romantically. I'm about to turn away, but then they move around a little and I see who the guy is.

It's Ben Hope.

I don't know how long I stand there, but at some point he opens his eyes and sees me. Becky looks too. She giggles and then she *realizes*. I got a drink on my way out, but it's fallen on the snow now and my hand is just cupping the air. They recoil from me, and then Ben hurries past me and into the house. Becky stays by the tree.

She raises her eyebrows at me when I reach her and says, "*What?*"

I wish I were dead. My hands clench and unclench.

She laughs. "*What*, for God's sake!"

Becky has betrayed me. Because she doesn't care.

"Everything I thought about you," I say, "is wrong."

"What are you talking about?"

"Am I hallucinating this?"

"Are you drunk?"

"You are a nasty *bitch*," I say. I think I'm shouting, but I can't really tell. I'm only 70 percent sure I'm saying any of this out loud. "I used to think that you were just forgetful, but now I have solid proof that you just *don't care*."

"Wh—"

"Don't try acting like you don't know what you've just done. Grow a backbone. Go on, try and defend yourself. I am literally dying to hear your justification. Are you going to tell me that I don't understand?"

Becky's eyes begin to fill with tears. As if she's actually *upset*. "I'm not—"

"That's it, isn't it? I'm your naive little friend whose sad little life makes you feel *better* about yourself. Well, you're absolutely spot-on there. I haven't got a single clue about anything. But you know what I do know? I know when someone is being a nasty bitch. Go ahead and cry your stupid little crocodile tears if you want to. You don't fucking care *at all*, do you?"

Becky's voice is sober now, if a little wobbly, and she begins to shout at me. "Well—you—you're the one being a nasty bitch! Jesus Christ, just calm down!"

I pause. This is bad. I need to stop. I can't. "I'm sorry—do you have any comprehension of the level of betrayal you have just reached? Do you have *any* concept of friendship? I didn't think it was possible for someone to be *that* selfish, but *clearly* I've been wrong all this time." I think I'm crying. "You've killed me. You've literally killed me."

"Calm *down*! Oh my *God*, Tori!"

"You have solidly proven that everyone and everything is shit. Well done. Gold star. Please delete yourself from my life."

And that is it. I am gone. I am gone. I guess everyone is like this. Smiles, hugs, years together, holidays, late-night confessions, tears, phone calls, one million words—they don't mean anything. Becky doesn't care. No one really cares.

The snowfall is blurring my vision, or maybe it's the tears. I stumble back to the house and, just as I enter, people start screaming and holding their phones above their heads. I can't stop crying, but I manage to get out my phone and find the Solitaire page and there is the post:

00:30 January 23rd

Solitairians.

We would like you to collaborate on our latest venture.

At our meetup tonight, there is a Higgs Year 12 named Ben Hope who has deliberately injured a Truham Year 11. Ben Hope is a known homophobe and a bully, who hides behind the facade of popularity.

We hope that you will join Solitaire in preventing such acts of violence in the future by giving him exactly what he deserves.

Act accordingly. Protect the unprotected. Justice is everything.

Patience Kills.

TWENTY-SEVEN

There is a tornado of people around me, screaming in all directions, and I can't go anywhere. After several minutes of pandemonium, the flow steadily softens in one direction rather than a whirlpool and I am torn out of the house in the current. Everyone is in the garden. Someone cries out: "Karma, motherfucker!"

Is this karma?

Two boys hold Ben Hope while several others hurl punches and kicks at him. Blood splatters onto the snow and the spectacle gets wild cheers every time a hit is made. Only a few meters away, Nick and Charlie are standing in the crowd, Nick's arm round Charlie, both of their expressions unreadable. Charlie steps forward, as if he's about to intervene, but Nick pulls him back, gesturing to his phone. Charlie nods and Nick presses three buttons—999—before holding it to his ear.

I couldn't stick up for Charlie, and now Solitaire's doing my job for me. I've never been able to do my job properly, I suppose.

Then again, maybe this isn't about Charlie.

I think back to what Michael said to me in Café Rivière.

Oh God.

Maybe it's about me.

I laugh, tears still falling, so hard that my stomach aches. Silly. Silly thought. Silly me. *Selfish*. Nothing is *ever* about me.

Another hit. The crowd shrieks with joy, waving their drinks in the air, like they're at a concert, like they're happy.

Nobody is trying to help.

Nobody

nobody.

I don't know what to do. If this were a film, I would be there, I would be the hero stopping this false justice. But this isn't a film. I am not the hero.

I start to panic. I turn back into the crowd and break out through the other side. My eyes won't focus. Sirens start to blare, distant in the town. Ambulance? Police? Justice is everything? Patience Kills?

Michael, out of nowhere, grabs me by the shoulders. He's not looking at me. He's looking at the scene, just like the rest of the crowd, watching but doing nothing, not caring.

I throw his hands off me, muttering crazily. "This is what we are. Solitaire. We could just—they just—they'll *kill* him. You think you've met bad people, and then you meet people who are worse. They're doing nothing—they're not—we're just as bad. We're just as bad for doing nothing. We don't care. We don't care that they could *kill* him—"

"*Tori.*" Michael takes hold of my shoulders again, but I step backwards and his arms drop. "I'll take you home."

"I don't want you to take me home."

"I'm your friend, Tori. This is what we do."

"I don't have any friends. You are not my friend. Stop pretending that you fucking *care.*"

Before he can argue, I'm gone. I'm running. I'm out of the house. I'm out of the garden. I'm out of the world. The giants and demons are rising and I am chasing them. I'm pretty sure I'm going to be sick. Am I hallucinating this? I am not the hero. It's funny because it's true. I begin to laugh, or maybe I'm crying. Maybe I don't care anymore. Maybe I'm going to pass out. Maybe I'll die when I'm twenty-seven.

PART 2

DONNIE: A storm is coming, Frank says. A storm that will swallow the children. And I will deliver them from the kingdom of pain. I will deliver the children back to their doorsteps. I'll send the monsters back to the underground. I'll send them back to a place where no one else can see them. Except for me, 'cause I am Donnie Darko.

DONNIE DARKO: THE DIRECTOR'S CUT (2004)

ONE

Lucas was a crier. It happened most days in primary school and I think it was one of the main reasons I was his friend. I didn't mind the crying.

It would come on slowly. He'd sport this odd expression for a few minutes before: not sad, but as if he were replaying a television program in his head, watching the events unfold. He'd look down, but not at the ground. And then the tears would start falling. Always silent. Never heaving.

I don't think that there was a particular reason for the crying. I think that was just his personality. When he wasn't crying, we played chess or lightsaber duels or Pokémon battles. When he was crying, we'd read books. This was the time in my life when I read books.

I always felt at my best when we were together. It's funny—I've never found that relationship with another person. Well, maybe Becky. In our early days.

When Lucas and I left primary school, we left with the assumption that we would continue to see each other. As all those who have left primary school can guess, this never came to fruition. I saw him only once more after that time—before now, of course. A chance meeting on the high street. I was twelve. He told me that he'd sent me an Easter egg in the post. It was May. I hadn't got any post since my birthday.

At home that evening, I wrote him a card. I said that I hoped that we could still be friends, and I gave him my email address, and I drew a picture of myself and him for good measure. I never sent that card. It stayed in the bottom of my top desk drawer for several years until I cleared out my room. When I found it, I tore it up and threw it away.

I think about all these things as I'm wandering the school on Monday. I can't find him. All this time, I've just been sitting around, moaning about how shit everything is, not bothering to try and make things better. I hate myself for that. I'm like all those people in the crowd at the Solitaire meetup, not bothering to help. I don't think I can be like that anymore.

Michael isn't anywhere to be seen either. He's probably decided to leave me alone for good now, which is fair enough. I screwed it all up again. Classic Tori.

Anyway, I want to talk to Lucas about Saturday, apologize for not meeting up with him like I said I would. Tell him he doesn't have to avoid me anymore.

Twice I think I see his lanky limbs swish round corridor corners, but as I run to catch him, I realize it's just another of the thin-faced sixth-form boys. He's not in the common room before school, at break, or at lunch. After a while, I forget who I'm looking for and just continue on walking forever. I check my phone several times, but there's only one message on my blog:

Anonymous: *Thought for the day: What is the point in studying literature?*

Becky and Our Lot have not talked to me all day.

$$\left(\cdots\right)$$

Ben Hope did not go to hospital. He wasn't anywhere near death. Some people seem to feel sorry for him, whereas others say he deserved what he got for being a homophobe. I am not sure what I think about it anymore. When Charlie and I talked about it, he seemed pretty shaken up.

"This is my fault," he said, grimacing. "It's my fault that Ben was angry in the first place, so it's my fault that Solitaire—"

"It's not anyone's fault," I told him, "except Solitaire's."

On Tuesday, Kent keeps me back after English. Becky seems to be quietly hopeful that I'm in some kind of severe trouble, but Kent says nothing until everyone is gone. He sits on his desk, arms folded, glasses angled at a nonchalant slant.

"Tori, I think we need to talk about your 'heroes of *Pride and Prejudice*' essay."

"..."

"It was a very angry essay."

"..."

"Why did you decide to write it in that way?"

"I really hate that book."

Kent rubs his forehead. "Yes. I got that impression."

He retrieves my essay from a cardboard folder and places it between us.

"*I am sorry, Mr. Kent,*" he reads, "*but I have not read* Pride and Prejudice. *I disagreed with the very first sentence and that was enough for me.*" Kent looks up at me briefly, before skipping to my second paragraph.

"*Alas, Elizabeth Bennet does not love Mr. Darcy while he is 'imperfect.' Only once his better character is revealed does she decide that she will accept Pemberley and the hundred billion a year. Fancy that. It seems that it is impossible, for almost everyone in this novel, to look past an exterior and try to dig out the greatness within others. Yes, all right, Elizabeth is prejudiced. I get it, Jane Austen. Well done.*"

"Yeah," I say. "All right."

"I'm not done," chuckles Kent. He skips to my conclusion. "*This is why Mr. Darcy is, in my eyes, a true hero. He struggles on, despite being so harshly treated and judged.* Pride and Prejudice *is one man's fight to be seen by others as he sees himself. Therefore, he is not typical. A typical hero is brave, confident, and dashing. Mr. Darcy is shy, haunted by himself, and unable to fight for his own character. But he loves, and I guess that is all that matters in the world of literature.*"

I should be embarrassed about this, but I'm really not.

He sighs again. "It's interesting that you identify with a character like Mr. Darcy."

"Why?"

"Well, most students choose Elizabeth as the strongest character."

I look at him squarely. "Mr. Darcy has to put up with everyone hating him for reasons that aren't even true, and he doesn't even complain about it. I'd call that pretty strong."

Kent chuckles again. "Elizabeth Bennet is thought to be one of the strongest women in nineteenth-century literature. I take it you're not a feminist."

"I am a feminist," I say. "I just don't like this book."

He smiles broadly and doesn't answer.

I shrug again. "It's just what I think."

He nods thoughtfully. "Well, that's fair. Don't write so colloquially in your exam though. You're smart and it'll get you a bad mark."

"All right."

He hands me back the essay.

"Listen, Tori." He scratches his chin, making a grating sound against his stubble. "I've noticed that you've been quite significantly underachieving in all of your AS subjects." He pauses and blinks. "I mean, you were doing really very well in Year 11. Especially in English."

"I got a B in my sociology mock last term," I say. "That's not that bad."

"You've been getting Ds in English, Tori. People who get two A*s in English GCSEs do not then get Ds at AS level."

". . ."

"Can you think of a reason why this has happened?" He stares at me cautiously.

"I suppose . . . I don't really like school . . . anymore."

"Why's that?"

"It's just . . . I just hate being here." My voice dies away. I look up at the classroom clock. "I need to go. I need to get to music."

He nods very slowly. "I think that a lot of people hate being here." He turns his head to the side and glances out of the window. "But that's life, isn't it?"

"Yeah."

"If you go on acknowledging that you hate it, you're never going to want to be here. You can't give up on it. You can't be defeatist about it."

"Yeah."

"Okay."

I run out of the door.

TWO

I find Lucas by the lockers at the end of school, and this time he really cannot avoid me.

He's with Evelyn and that guy with the quiff. They're all pinching their noses because Solitaire stink-bombed the entire school approximately one hour ago. Classic, disgusting, and unnecessary; however, most people in school today seem to be generally supportive of this particular prank. The smell in this corridor is moldy egg. I cover my mouth and nose with my jumper.

Lucas, Evelyn, and Quiff Guy are in conversation—serious conversation—but because I've recently turned into a rude and arrogant person, I don't give a crap that I'm going to interrupt.

"Why are you avoiding me?" I call.

Lucas nearly drops several large ring binders and stares round Evelyn's head. He moves his hand away from his nose. "Victoria. God."

Evelyn and the guy turn and study me suspiciously before slinking away. I step towards Lucas. He's got his bag slung over his shoulder.

"Are you sure Evelyn isn't your girlfriend?" I ask, still holding my jumper over part of my face.

"What?" He laughs nervously. "Why do you think that?"

"I always see you with her. Are you her secret boyfriend?"

He blinks several times. "Uh, no. No."

"Are you lying?"

"*No.*"

"Are you angry because I forgot we were going to meet up on Saturday?"

"No. No, I promise I'm not."

"Then why are you avoiding me? I haven't seen you since . . . I haven't seen you this week."

He shoves the ring binders into the locker and withdraws a sizeable art sketchbook. "I'm not avoiding you."

"Don't lie."

He flinches.

I get it. Lucas has tried so hard since term started to be friends with me again. And I've been such an arse about it. Just because I hate making friends, I've been rude to him, I've ignored him, *I've* avoided him, and I haven't made a single bit of effort for him. That's me, as usual, being an utter dick to everyone for no apparent reason. I get it. I get that I don't exactly *engage* with people. But, since Saturday, I've felt that *not* engaging can be just as bad as the alternative.

Now Lucas doesn't seem to even want to know me.

"Look," I say, dropping my jumper, feeling desperation sink into my soul, "we were best friends once, weren't we? I don't want you to avoid me. I'm sorry I forgot about Saturday. I forget stuff like that. But you're one of three people who I've ever been friends with and I don't want to not talk to you anymore."

He runs a hand through his hair. It's halfway down his forehead.

"I—I don't know what to say."

"Just *please* tell me why you avoided me on Saturday night?"

Something's different. His eyes shift from side to side. "I can't be around you." Then quieter: "I can't do this."

"What?"

He slams the locker shut. It makes a noise that's far too loud. "I've got to go."

"Just—"

But he's already walked away. I stand by his locker for a minute or so. The moldy egg smell appears to be intensifying, as does my hatred for Solitaire. Lucas forgot to lock his locker properly, so I can't resist opening it and having a look inside. There are three ring binders in there: English literature, psychology, and history, along with a bunch of sheets. I pick one up. It's a psychology sheet about coping with stress. There's a picture of a girl holding her head in both hands, a bit like that famous painting *The Scream*. One of the suggestions is regular exercise, and another is writing down your problems. I replace the sheet and shut Lucas's locker.

THREE

Grandma and Grandad have come round. The first time in months. We're all at the dinner table and I'm trying not to catch anyone's eye, but I keep seeing Mum glance concernedly towards Grandad and then glance concernedly towards Charlie. Dad's sitting between Charlie and Oliver. I'm at the head of the table.

"Your mum's told us you've got back into the rugby team, Charlie," says Grandad. When he talks, he leans forward like we can't hear him, even though he speaks twice as loud as everyone else. I think that this is very stereotypical of Grandad. "It's a blessing they let you back in. You really messed them around, what with all that time off."

"Yeah, it was really nice of them," says Charlie. He's holding his knife and fork in his hands by the side of his plate.

"It feels like we haven't seen Charlie for years," says Grandma, "doesn't it, Richard? Next time we see you, you'll probably have a wife and children."

Charlie forces himself to laugh politely.

"Would you pass me the Parmesan, Dad?" asks Mum.

Grandad passes the Parmesan. "A rugby team always needs a skinny one like yourself. To do the running, you understand. If you'd have eaten more earlier on, you would have grown big enough to be one of the proper players, but I suppose it's too late for that now. I blame your parents personally. More dark vegetables at an early age."

"You haven't told us about your Oxford trip, Dad," says Mum.

I look at the plate. It's lasagna. I haven't eaten anything yet.

I discreetly retrieve my phone from my pocket and I have a message. I'd texted Lucas earlier.

(15:23) **Tori Spring**

look I'm really really sorry

(18:53) **Lucas Ryan**

It's fine x

(19:06) **Tori Spring**

quite clearly it's not

(19:18) I'm so sorry

(19:22) **Lucas Ryan**

It's not even about that tbh x

(19:29) **Tori Spring**

well why are you avoiding me then

Dad's finished his dinner, but I've been taking it slow for Charlie.

"How are you getting along, Tori?" asks Grandma. "Enjoying sixth form?"

"Yes, yeah." I smile at her. "It's great."

"They must treat you like adults now."

"Oh, yes, yeah."

(19:42) **Tori Spring**

you at least need to tell me why

"And your lessons are interesting?"

"Yes, very."

"Thought much about university?"

I smile. "No, not really."

Grandma nods.

"You should start thinking," Grandad grumbles. "Important life decisions. One wrong move and you could end up in an office for the rest of your life. Like me."

"How's Becky?" asks Grandma. "She's such a lovely girl. It would be nice if you could keep in touch when you leave."

"She's fine, yeah. She's good."

"Such beautiful long hair."

(19:45) **Lucas Ryan**

Can you meet me in town tonight? x

"How about you, Charlie? Have you been thinking about sixth form? Subjects-wise?"

"Erm, yeah, well, I'll definitely do classics, and probably English, but apart from that I'm not really sure. Maybe music or something. Or psychology."

"Where are you going to apply?"

"Higgs, I think."

"Higgs?"

"Harvey Greene. Tori's school."

Grandma nods. "I see."

"An all-girls' school?" Grandad scoffs. "You won't find any discipline there. A growing boy needs discipline."

My fork makes a loud noise on my plate. Grandad's eyes flicker towards me, and then back at Charlie.

"You've made some good strong friends at that school. Why are you leaving them?"

"I'll see them outside of school."

"Your friend Nicholas, he's at Truham sixth form currently, is he not?"

"Yeah."

"So you don't want to be with him?"

Charlie nearly chokes on his food. "It's not that. I just think that Higgs is a better school."

Grandad shakes his head. "Education. What's that compared to friendship?"

I can't take any more of this and I'm getting much too angry so I ask to be excused with a stomachache. As I leave, I hear Grandad say:

"Girl's got a weak stomach. Just like her brother."

I arrive first. I sit at a table outside Café Rivière. We agreed to meet at 9 p.m., and it's just gone ten to. The street is empty and the river quiet, but a faint echo of one of those indie bands—maybe Noah and the Whale or Fleet Foxes or Foals or the xx or someone like that, I can never tell the difference anymore—is drifting out of an open window above my head. The music continues to play while I wait for Lucas.

I wait until 9 p.m. Then I wait until 9:15 p.m. Then I wait until 9:30 p.m.

At 10:07 p.m., my phone vibrates.

(22:07) **Lucas Ryan**

Sorry x

I look at the message for a long time. At the single word without a full stop, at the tiny, meaningless x.

I place my phone on the table and look up at the sky. The sky always seems to be lighter when it's snowing. I breathe out. A cloud of dragon breath sails above my head.

Then I stand up and start to walk home.

FOUR

In Wednesday assembly, the sixth-formers spread themselves along five sectioned-off rows of the hall seating. You have to fill up all the gaps, otherwise not everyone will fit in the hall, so you don't get to choose where you sit. This is how I end up accidentally sitting between Rita and Becky.

As people are filing into the seating rows, Ben Hope, back at school with a moderately bruised face, stares directly at me. He doesn't seem angry or scared, and he doesn't even try to ignore me. He just looks sad. Like he's about to cry. Probably because he's not going to be popular anymore. I haven't seen Ben and Becky together yet, which is a sign that maybe Becky actually listened to my explosion. I think about Charlie. I wonder where Michael is. I wish Ben didn't exist.

Kent's taking the assembly. He's talking about women. Most of our assemblies are about women.

"—but I'm going to tell you the absolute truth. You, as women, are at an automatic disadvantage in the world."

Becky, on my right, keeps changing which side she crosses her legs. I make a conscious effort not to move.

"I don't think . . . that many of you realize how fortunate you have been so far."

I start counting Kent's pauses under my breath. Becky doesn't join me.

"Going to . . . the *best* . . . girls' grammar school in the county . . . is an unbelievable privilege."

I can see Lucas two rows in front of me. He managed to catch my eye as he was sitting down on the way in and I didn't bother trying to look away. I just stared. I don't even feel angry, really, about him standing me up last night. I don't feel anything.

"I know that many of you . . . complain about the hard work, but until you've faced the real world, the world of work, you can't understand the meaning . . . of hard work."

Rita taps me suddenly on the knee. She holds out her hymn sheet. Underneath the lyrics to "Love Shine a Light" she has written:

You're isolating yourself!!!!!!

"You are going to face a phenomenal shock once you leave this school. This school, where *all* are treated as equals."

I read it several times, then study Rita. She's just someone I know. I'm not really friends with her.

"You are going to have to work harder than men . . . to get to where you want to be. *That* is the simple truth."

She shrugs at me.

"Therefore I hope that, while you're at this school, you'll think about, and be appreciative of, what you've got. You are all very lucky. You have the potential to do anything you want to do and be anything you want to be."

I fold up the hymn sheet into a paper plane, but I don't fly it, because you can't do that in assembly. Everyone stands and sings "Love Shine a Light" and the lyrics nearly make me laugh out loud. On my way out, I drop the paper plane discreetly into Becky's blazer pocket.

$$\left(\cdots\right)$$

I don't sit with anyone at lunch. I end up not having any lunch actually, but I don't mind. I walk around the school. At many points during the day, I wonder where Michael could be, but at other times I'm fairly sure that I don't care.

I haven't seen Michael all week.

I have been thinking a lot about his skating. National Youth Speed Skating Semifinals.

I wonder why he didn't tell me about it.

I wonder why he isn't here.

I'm sitting against the tennis courts, surrounded by seagulls, which is odd, because they should have migrated by now. It's Period 5. Music. I always skip Wednesday Period 5 because that is our performance practice lesson. I am watching as every girl in Year 7 makes her way out of the main school building and onto the field, some running, most laughing, and each with a collection of party poppers in her hands. I can't see any teachers.

I don't know what Solitaire has said to Year 7, but it is clear to me that this is their doing.

I take out my phone and load up Google. I type in *Michael Holden*, and then I type in the name of our town. Then I press Enter.

Like magic, my Michael Holden appears in the search results.

The first result is an article from our county newspaper, entitled "Local Teen Wins National Speed Skating Championship." I click on it. It takes a while to load. My knees start to bob up and down in anticipation. Sometimes I hate the internet.

The article is about three years old. There is an accompanying picture of fifteen-year-old Michael, but he doesn't look so very different. Maybe his face is a little less defined. Maybe his hair is a little longer. Maybe he's not quite so tall. In the picture, he is standing on a podium with a trophy and a bunch of flowers. He is smiling.

Local teen Michael Holden has skated to victory at this year's National Under-16 Speed Skating Championships . . .

Holden's previous victories include Regional Under-12 Champion, Regional Under-14 Champion, and National Under-14 Champion . . .

The head of the UK's Speed Skating authority, Mr. John Lincoln, has spoken out in response to Holden's undeniably extraordinary run of victories. Lincoln claimed, "We have found a future international competitor. Holden clearly displays the commitment, experience, drive, and talent to bring the UK to victory in a sport that has never received satisfactory attention in this country."

I head back to the search results page. There are many more articles of a similar nature. Michael won the Under-18 Championships last year.

I guess this is why he was angry when he came second in the semifinal. And fair enough. I think I would be angry, if I were him.

I sit there, staring at Google, for some time. I wonder whether I feel star-struck, but I don't think that's really it. It just seems momentarily impossible for Michael to have this spectacular life that I don't know about. A life where he's not simply running around with a smile on his face doing stuff that has no point.

It's so easy to assume you know everything about a person.

I click off my phone and lean back against the wire fence.

The Year 7s have now congregated. A teacher runs out of school towards them, but she's too late. The Year 7s shout a countdown from ten, and then they lift their party poppers into the air and let loose, and it sounds like I've wandered into a World War II battlefield. Soon everyone is screaming and jumping, the streamers spiraling through the air like some crazy rainbow hurricane. Other teachers begin to show, also screaming. I find myself smiling, and then I begin to laugh, and then instantly feel disappointed in myself. I shouldn't be enjoying anything that Solitaire is doing, but also this is the first time in my life that I have ever felt a positive emotion towards Year 7.

FIVE

I'm on my way home on the bus when Michael finally decides to make his dramatic reappearance. I'm sitting in the second seat from the back on the left downstairs, when he spontaneously cycles up beside me on his moldy old bike so that he is rolling down the road at the same speed as the bus. The window that I'm looking out of is all grimy and the snow has dried water droplets into it, but I can still see his smug face in profile, grinning in the wind like a dog hanging its head out of the car.

He turns, searching along the windows, eventually realizing that I am in fact directly adjacent to him. Hair billowing, coat flapping behind him like a cape, he waves, freakishly, and then slaps his hand so hard on the window that every stupid kid on the bus stops throwing whatever they're throwing and looks at me. I raise my own hand and wave, feeling quite ill.

He keeps this up until I get off the bus, ten minutes later, by which time it has started to snow again. I tell Nick and Charlie that they can go on without me. When we're alone, we sit on a garden wall, Michael propping his bike up against it. I notice that he isn't wearing his school uniform.

I look to my left, up at his face. He's not looking at me. I wait for him to start the conversation, but he doesn't. I think he's challenging me.

It's taken longer than it should for me to recognize that I want to be around him.

"I'm—" I say, forcing the words out, "—sorry."

He blinks as if confused, turns to me, and smiles gently. "It's okay," he says.

I nod a little and look away.

"We've done this before, haven't we?" he says.

"Done what?"

"The awkward apology thing."

I think back to the "manically depressed psychopath" comment. This isn't the same though. That was me being stupid and his anger getting the better of him. That was just words.

I didn't know Michael at all back then.

Michael still has that spark. That light. But there's more there now. Things that cannot be seen, only found.

"Where've you been?" I ask.

He looks away and chuckles. "I got *suspended*. For Monday afternoon, yesterday, and today."

This is so ridiculous that I actually laugh. "Did you finally give someone a nervous breakdown?"

He chuckles again, but it's weird. "That could probably happen, to be fair." His face changes. "No, yeah, I—er—I swore at Kent."

I snort. "You *swore*? You got suspended because you *swore*?"

"Yep." He scratches his head. "Turns out Higgs has some sort of policy on that."

"The Land of Oppression." I nod, quoting Becky. "So how did that happen?"

"It sort of started in history, I guess. We had our mock-mocks a couple of weeks ago, and we got our marks on Monday, and my teacher held me back after the lesson because predictably I did really badly. I think I legitimately failed. So she started having a real go at me, you know, raving on about how much of a disappointment I am and how I don't even *try*. That's when I started to get pretty annoyed, because, like, I clearly tried. But she kept going on and on, and she held up my essay and pointed at it and was like, 'What do you think this is? Nothing in this makes sense. Where's your Point Evidence Explanation? Where's your PEE?' Basically, she ended up taking me to Kent's office like I was some primary-school kid."

He pauses. He isn't looking at me.

"And Kent started his big speech about how I should be better than this and I'm not committing enough to schoolwork and I'm not putting in enough effort. And I tried to defend myself, but you know what Kent's like—as soon as I started trying to reason with him, he got all aggressive and patronizing, which made me even *more* angry, because, you know, teachers simply *cannot* admit to a student that they could *possibly* be wrong, and then, like, I didn't *mean* to, but I was like, 'You don't even fucking *care* though, do you?' And, erm, yeah. I got suspended."

This reminds me of the Michael that Nick described the first day of term. But instead of finding this story a little strange, I actually feel pretty impressed.

"What a rebel," I say.

He gives me a long look. "Yes," he says. "I'm awesome."

"Teachers really *don't* care though."

"Yeah. I should have known that really."

We both return to staring at the row of houses opposite. The windows are all orange from the setting sun. I scuff my shoes on the snowy pavement. I kind of want to ask him about his skating, but at the same time I feel like that's *his* thing. His special, private thing.

"I've been pretty bored without you," I say.

There's a long pause.

"Me too," Michael says.

"Did you hear about what the Year 7s did today?"

"Yeah . . . that was hilarious."

"I was there. I always sit on the field Wednesday Period 5 so I was literally right there. It was like . . . it was raining streamers or something."

He seems to stop moving. After a few seconds, he turns his head slowly towards me.

"*That* was a lucky coincidence," he says.

It takes me a minute to get what he's saying.

It's ridiculous. Solitaire would have no way of knowing that I always skip that lesson and sit on the field. Teachers hardly notice most of the time. It's *ridiculous*. But I start thinking about what Michael said before. About *Star Wars*. "Material Girl." The cats. The violin. And the Ben Hope attack—that was about *my* brother. But it's impossible. I'm not special. It's entirely impossible. But—

There have been *a lot* of coincidences.

"Yes," I say. "Just a coincidence."

We both stand up and start to walk along the gradually whitening path, Michael pushing his bike along beside him. It leaves a long gray line behind us. Little white dots of snow rest in Michael's hair.

"What now?" I ask. I'm not quite sure which "now" I'm talking about. This minute? Today? The rest of our lives?

"Now?" Michael considers my question. "Now we celebrate and rejoice in our youth. Isn't that what we're supposed to do?"

I find myself grinning. "Yes. That is what we're supposed to do."

We walk a little farther. The snow grows from a light sprinkling to flakes as large as five-pence pieces.

"I heard about what you said to Becky," he says.

"Who told you?"

"Charlie."

"Who told *Charlie*?"

He shakes his head. "I don't know."

"When did you talk to Charlie?"

He avoids my eye. "The other day. I just wanted to make sure you were all right—"

"What, do you think I'm *depressed* or something?"

I say this much too angrily.

I don't want people to be worried about me. There's nothing *to* worry about. I don't want people to try and understand why I'm the way I am, because *I* should be the first person to understand that. And I *don't* understand yet. I don't want people to interfere. I don't want people in my head, picking out this and that, permanently picking up the broken pieces of me.

If that's what friends do, then I don't want any.

He smiles. A proper smile. Then he laughs. "You really cannot accept that people care!"

I don't say anything. He's right. But I don't say anything.

He stops laughing. Several minutes pass in silence.

I start to think about four weeks ago, when I didn't know Michael. When Solitaire hadn't happened. I am aware that I feel sadder about things now. A lot of things around me have been very sad, and I seem to be the only one who can see it. Becky, for example. Lucas. Ben Hope. Solitaire. Everyone is okay with hurting people. Or maybe they cannot see that they're hurting people. But I can.

The problem is that people don't act.

The problem is that *I* don't act.

I just sit here, doing nothing, assuming that someone else is going to make things better.

Eventually, Michael and I end up at the edge of town. It's getting dark now, and more than one streetlamp flickers on as we pass, casting a yellow glow across the ground. We walk down a wide alley between two large houses and break out into the fields, slick with snow, which stretch between the town and the river. Whites, grays, blues; everything is a blurry mist, rain on the windscreen, a painting.

I stand there. It all kind of stops, like I've left earth. Like I've left the universe.

"It's beautiful," I say. "Don't you think the snow is beautiful?"

I expect Michael to agree with me, but he doesn't.

"I don't know," he says. "It's just cold. It's romantic, I guess, but it just makes things cold."

SIX

"So, Tori." Kent scans my next essay. "What was your opinion this time?"

It's Friday lunchtime. I didn't really have anything to do so I came to give in my next English essay early: "To what extent is marriage the central concern of *Pride and Prejudice*?" It appears that Kent is talkative today—my least favorite character trait.

"I wrote a normal essay."

"I thought you might." He nods. "I still want to know what you thought."

I try to think back to when I wrote it. Monday lunch? Tuesday? All the days blur into one.

"Do you think marriage is the central concern?"

"It's *a* concern. Not the *central* concern."

"Do you think that Elizabeth cares about marriage at all?"

I picture the film. "I think she does. But it doesn't really occur to her when she's with Darcy. Like, she doesn't connect the two together. Darcy and marriage. They're two separate problems."

"Then what would you consider to be *the* central concern of *Pride and Prejudice*?"

"Themselves." I put my hands in my blazer pockets. "They spend the whole thing trying to merge who they really are and who they're seen as."

Kent nods again as if he knows something that I don't. "That's interesting. Most people say that love is the main theme. Or the class system." He puts my essay in a cardboard folder. "Do you read many books at home, Tori?"

"I don't read."

This seems to surprise him. "Yet you decided to take English literature A level."

I shrug.

"What do you do for fun, Tori?"

"Fun?"

"Surely you have a hobby. Everyone has a hobby. I read, for example."

My hobbies are drinking diet lemonade and being a bitter asshole. "I used to play the violin."

"Ah, you see? A hobby."

I don't like the implications of the word *hobby*. It makes me think of crafts. Or golf. Something that cheerful people do.

"I gave it up though."

"Why?"

"I don't know. I just didn't enjoy it much."

Kent nods for the hundredth time, tapping his hand on his knee. "That's fair. What *do* you enjoy?"

"I like watching films, I guess."

"What about friends? Don't you like being with them?"

I think about it. I should enjoy being with them. That's what people do. They hang around with friends for fun. They have adventures and they travel and they fall in love. They have fights and they lose each other, but they always find each other again. That's what people do.

"Who would you consider to be your friend?"

I again take my time to think and make a list in my head.

1. Michael Holden—Most qualified candidate for friend status.
2. Becky Allen—Was best friend in past, but obviously no more.
3. Lucas Ryan—See above.

Who else was my friend before this? I can't really remember.

"Things certainly are a lot easier the fewer friends you have." Kent sighs, folding his arms against his tweed jacket. "But then friendship comes with a lot of benefits."

I wonder what he's talking about. "Are friends really that important?"

He clasps his hands together. "Think about all the films you've seen. Most of the people who do well, and turn out happy, have friends, yes? Often it's just one or two very close friends. Look at Darcy and Bingley. Jane and Elizabeth. Frodo and Sam. Friends are important. People who are alone are usually the antagonists. You can't always rely just on yourself, even though it can seem like an easier way to live."

I disagree, so I choose not to say anything.

Kent leans forward. "Come on, Tori. Snap out of it. You're better than this."

"Better than what? Sorry my grades haven't been good."

"Don't be dumb. You know this isn't about that."

I frown at him.

He frowns right back—a sarcastic frown. "Get a grip. It's time for you to stand up. You can't continue to let life's chances just drift by."

I stand up out of the chair and turn round to leave.

As I open the door, he murmurs: "Nothing's going to change until you decide you want it to change."

I shut the door behind me, wondering if I just imagined this entire conversation.

SEVEN

Last period is a free period so I sit in the common room. I keep looking at Becky, who's working at another table, but she doesn't look at me. Evelyn is also there. She stays on her phone for the entire hour.

I check my blog and there's a message:

Anonymous: *Thought for the day: Why do people believe in God?*

I check the Solitaire blog, and the top post at the moment is a gif of a little boy blowing bubbles out of one of those plastic pots. A barrage of bubbles bursts into the air and up into the sky, and the camera looks up at them and sunlight shines through, lighting them up pink and orange and green and blue. Then the gif repeats, and you see the little boy again, blowing the bubbles into the sky, the boy, the bubbles, the sky, the boy, bubbles, sky.

When I get home, even Mum notices that something's changed and she tries half-heartedly to get it out of me, but I just end up back in my room. I walk around for a little bit and then lie down. Charlie comes into my room and asks me what's wrong. Just as I'm about to tell him, I start crying and it's not even silent tears this time, it's proper bawling, and I hate myself so much for it that it makes me literally barricade my face from the air with my arms and cry so hard that I stop breathing properly.

"I've got to do something," I keep saying. "I've got to do something."

"Do something about what?" asks Charlie, clutching his knees to his chest.

"Just—I don't know—everyone—everything's gone crazy. Everyone's gone crazy. I've ruined everything with Becky and I keep ruining every-thing with Michael and I don't even know who Lucas *is*, not really. My life was so normal before. I used to hate being so bored, but I want that back. I didn't care about anything before. But then—on Saturday—all those people, like, no one gave a single *shit* about it. They didn't care that Ben Hope could have been kicked to death. And I know he wasn't. But, like, I don't—I *can't* be like that anymore. I know it doesn't make any sense. I know I'm probably just stressing about nothing. I know, I'm shit, I'm a ridiculous excuse for a human being. But before Solitaire, everything was fine. I was fine. I used to be fine."

Charlie just nods. "All right."

He sits with me while I'm raving and crying and when I calm down I pre-tend I need to sleep so he goes away. I lie with my eyes open and think about everything that has happened in my entire life and it doesn't take me very long to get to where I am now. I decide sleeping is impossible so I start searching through my room for nothing in particular. I find my box of spe-cial things in my desk drawer—a box of keepsakes, I guess—and on the top is a diary that I kept in the summer of Year 7. I read the first page:

Sunday August 24th

Up at the crack of 10:30 a.m. Becky et moi went to the cinema today and saw Pirates of the Carribean (is that how you spell it???) 2 and OMG it was SO GOOD. Becky thinks Orlando Bloom is the fittest. Then we went to get pizza in the high street she had Hawaiian but obviously mine was plain cheese. YUM! She's coming round next week for a sleepover too, which is going to be so so fun. She says she needs to tell me about a boy that she likes!! And we're going to eat so much food and stay up all night and watch films!!!!!

I put the diary back into the bottom of the drawer and sit calmly for sev-eral minutes. Then I get it out again and find a pair of scissors and start shredding it, cutting up the pages and the hard cover, slashing and ripping, until there's just a confetti-like pile of paper shavings in my lap.

Also in the treasure box is an empty bubbles pot. Becky gave it to me for my birthday a long time ago. I used to love bubbles, even if I could never let go of the fact that they're always empty inside. And then I remember the gif on the Solitaire blog. That's another thing, then. Another thing to add to the list: the violin video and *Star Wars*, all that bullshit. I look at the bubbles pot, feeling nothing. Or everything. I don't know.

No. I *do* know.

Michael was right. He's been right this whole time. Solitaire. Solitaire is . . . Solitaire is talking to me. Michael was *right*.

It doesn't make any sense, but I know it's me. It's all been about me.

I run into the bathroom and throw up.

When I return, I shove away the box, shut the drawer, and open another. This one is full of stationery. I test out all of my pens with wild squiggles on the pieces of paper and chuck those that don't work under my bed, which is most of them. I'm humming loudly to cover up the sounds I'm hearing from the window, because I know that I'm making them up. My eyes keep tearing up then calming down then tearing up again, and I keep rubbing them so hard that I see sparkles even when they're open.

I grab the scissors again and spend at least half an hour sitting in front of my mirror and trimming my split ends obsessively. Then I find a big black marker and I get this sudden urge to write something. So on my own arm, in the big black marker, I write *I AM VICTORIA ANNABEL SPRING*, partly because I can't think of anything else to write, and partly because I'm feeling as if I need to remind myself that I actually have a middle name.

Solitaire is talking to me. Maybe deliberately, maybe not. But I've decided it's on me, now, to do something about it. It's all on me.

I move to my bedside table. I take out a few old pens and a few books I haven't read, and my makeup wipes and my current diary, which I don't write in anymore. I open it up, read a few of the entries and close it again.

It's very sad. Very clichéd teenager. I disgust myself. I close my eyes and hold my breath for as long as possible (forty-six seconds). I cry, consistently and pathetically, for a full twenty-three minutes. I turn on my laptop and scroll through my favorite blogs. I don't post anything on my own blog. I can't remember the last time I did that.

EIGHT

It's been a weird weekend. Not really knowing what to do, I stayed in bed for most of it, scrolling through the internet, watching TV, etc., etc. Nick and Charlie came to have a "chat" after lunch on Sunday and made me feel pretty bad for being a lazy slob. So my weekend concludes with Nick and Charlie dragging me to a local music festival at the Clay, which is a grassless field just over the river bridge, bordered by a scattering of trees and broken fences.

Nick and Charlie and I walk across the mud towards the crowds surrounding the stage. It's not quite snowing yet, but I can feel it coming. Whoever thought that January was a good month for a music festival was probably a sadist.

The band, apparently some London indie band, is so loud that you can hear them from the other end of the high street. While there aren't any actual lights, every other person appears to be holding a flashlight or carrying a glow stick, and towards the edge of the field is a violent bonfire. I feel significantly underprepared. I think about running back over the bridge and back up the high street, all the way home.

No. No running home.

"Are you all right?" shouts Charlie over the music. He and Nick are several paces ahead, Nick with his phone's flashlight shining in my direction, blinding me.

"Are you sticking with us?" Nick points at the stage. "We're going to go watch."

"No," I say.

Charlie just looks at me as I walk off. Nick pulls him away and they disappear into the crowd.

I disappear into the crowd too.

💬

It's pretty hot and I can't see much—just the green and yellow of glow sticks and the lights of the stage. This band has been on for at least half an hour and the Clay is now more like the Swamp. Mud splatters my jeans. I keep seeing people I know from school and, every time I do, I give them a large, sarcastic wave. In the middle of the crowd, Evelyn shakes me by the shoulders and screams that she's looking for her boyfriend. It really makes me dislike her.

After a while, I realize that I keep treading on bits of paper. They're literally *everywhere*. I'm alone in the crowd when I decide to pick one up and look at it properly, lighting it up with my phone's flashlight.

It's a flyer. Black background. There's a symbol in the middle in red: an upside-down heart, drawn in a scrawly sort of way so that it looks like the letter *A*, with a circle around it.

So that it sort of looks like the symbol for anarchy.

Beneath the symbol is the word:

FRIDAY

My hands begin to shake.

Before I have time to think any more about what this might mean, I'm pushed right next to Becky, where she's jumping up and down near the barrier with Lauren and Rita. Our eyes meet.

Lucas is there too, behind Rita. He's wearing this shirt with little metal edges on the collar, underneath a grandad jumper and a large denim jacket. He's also wearing Vans and rolled black jeans. Just looking at him makes me feel really sad.

I shove the FRIDAY flyer into my coat pocket.

Lucas sees me over Rita's shoulder and kind of cowers backwards, which must be pretty difficult in a crowd as packed as this. I point at my chest, not dropping my eyes. Then I point at him. Then I point towards the empty end of the field.

When he doesn't move, I grab him by the arm and start to pull him backwards, out and away from the crowds and the throbbing speakers.

I'm reminded of when we were ten, or nine, or eight, in a similar situation—me pulling Lucas along by the arm. He never did anything by himself. I was always very good at doing things by myself. I guess I sort of *enjoyed* looking after him. There comes a point, though, when you can't keep looking after other people anymore. You have to start looking after yourself.

Then again, I guess I don't do either of those things.

"What are you doing here?" he asks. We've broken out from the crowd and stopped a little way in front of the bonfire. Various groups of people wander past with drink bottles in their hands, laughing, though the area around the fire is largely empty.

"I'm doing things now," I say. I take hold of his shoulder and lean forward, quite seriously. "Why—*when* did you turn into a hipster?"

He gently removes my hand from his shoulder. "I'm serious," he says.

The band has stopped. There is momentary quiet, the air filled only with voices merging into one swirling noise. There are several of those flyers at my feet.

"I sat outside the café for a whole hour," I say, hoping to make him feel really bad. "If you don't tell me now why you're avoiding me, then, like, we might as well just get it over with and stop being friends."

He stiffens and turns red, visible even in the dim light. It dawns on me that we're never going to be best friends again.

"It's . . ." he says, "it is very difficult . . . for me . . . to be around you . . ."
"*Why?*"

It takes him a while to answer. He smooths his hair to one side, and rubs his eye, and checks his collar isn't turned up, and scratches his knee. And then he starts to laugh.

"You're so funny, Victoria." He shakes his head. "You're just so funny." At this, I get a sudden urge to punch him in the face. Instead, I descend into hysteria.

"For fuck's *sake!* What are you *talking* about?!" I begin to shout, but you can't really tell over the noise of the crowd. "You're *insane*. I don't know why you're saying any of this to me. I don't know why you decided you wanted to be BFFs all over again and now I don't know why you won't even look me in the eye, I don't understand *anything* you're doing or saying, and it's *killing* me, because I already don't understand a single thing about me or Michael or Becky or my brother or *anything* on this shitty planet. If you secretly hate me or something, *you need to spit it out*. I am asking you to give me *one* straight answer, *one* sentence that might sort at least *something* out in my head, but NO. You don't care, do you?! You don't give a SINGLE SHIT for my feelings or anyone else's. You're just like everyone else."

"You're wrong," he says. "You're wro—"

"Everyone's got such dreadful *problems*." I shake my head wildly, holding on to it with both hands. I start speaking in a posh voice for no reason. "Even you. Even perfect, innocent Lucas has *problems*."

He's staring at me in a kind of terrified confusion and it's absolutely hilarious. I start to crack up.

"Maybe, like, *everyone* I know has problems. Like, there are no happy people. *Nothing* works out. Even when it's someone who you think is perfect. Like my brother!" I grin wildly at him. "My brother, my little brother, he's soooo perfect, but he's—he doesn't like food, like, literally doesn't like food, or, I don't know, he loves it. He loves it *so* much that it has to be perfect all the time, you know?"

I grab Lucas by one shoulder again so he understands.

"And then one day he got so fed up with himself, he was like, he was so annoyed, he hated how much he loved food, yeah, so he thought it would be better if there wasn't any food." I start laughing so much that my eyes water. "But that's so silly! Because you've got to eat food or you'll die, won't you? So my brother, Charles, Charlie, he, he thought it would be better if he just got it over with then and there! So he, last year, he"—I hold up my wrist and point at it—"he *hurt* himself. And he wrote me this card afterwards, telling me he was really sorry and he didn't mean it to happen. But it did happen."

I shake my head and laugh and laugh. I know I'm exaggerating all of this. I know Charlie just had one really awful night, and I know I'm making it sound way more dramatic and way more horrific than it actually was. But my brain won't stop taking clouds and turning them into hurricanes.

"And you know what just makes me want to *die*? The fact that, like, all that time, I *knew* it was coming, but I didn't do *anything*. I didn't even say anything to anyone about it, because I thought I'd been *imagining* it."

There are tears running down my face.

"And you know what's *literally hilarious*? The card had a picture of a *cake* on it!"

He's not saying anything and he doesn't find it hilarious, which strikes me as odd. He makes this pained sound and turns at a sharp right angle and strides away. I wipe the tears of laughter from my eyes and then I take that flyer out of my pocket and look at it, but the music has started again and I'm too cold and my brain doesn't seem to be processing anything. Only that goddamn picture of that goddamn cake.

NINE

"Victoria? Tori? Are you there?"

Somebody is talking to me on the phone.

"Where are you? Are you all right?"

I am alone on the outskirts of the crowd. The music is gone. Everyone is waiting for the next band, and more and more people begin to join the crush, and it only takes a minute or two for me to be once again trapped in the heaving mass of bodies. The ground is covered in those flyers and people have started to pick them up. Everything is happening very fast.

"I'm fine," I say at last. "Charlie, I'm fine. I'm just on the field."

"Okay. Good. Nick and I are heading back to the car now. You need to come too."

There's a rustling as Nick takes the phone from Charlie.

"Tori. Listen to me. You need to get back to the car *right now.*"

But I can barely hear Nick.

I can barely hear Nick because something else is happening.

There's a huge LED screen on the stage. Up until this point, it has been displaying decorative moving shapes, and occasionally the names of the songs being played.

Now it's gone black, leaving only the dots of the glow sticks spread across the dark crowd. I begin to be jostled closer to the screen, the figures around me irresistibly drawn towards it. I turn away, intending to start to push out of the crowd, and that's when I see it—there's a figure, a boy figure, staring blankly from across the river. Is that Nick? I can't tell.

"Something's . . . something's happening . . ." I say into the phone, twisting back towards the screen.

"Tori, you NEED to get back to the car. It's going to get INSANE out there."

The LED screen changes. It shines pure white, then blood red, then back to black.

"Tori? Hello? Can you hear me?"

There's a tiny red dot in the center of the screen.

"TORI?!"

It magnifies and takes shape.

It's the upside-down heart.

The crowd screams as if Beyoncé has just graced the stage.

I press the red button on my phone.

And then a distorted, genderless voice begins.

"GOOD EVENING, SOLITAIRIANS."

Everyone puts their arms in the air and shrieks—with glee, with fear, I don't know anymore, but they're *loving it*. Bodies edge forward, crushing against each other, everyone sweating, and soon I'm struggling even to breathe.

"ARE WE HAVING A GOOD TIME?"

The ground vibrates as voices screech across the air. The flyer I picked up is in my hand. I can't see Lucas, or Becky, or anyone I know. I need to get out. I throw my elbows outwards and turn one-eighty degrees and begin to barge my way through the howling crowd—

"WE'VE *POPPED IN* TO TELL YOU ABOUT A *SPECIAL EVENT* WE'RE PLANNING."

I push against the bodies, but I don't seem to be moving. People are staring upwards at the screen as if hypnotized, shouting indiscernible strings of words—

And then I see him again. I peek through the gaps in the heads of the crowd. There, across the river. The boy.

"WE WANT IT TO BE A BIG SURPRISE. *THIS COMING FRIDAY*. IF YOU ATTEND HARVEY GREENE GRAMMAR SCHOOL, *HIGGS SCHOOL*, YOU HAD BETTER BE ON YOUR GUARD."

I squint, but it's so dark, and the crowd is so loud and so happy and so terrifying, and I can't see who it is. I swivel my body back to the LED screen, elbows and knees digging into me at every angle, and there's a countdown timer now showing, with the days, hours, minutes, and seconds—the crowd has started to fist-pump—04:01:26:52, 04:01:26:48, 04:01:26:45.

"IT'S GOING TO BE SOLITAIRE'S BIGGEST OPERATION YET."

And with that, all at once, at least twenty fireworks go off within the crowd, shooting upwards from the bodies like meteors and raining sparks down onto their heads, one of which is only five meters away from me. Those closest release petrified screams, jumping backwards and away from harm, but most of the screams are still screams of happiness, screams of excitement. The crowd begins to sway and shake and I'm buffeted in every direction, my heart pounding so hard I think I might be dying, yes, I'm dying, I'm going to die—until eventually I burst out the edge of the crowd and find myself right on the riverbank.

I gaze in horror at the crowd. Fireworks of all shapes and colors are continuously exploding among the bodies. At the edge, I see several people fleeing, one or two on fire. A few meters away a girl collapses and has to be dragged away by her wailing friends.

Most of them seem to be enjoying themselves though. Entranced by the rainbow lights.

"Tori Spring!"

For a moment, I think it's the Solitaire voice speaking, speaking to *me*, and my heart stops completely. But it's not. It's *him*. I hear him scream it. I turn round. He's across the river, which is narrow here, his face lit up by his phone like he's about to tell a scary story, out of breath, in just a T-shirt and jeans. He begins to wave at me. I swear to God he must have an internal central-heating system.

I stare across at Michael.

He's got a flask of something in one hand.

"Is that . . . is that *tea*?!" I shout.

He raises the flask and studies it, as if he'd forgotten all about it. He looks back at me and his eyes sparkle and he bellows into the night: "Tea is the elixir of life!"

A fresh wave of screams ripples through the group near me, and I spin round, only to find people backing away, squealing and pointing at a small light on the ground only two steps away from me. A small light slowly fizzling towards a cylinder, dug into the ground.

"WE WOULD ESPECIALLY LIKE TO THANK THE CLAY FESTIVAL COMMITTEE WHO DEFINITELY DID NOT ALLOW US TO BE HERE."

It takes me precisely two seconds to realize that, if I do not move, a firework is going to go off in my face.

"TORI." Michael's voice is all around me. I seem to be incapable of movement. "TORI, JUMP INTO THE RIVER RIGHT NOW."

I turn my head towards him. It's almost tempting to just accept my fate and be done with it.

His face is locked in an expression of pure terror. He pauses and then he jumps into the river.

It is zero degrees out here.

"Holy," I say, before I can stop myself, "shit."

"KEEP AN EYE ON THE BLOG. AND KEEP AN EYE ON EACH OTHER. YOU ARE ALL IMPORTANT. PATIENCE KILLS."

The light is nearing the cylinder. I have perhaps five seconds. Four.

"TORI, JUMP INTO THE RIVER!"

The screen cuts to black and the shrieking reaches its highest point. Michael is wading towards me, one hand outstretched, one holding his flask over his head. My only option.

"TORI!!!"

I leap from the bank into the river.

Everything seems to slow. Behind me, the firework explodes. As I'm in midair, I see its reflection in the water, yellows and blues and greens and purples dancing across the waves, and it's almost beautiful, but only almost. I land with a splash so cold that my legs nearly give way.

And then I feel the pain on my left arm.

I look at it. I take in the flames creeping up my sleeve. I hear Michael scream something, but I don't know what. And I plunge my arm into the icy water.

"Oh my God." Michael is wading out, holding his flask over his head. The river is at least ten meters wide. "Sweet merciful FUCK, it's freezing!"

"AND REMEMBER, SOLITAIRIANS: JUSTICE IS EVERYTHING."

The voice cuts out. Across the river, the crowds are hurrying through town to their cars.

"Are you all right?" shouts Michael.

I hesitantly lift my arm from the water. My coat sleeve is entirely burned away, and my jumper and shirtsleeves are in tatters. The skin peeking through is bright red. I press on it with my other hand. It hurts. A lot.

"Holy fucking shit." Michael tries to wade faster, but I can see him physically shaking.

I step forward, farther into the river, my body vibrating uncontrollably, maybe from the cold or maybe from the fact that I just escaped death or maybe from the searing pain on my arm. I start to mumble deliriously. "We'll kill ourselves. We're both killing ourselves."

He cracks a grin. He's about halfway. The water is up to his chest. "Well, hurry up then. I don't feel like dying of hypothermia today."

The water has risen to my knees, or maybe I've stepped forward again. "Are you drunk?!"

He raises his arms above his head and screams: "I AM THE SOBEREST INDIVIDUAL ON THIS WHOLE PLANET!"

The water's at my waist. Am I walking forward?

He's two meters away. "I'm just going outside!" he calls in a singsong voice. "I may be some time!" Then: "Mother of God, I literally am going to freeze to death."

I'm thinking exactly the same thing.

"What's wrong with you?" he asks. No need to shout now. "You just—you just stood there."

"I nearly died," I say, not really hearing him properly. I think I might be going into shock. "The firework."

"It's okay. You're okay now." He lifts my arm and takes a look at it. He swallows and tries not to swear. "Okay. You're okay."

"There are people—there are lots of hurt people—"

"Hey." He finds my other hand in the water and bends a little so our eyes are parallel. "It's okay. Everyone's going to be okay. We'll go to the hospital."

"Friday," I say. "Solitaire is . . . on Friday."

We look back and the sight is magnificent. It's raining flyers. They're hailing down into the crowd from the large fans set up onstage, and the fireworks are still erupting across the field, each one eliciting a wave of shrieks from the festivalgoers. It's a storm, an honest-to-God storm. The sort of storm you go outside in just for the thrill of the risk of death.

"I've been looking for you," I say. I cannot feel most of my body.

For some reason, he puts his hands on either side of my face and leans forward and says, "Tori Spring, I have been looking for you *forever*."

The fireworks keep going, never-ending, and Michael's face keeps flashing in rainbow colors and the light gleams from his glasses and several flyers swirl around us like we're trapped in a hurricane and the black water strangles us and we're so close and there are people shouting at us and pointing but I really couldn't give a crap and the cold has dissolved into some kind of numb ache but it barely registers and I think the tears freeze on my cheeks and I don't really know what happens but through some kind of planetary force I find myself holding him like I don't know what else to do and he's holding me like I'm sinking and I think he kisses the top of my head and it might just be a snowflake but he definitely whispers, "Nobody cries alone" or it might be "Nobody dies alone" and I feel that as long as I stay here there might be some kind of tiny chance that there is something remotely good in this world and the last thing I think before I pass out from the cold is that if I were to die, I would rather be a ghost than go to heaven.

TEN

It might be Monday. Last night was a blur. I remember waking up on the river-bank in Michael's arms, I remember the icy sting of the water and the smell of his T-shirt, and I remember running away. I think that I'm scared of some-thing, but I can't tell what it is. I don't know what to say.

I went to the hospital. Nick and Charlie made me. I've got a big bandage on my arm now, but it's okay, it doesn't really hurt much at the moment. I have to take it off this evening and put this cream stuff on it. I'm not looking forward to that.

It sort of reminds me about Solitaire every time I look at it. It reminds me what they're capable of.

Everyone looks very happy today and I don't like it. The sun is out on a murderous rampage and I had to wear sunglasses on my way to school because the sky, a great flat swimming pool, is trying to drown me. I sit in the common room and Rita asks me what happened to my arm, and I tell her that Solitaire did it. She asks if I'm all right. The question makes me tear up so I tell her that I'm fine and run away. I'm fine.

I get flashes of life around me. Some anon group of girls leaning back in their chairs. Some Year 12 looking out of the window while her friends laugh around her. A laminated picture of a mountain featuring the word *Ambition*. A blinking light. But I think what calms me down is the knowledge that I'm going to find out who Solitaire is and what they are planning for Friday, and I'm going to stop them.

By breaktime, I have counted sixty-six Solitaire posters in the school reading, FRIDAY: JUSTICE IS COMING. Kent, Zelda, and the prefects are in uproar, and you can no longer pass through a corridor without being over-taken by one of them as they snatch posters from the walls, muttering angrily to themselves. Today, there are two new posts on the Solitaire blog: a photograph of last week's assembly where a Solitaire poster popped up on the projector screen, and a picture of the Virgin Mary. I will print both of these out and stick them on my bedroom wall, where I have already stuck all of Solitaire's previous posts. My wall is nearly completely covered.

First, Solitaire beat up a boy. And then they seriously injured a bunch of people, all for the purpose of putting on a good show. And everybody in the town is absolutely in love with them.

It's clear to me now that if I do not stop Solitaire, nobody else will.

At lunch, I sense that I'm being followed, but when I reach the IT depart-ment I reckon I've outsmarted them. I take a seat in C15, the room directly opposite C16, where I met Michael. There are three people with me in the room. Some Year 13 is scrolling down the University of Cambridge website and a pair of Year 7s are playing the Impossible Quiz with immense concen-tration. They don't notice me.

I boot up the computer and scroll up and down the Solitaire blog for forty-five minutes.

$$\left(\cdots\right)$$

At some point, my follower walks into C15. It's Michael, obviously. Since I'm still feeling guilty for running away again, and unwilling to talk about it, I dive past him and out of the room, and begin to walk swiftly in no particu-lar direction. He catches up to me. We're walking very fast.

"What are you doing?" I ask.

"I'm walking," says Michael.

We turn a corner.

"Maths," he says. We're in the maths corridor. "They make the displays so beautiful here because otherwise no one would like maths. Why would people think that maths is fun? All maths does is give you a false sense of achievement."

Kent exits a classroom a few paces ahead of us.

"All right, Mr. Kent!" says Michael. Kent gives him a vague nod and passes by us.

"I definitely think he writes poetry," Michael continues. "You can tell. In his eyes and the way he folds his arms all the time."

I come to a halt. We've made a full circle around Higgs's first floor. We stay very still, sort of looking at each other. He has a mug of tea in his hand. There's a weird moment where I think we both want to hug each other, but I quickly end it by turning round and walking back into C15.

I sit at the computer I'd been staring at, and he takes the seat next to me.

"You ran off again," he says.

I don't look at him.

"You didn't reply to my texts last night after you ran off," he says. "I had to message Charlie to find out what had happened to you."

I say nothing.

"Did you get my texts? My voicemails? I was kind of worried you'd caught hypothermia or something. And your arm. I was really worried."

I don't remember there being any texts. Or voicemails. I remember Nick shouting at me for being an idiot, and Charlie sitting next to me in the back of the car rather than next to Nick in the passenger seat. I remember arriving at A&E and waiting for hours. I remember Nick falling asleep on Charlie's shoulder, and Charlie and me playing twenty questions, and him winning every time. I remember not sleeping last night. I remember telling Mum that I would be going to school and that was final.

"What are you doing?" he asks.

What am I doing. "I am . . ." I am thinking. I am looking at myself in the black computer monitor. "I'm . . . I'm doing something. About Solitaire."

"Since when are you interested in Solitaire?"

"Since—" I go to answer him, but I don't know the answer.

He doesn't frown, or smile, or anything.

"Why wouldn't I be interested?" I ask. "*You're* interested. You're the one who said that Solitaire was targeting me."

"I just thought you weren't," he says, his voice a little wobbly. "It's not like you to . . . I just didn't think . . . you didn't care that much, you know, originally."

That may be true.

"*You're* still interested . . . right?" I ask, scared of the answer.

Michael looks at me for a long time. "I'd like to know who's behind it all," he says, "and I know what happened to Ben Hope was pretty nasty, and then last night . . . I mean, that was just downright idiotic. It's a miracle nobody died. Did you see the article on BBC News? The Clay Festival organizers are passing it off as if it were their final act gone wrong or something. Solitaire didn't even get a mention. I guess the organizers didn't want anyone to know they'd been hijacked. And who's going to listen to a bunch of kids going on about some blog that organized it?"

Michael's staring at me as if he's scared of me. I must have a very strange expression on my face. He tilts his head.

"When was the last time you slept?"

I don't bother to answer. We sit silent for a moment before he tries again.

"You know, this is a very generic thing to say, but . . ." He pauses. "If you want to, er, like, talk about anything, like . . . you know . . . people always need people to talk to. . . . You don't talk much. I'm always here . . . like . . . to talk. You do know that, don't you?"

The sentence is so broken up that I don't really grasp its concept, so I just nod enthusiastically. Judging by his slightly relieved smile, that seems to satisfy him. At least until he goes on to ask: "Are you going to tell me why you've changed your mind? Why you're being obsessive?"

It doesn't strike me that I'm obsessing. I don't think that's the word I'd use. "Someone has to."

"Why?"

"It's important. No one cares about the important things anymore." I drift off. "We're so used to disaster that we accept it. We think we deserve it."

His smile, fleeting, fades. "I don't think anyone deserves disaster. I think a lot of people wish for disaster because it's the only thing left with the power to turn heads."

"Attention-seekers?"

"Some people don't get any attention," he says, and here again is the boy from the ice rink: serious, genuine, morose, old, and silently *angry*. "Some people get *no* attention. You can understand why they'd go seeking it. If they're waiting forever for something that might never come."

He starts fishing for something in his bag and after a few moments withdraws a can, holding it out to me. It's a really obscure brand of diet lemonade. One of my favorites. He smiles, but it's forced. "I was at the shop and thought of you."

I look at the can, feeling something very strange in my stomach. "Thanks." Another long pause.

"You know," I say, "when that firework was about to go off, I actually thought I was going to die. I thought . . . I was going to burn and die."

He gazes at me. "But you didn't."

He really is a good person. Far too good to be hanging around someone like me.

I almost laugh at myself for thinking something so clichéd. I think I've said before how things are clichéd because they're true. Well, there's one thing that I know is true, and that is that Michael Holden is too good for me.

Later, 7 p.m., dinner. Mum and Dad are out somewhere. Nick and Charlie are at opposite ends of the table. I am next to Oliver. We're eating pasta with some meat in it. I'm not sure what the meat is. I cannot concentrate.

"Tori, what's the matter?" Charlie waves his fork at me. "What's going on? Something's going on."

"*Solitaire* is going on," I say, "yet no one cares. Everyone is sitting around talking about things that do not matter and pretending that it's still some big hilarious joke."

Nick and Charlie look at me like I'm crazy. Well, I am.

"It's pretty weird that Solitaire hasn't been reported on, I guess," says Nick. "Like, even with that stuff at the Clay. Solitaire didn't even come into it. People don't seem to be taking Solitaire seriously—"

Charlie sighs, cutting him off. "Whether Solitaire does or does not pull off something spectacular, there's no reason for Tori or anyone else to get involved. It's not our problem, is it? Shouldn't the teachers or, like, the police be doing something about it? It's their own fault for not bothering to do anything."

And that's when I know I've lost him as well.

"I thought that you two were . . . better than all this."

"All what?" Charlie raises his eyebrows.

"All this stuff that people spend their time bothering with." I scrunch up my hands, placing them on my head. "It's all fake. Everyone is faking. Why does no one *care* about *anything*?"

"Tori, seriously, are you all r—"

"YES," I probably scream. "YES, I'M ALL RIGHT, THANKS. HOW. ABOUT. YOU?"

And then I get myself out of there just before I start to cry.

Obviously, Charlie tells Mum and Dad. When they get home, I'm not sure what time, they knock on my door. When I don't answer, they come in.

"What?" I say. I'm sitting upright on my bed and have been trying to choose a film to watch for the last thirty-seven minutes. On the television, some news guy is talking about the suicide of a Cambridge student, and my laptop is on my legs, like a sleeping cat, my blog home page emitting its dim blue glow.

Mum and Dad take a long look at my back wall. You can't see any parts of the paint anymore. It's just a patchwork of Solitaire printouts, hundreds of them.

"What's the matter, Tori?" asks Dad, averting his eyes from the display.

"I do not know."

"Did you have a bad day?"

"Yes. Always."

"Come on now, there's no need to be so melodramatic." Mum sighs, apparently disappointed in something. "Cheer up. Smile."

I make a fake hurling sound. "Dear God."

Mum sighs again. Dad imitates her.

"Well, we'll leave you to your misery then," he says, "if you're going to be sarcastic."

"Ha. Ha. Sarcastic."

They roll their eyes and leave. I start to feel sick. I think it's my bed. I don't know. I don't even know. So my ingenious solution to this is to pathetically flop off the bed and onto the floor, propping myself sluggishly up against my Solitaire wall. My room is half-dark.

Friday. Friday. Friday Friday Friday Friday Friday Friday Friday Friday Friday Friday Friday Friday Friday Friday Friday Friday Friday Friday.

ELEVEN

"Mum," I say. It's Tuesday, 7:45 a.m., and I have no skirt. This is one of those situations where talking to my mum is unavoidable. "Mum, can you iron my school skirt?"

Mum doesn't say anything because she's on the kitchen computer in her dressing gown. You'd think she was ignoring me deliberately, but she really is that engrossed in whatever dumb email she's writing.

"Mum," I say again. "Mum. Mum. Mum. Mum. Mum. Mu—"

"*What?*"

"Can you iron my school skirt?"

"Can't you wear your other one?"

"It's too small. It's been too small since we bought it."

"Well, I'm not ironing your school skirt. You iron it."

"I have never ironed anything in my life and I have to leave in fifteen minutes."

"That's annoying."

"Yes, it is, Mum." She doesn't answer me. Jesus Christ. "So I guess I'm going to school with no skirt."

"I guess you are."

I grate my teeth together. I have to catch a bus in fifteen minutes and I'm still in my pyjamas.

"Do you care?" I ask. "Do you care that I have no skirt?"

"At the moment, Tori, *no*. It's in the airing cupboard. It's just a bit crinkled."

"Yeah, I found it. It's supposed to be a pleated skirt, Mum. Currently, there are no pleats."

"Tori. I'm really busy."

"But I don't have a skirt to wear to school."

"Wear your other skirt then, for Christ's sake!"

"I literally just told you, it's too sma—"

"Tori! I really don't care!"

I stop talking. I look at her.

I wonder if I'll end up like her. Not caring whether my daughter has a skirt to wear to school.

And then I realize something.

"You know what, Mum?" I say, starting to actually laugh at myself. "I don't even think I care either."

So I go upstairs and put on my gray school skirt that is too small, and put my old PE shorts on over my tights so you can't see anything, and then I attempt to sort out my hair, but oh, guess what, I don't care about that either, and then I go to put some makeup on but no, wait, I also don't care what my face looks like, so I go back downstairs and pick up my schoolbag and leave the house with Charlie, basking in the light and glory that comes from not giving a damn about anything in the entire universe.

I'm feeling kind of like a ghost today. I sit on a swivel chair in the common room, fiddling with the bandage on my arm, and watch, out of the window, some Year 7s chucking snowballs at each other. They're all smiling.

"Tori," calls Becky from a little way across the room. "I need to talk to you."

Begrudgingly, I rise from the chair and weave through the sixth-form crowd to get to her. Wouldn't it be nice to be able to walk through people?

"How's your arm?" she asks. She's acting super awkward. I'm past that now—I'm past awkward. Why should I care what anyone thinks anymore? Why should I care about anything anymore?

"It's fine," I say. An obligatory answer to an obligatory question.

"Look, I'm not going to apologize, yeah? I wasn't in the wrong." She talks as if she's blaming me for being angry at her. "I'm just going to come out and say what we've *both* been thinking." She stares me straight in the eye. "We haven't been acting like friends recently, have we?"

I say nothing.

"And I'm not just talking about after what happened at . . . what happened. It's been going on for months. It's like you—it's like you don't really want to be friends with me. It's like you don't like me."

"It's not that I don't like you," I say, but I don't know how to continue. I don't know what it is.

"If we're . . . if we can't act like friends, then there's no real point in us carrying on being friends."

As she's saying this, her eyes get a little watery. I can't think of anything to say. I met Becky on the first day of Year 7. We sat next to each other in form and in science. We passed notes and we played MASH and I helped her decorate her locker with pictures of Orlando Bloom. She lent me money for cookies at breaktime. She always spoke to me, even though I was one of the quiet ones. Five and a half years later, here we are.

"I don't think that we're compatible," she says. "I don't think that it's possible for us to be friends anymore. You've changed. I might have changed too, but you definitely have. And that's not necessarily a bad thing, but it's true."

"So is it my fault we're not friends anymore?"

Becky doesn't react. "I'm not sure that you need me anymore."

"Why is that?"

"You don't like being around me, do you?"

I laugh, exasperated, and I forget everything else except her and Ben, her and Ben, her and the guy that beat up my brother.

"Are you trying to gain sympathy here? Are you breaking up with me? This isn't a rom-com, Becky."

She frowns, disappointed. "You're not taking me seriously. Stop with all this crap," she says. "Just stop, yeah? *Cheer up.* I know you're a pessimist, but this is getting out of hand. Go and hang around with Michael some more."

"What," I scoff, "so he can *fix me*? So he can teach me how to stop being me?" I laugh loudly. "He shouldn't be hanging around with someone like me."

She stands up. "You should try to find people who are more like you. They'll be better for you."

"There is no one like me."

"I think you're breaking down."

I cough loudly. "I'm not a *car.*"

And she is furious, like, Jesus, actual rage is steaming from her face. It takes all her effort not to shout her last word: *"Fine."*

Becky thunders over to a crowd who I used to consider myself part of. I should feel like I've lost something, but instead I feel nothing. I put on my headphones and start listening to some sad album, something really self-pitying, and I roll over facts in my head: The top post on the Solitaire blog today is a screencap from *Fight Club*. You have a one in twenty thousand chance of being murdered. Charlie couldn't eat this morning—he cried when I tried to make him so I gave up. It was probably my fault for being angry at him yesterday. I have three unread texts from Michael Holden and twenty-six unread messages on my blog.

It's later. I've come back to C16—the decaying computer room on the first floor where I found that Post-it note. I can tell that nobody has been in here. The sun lights up the dust floating in the air.

As I'm looking out of the window, my face pressed against the glass, I notice that there's a tall metal staircase just outside to my left, its top step parallel to the window I'm staring through. It leads onto the concrete roof of the art conservatory—a newly built classroom that juts out from the ground floor—and spirals all the way down to the ground. I don't think I've ever seen this staircase before.

I exit C16, trot down to the ground floor, go outside, and scale the metal staircase all the way to the top.

Even though I'm not on the roof of the school itself, standing on the roof of the art conservatory is fairly dangerous. I sneak a look onto the grass below. It slopes down slightly towards the field.

I look out. The slushy field opens out into the distance. The river slowly tumbles on.

I sit down so that my legs are hanging off the edge. No one can see or find me here. It's Period 4 on Tuesday, nearly lunchtime, and I'm skipping music for the hundredth time. It doesn't matter.

I bring up the Solitaire blog on my phone. The countdown timer is at the top of the screen. I find myself checking it continually. 02:11:23:26. Two days, eleven hours, twenty-three minutes, twenty-six seconds until Thursday turns into Friday. Solitaire antics today have been focused around the number 2: on hundreds of posters, on Post-its on every surface, written on all whiteboards, popping up on the computers. From here I can see that the number 2 is painted in red directly onto the snow of the field. It looks a bit like blood.

A little way away from the number 2 on the field is a large wooden object. I stand up and step backwards. I realize that it's Kent's lectern, from which he leads our school assemblies. A small congregation of students have gathered outside, staring, like me, clearly waiting for something exciting to happen. At the front of the crowd, Quiff Guy is standing with a camera in his hands.

I fold my arms. My blazer flaps out behind me in the wind. I suppose I look very dramatic, standing here on the roof.

Painted on the front of the lectern is Solitaire's anarchy symbol.

The side that Kent would stand at when speaking is directed away from us, staring wistfully out over the snowy field and down into the town and river beyond. Music, Ludovico Einaudi, begins to play out of the outside tannoy, blending into the sigh of a steady breeze. A piece of paper, one of Kent's past assemblies clipped onto the lectern, somehow lifts up and flickers as if it's gesturing "come here" to the town and the river.

Then the lectern catches fire.

It's over in less than thirty seconds, but it feels longer. A spark from its base sends the entire wooden body into flames and they double the size of the lectern, magnifying it, expanding it. It's sort of beautiful. The reddish orange of the spectacle sends a dim glow across the snow so that the entire field is slightly alight, wavering up and down. The wind is so strong that the fire begins to vortex round the wood, shooting shards of blackened charcoal outwards in every direction, a tunnel of smoke coughing upwards. Slowly, the darkness creeps across the pale wood. It cracks. The lectern takes its last lingering look out at what freedom might have been. Then, all at once, the entire frame crumbles into a destroyed heap and the once-blazing fire subsides. What is left is little more than a pile of soot and ash.

I am paralyzed. The scattering of students on the field are shrieking and screaming, but not with fear. One small girl steps out and retrieves a broken piece of the lectern, bringing it back to her friends. Teachers begin to show, barking reprimands and shooing people away, and I watch as the girl drops the piece of lectern on the snow.

Once the field is clear, I tear down the stairs and run across the snow to rescue it. I study the piece of burnt wood. I then stare back towards the pile of remains, then the grayish snow, then the long and omnipresent river, and then I think about the sea of anonymous students who had been so excited to watch this. It reminds me of the people who watched the beating-up of Ben Hope, jeering, laughing at pain. The crowd that had jumped up and down like children at the fireworks at the Clay, while the injured ran, terrified, burning.

I close my fist. The piece of wood dissolves into black dust.

TWELVE

When I get to school on Wednesday, I watch out for Michael Holden in the common-room crowds. I wonder whether seeing him will make me feel better or worse. It could go either way. I know I'm dragging him down. Seeing me cannot make Michael Holden feel better. He deserves to have a friend who loves life and laughter, who loves having fun and adventures, someone to drink tea with and argue about a book and stargaze and ice-skate and dance with. Someone who isn't me.

Becky, Lauren, Evelyn, and Rita are sitting in our spot in the corner. No Ben, no Lucas. Like the beginning of the year all over again. I stand at the door to the common room, kind of staring at them. Evelyn is the only one who sees me. She catches my eye, then quickly looks away. Even if I could quietly overlook her exceedingly irritating hair and clothing choices like a decent and accepting human being should, Evelyn has always done many things that I don't approve of, such as thinking she's better than people, and pretending to know more than she does. I wonder whether she dislikes me as much as I dislike her.

I take a seat in a swivel chair, away from Our Lot, thinking about all my personal attributes. Pessimist. Mood-killer. Unbearably awkward and probably paranoid. Deluded. Nasty. Borderline insane, manically depressed psychopa—

"Tori."

I spin round on the chair. Michael Holden's found me.

I look up at him. He's smiling, but it looks weird. Fake. Or am I imagining that?

"It's Wednesday today," I say instantly, unwilling to build up our conversation with small talk, but doing it anyway.

He blinks but doesn't act too taken aback. "Yes. Yes, it is."

"I suppose," I say, curling onto the desk with my head on my arm, "I don't like Wednesday because it's the middle day. You feel like you've been at school for ages, but it's still ages until the weekend. It's the most . . . disappointing day."

As he takes this in, something else kind of weird crosses his expression. Almost like panic or something. He coughs. "Can we, er, talk somewhere quieter?"

I really do not want to get up.

But he persists. "Please? I've got some news."

As we're walking, I stare into the back of his head. In fact, I just stare at his whole body. I've always thought of Michael Holden as this kind of entity, this sparkling orb of wonder, and yet now, looking at him walking along in his average school uniform, hair kind of soft and messy compared to how he had it gelled when I first met him, I find myself thinking about the fact that he's just a normal guy. That he gets up and goes to bed, that he listens to music and watches TV, that he revises for exams and probably does homework, that he sits down to dinner, that he showers and brushes his teeth. Normal stuff.

What am I talking about?

He takes me to the school library. It's not as quiet as he'd hoped. There are lower-school girls swarming round the desks in exactly the same way that the sixth-formers do in the common room except with much more enthusiasm. There are not many books; it's actually more of a large room with a few bookshelves than a library. The atmosphere is quite strange. I'm almost glad that it's so bright and happy in here. It's an odd feeling because I never like bright and happy things.

We sit down in the middle of the nonfiction row. He's looking at me, but I don't want to look back anymore. Looking at his face makes me feel funny.

"You were hiding yesterday!" he says, trying to make it sound like a cute joke. As if we're six years old.

For a second, I wonder if he knows about my special beautiful place on the art conservatory roof, but that's impossible.

"How's your arm?" he asks.

"It's fine," I say. "Didn't you have something to tell me?"

And the pause he leaves then—it's like he has everything he wants to tell me, and nothing.

"Are you al—" he begins, then changes his mind. "Your hands are cold."

I stare blankly at my hands, still avoiding his eyes. Had he been holding my hand on the way here? I curl my palms into fists and sigh. Fine. Small talk it is. "I watched all three *Lord of the Rings* last night and *V for Vendetta*. Oh, and I had a dream. I think it was about Winona Ryder."

And I can feel the sadness pouring out of him all of a sudden, and it makes me want to get up and run away and keep running.

"I also found out that approximately one hundred billion people have died since the world began. Did you know that? One hundred billion. It's a big number, but it still doesn't seem like quite enough."

There's a long silence. A few of the lower-school groups are looking at us and giggling, thinking we're having some kind of deep, romantic conversation.

Finally, he says something productive: "I guess neither of us has been sleeping much."

I decide to look at him then.

It shocks me a little.

Because there's none of the usual Michael in that calm smile.

And I think of the time at the ice rink when he'd been so angry,

but it's different to that.

And I think of the sadness that's been in Lucas's eyes since the day I met him,

but it's different to that too.

Split between the green and the blue, there is an indefinable beauty that people call humanity.

"You don't have to do this anymore." I'm whispering, not because I don't want people to hear, but I seem to have forgotten how to increase the volume in my voice. "You don't have to be my friend. I don't want people to feel sorry for me. I'm literally one hundred and ten percent fine. Really. I understand what you've been trying to do, and you are a very nice person, you're the perfect person actually, but it's okay, you don't have to pretend anymore. I'm fine. I don't need you to help me. I'll do something about all this and then I'll be all right and it'll all go back to normal."

His face doesn't change. He reaches towards me with his hand and brushes what must be a tear from my face—not in a romantic way, but as if I had a malaria-carrying mosquito perched on my cheek. He looks at the tear, somewhat confused, and then holds his hand up to me. I hadn't realized I was crying. I don't really feel sad. I don't really feel anything.

"I'm not a perfect person," he says. His smile is still there, but it's not a happy smile. "And I don't have any friends except for you. In case you haven't heard, most people know that I'm the king of freaks; I mean, yeah, sometimes I come across as charming and eccentric, but eventually people realize that I'm just trying too hard. I'm sure Lucas Ryan and Nick Nelson can tell you all kinds of wonderful stories about me."

He leans back. He looks annoyed, to be honest.

"If *you* don't want to be friends with *me*, I completely understand. You don't have to make some excuse about it. I know that I'm the one who always comes to find you. I'm the one who always starts our conversations. Sometimes you don't say anything for ages. But that doesn't mean that our friendship is all about *me* trying to make *you* feel better. You know me better than that."

Maybe I don't want to be friends with Michael Holden. Maybe that's better.

We sit together for a while. I randomly select a book from the shelf behind me. It's called *The Encyclopaedia of Life* and it can only be about fifty pages long. Michael reaches out his hand towards me, but doesn't, as I anticipate, take my own hand. Instead, he takes hold of a strand of my hair, which, I guess, had sort of been in my face, and he tucks it carefully behind my left ear.

"Did you know," I say at some point, for some inexplicable reason, "that most suicides happen in the springtime?" Then I look at him. "Didn't you say you had news?"

And that's when he gets up and walks away from me and out of the library door and out of my life, and I am 100 percent sure that Michael Holden deserves better friends than the pessimist, introvert psychopath Tori Spring.

THIRTEEN

The song repeating itself over the tannoy throughout Thursday is "The Final Countdown" by Europe. Most people enjoy this for the first hour, but by second period, no one is screaming "IT'S THE FINAL COUNTDOWWWWN" in the hallways anymore, much to my delight (if that's possible for me). Zelda and her entourage are once again strutting through the hallways, tearing posters from the walls, and today these include pictures of Nelson Mandela, Desmond Tutu, Abraham Lincoln, Emmeline Pankhurst, and, oddly enough, former Christmas chart-toppers Rage Against the Machine. Perhaps Solitaire is attempting to offer us some sort of positive encouragement.

It has been snowing violently since I woke up. This, of course, sparks mass hysteria and insanity in everyone in the lower school, and a kind of collective depression in everyone in the upper school. Most of the students have gone home by break, and lessons are officially canceled. I could easily walk home. But I don't.

Tomorrow is the day.

At the start of what would have been Period 3, I exit the school building and head towards the art conservatory. I sit down, leaning against the little grass slope that leads up to the room's concrete wall, and the roof above me overhangs a little so I'm not really getting snowed on. It's cold though. Like, numbingly cold. On my way outside, I picked up a large heater from the music block and plugged it in via a classroom window a few meters away. I've got it nestled into the snow next to me, blasting clouds of warmth around my body. I have three shirts on, both of my school jumpers, four pairs of tights, boots, blazer, coat, hat, scarf and gloves, and shorts under my skirt.

If I don't find out what's happening tomorrow before tomorrow, then I'll have to come to school and find out on the day. Solitaire is going to do something to Higgs. It's what they've been doing so far, isn't it?

I feel strangely excited. It's probably because I haven't slept for quite a long time.

Last night I watched a film called *Garden State*. Not all of it, but most of it. It's about this guy, Andrew, and you're never quite sure whether Andrew's life is truly depressing or not. It seems like he has no decent friends or family, but then he meets this girl (typically happy-go-lucky, quirky, and beautiful ManicPixieDreamGirl Natalie Portman, of course), who teaches him how to live properly again.

You know, now that I think about it, I'm not so sure that I liked the film that much after all. It was very clichéd. Pretty misogynistic, actually, since Natalie Portman's character didn't have much of a purpose other than to cheer up the main guy. To be honest, I may have just got myself caught up in the artistic effects. It was good at the beginning, especially when Andrew dreamt that he was in a plane crash. And the shot where he wears a shirt that matches the wallpaper print behind him so he sort of fades away. I liked those bits a lot.

I keep typing Michael's number into my phone and then deleting it. After about ten minutes of this, I realize that I know his number by heart. Then I accidentally press the green call button.

I swear resignedly at myself.

But I don't hang up.

I bring the phone up to my ear.

I hear the little click of the call being answered, but he doesn't say hello or anything. He listens. I think I hear him breathing, but it might just be the wind.

"Hello, Michael," I finally say.

Nothing.

"I'm going to talk, so you can't hang up."

Nothing.

"Sometimes," I say, "I can't tell whether people are real or not. Lots of people pretend to be nice to me, so I'm never sure."

Nothing.

"I'm just—"

"I'm fairly angry at you, Tori, to be honest."

He speaks. The words circle round my head and I want to roll over and throw up.

"You don't see me as a person at all, do you?" he says. "I'm just some tool who's always turning up to stop you hating yourself so much."

"That's wrong," I say. "That's completely wrong."

"Prove it."

I try to speak, but nothing comes out. My proof is shrouded by something like snow, and I can't get it out. I can't explain that yes, he stops me hating myself so much, but no, that isn't why I want to be his friend more than I've ever wanted anything.

He laughs weakly. "You're pretty hopeless, aren't you? You're as bad as I am at feelings."

I try to think about when Michael might have expressed his feelings, but the only time I can think of is at the ice rink, that anger, so crazy that he might explode.

"Can we meet up?" I ask. I need to talk to him. In the real world.

"Why?"

"Because . . ." Once again, my voice is trapped in my throat. "Because . . . I like . . . being . . . with you."

There's a long pause. For a brief moment, I wonder if he's hung up. Then he sighs.

"Where are you right now?" he asks. "Have you gone home?"

"On the field. By the art conservatory."

"But it's literally *Hoth* out there."

A *Star Wars* reference. It takes me so by surprise that I once again fail to say anything in reply.

"I'll see you in a minute," he says.

I hang up.

He's here in almost exactly a minute, which is impressive. He's not wearing a coat or a scarf or anything over his uniform. I think that he may secretly be a radiator.

Several meters away, he absorbs the situation. I suppose it's funny and that's why he laughs.

"You took a heater *outside*?"

I look at the heater. "I am freezing."

He thinks I'm insane. He's not wrong.

"That is genius. I don't even think *I* would do that."

He sits next to me, leaning against the art conservatory's outer wall. We stare over the field. It's uncertain really where the field stops and the sheet-like snowflakes begin. The snow is falling slowly and vertically. I would say that there is total peace on earth, except that every now and then a solitary snowflake flies into my face.

At some point, he glances down at my left arm, which is resting on the snow between us. He doesn't say anything about it.

"You had news to tell me," I say. It's pretty amazing that I even remember this. "But you didn't tell me."

His head turns to me, his smile absent. "Er, yeah. Well, it's not too important."

That means that it is important.

"I just wanted to tell you that I have another race in a few weeks," he says, a little embarrassed. "I'm going to the World Junior Speed Skating

Championships." He shrugs and smiles. "I mean, the British never win, but if I get a good enough time score there, I might qualify for the Winter Olympics."

I spring forward from the wall. "Holy shit."

He shrugs again. "I mucked up Nationals a couple of weeks ago, but . . . I got better times than that before so they decided to let me go."

"Michael," I say, "you're literally extraordinary."

He laughs. "Extraordinary is only an extension of ordinary," he says.

He's wrong though. He is extraordinary, extraordinary as in magnificent, as in miraculous.

"So would you like to?" he asks.

"Like to what?" I ask.

"Would you like to come? To watch? I'm allowed to take someone, and usually it's a parent, but, you know . . ."

And without thinking, without wondering whether my parents would say yes, without even worrying about Charlie—

"Yeah," I say. "Okay."

He grins at me, and then I see a new expression that makes my chest hurt—a kind of raw gratitude, as if me going with him was the only thing that mattered.

I open my mouth to begin a serious conversation, but he sees it coming and holds up a finger to stop me.

"We are severely wasting this snow," he says. I can see myself in his glasses.

"Wasting?"

He jumps to his feet and walks into the blizzard. "Snow shouldn't be just to *look at*, should it?" he says, rolling a snowball in his hands and tossing it from one to the other.

I say nothing because I think that's exactly what snow should be for.

"*Come on.*" He's smiling, gawking at me. "Throw a snowball at me."

I frown. "Why?"

"For *no reason!*"

"There's no point."

"The point *is* that there's no point."

I sigh. I am not going to win this argument. Begrudgingly, I stand up, step out into the Arctic, and, with little enthusiasm, collect a ball of snow in my hands. Luckily, I'm right-handed, so my injured arm doesn't really put me at a disadvantage. I throw it towards Michael, where it lands about three meters to his right. He looks at it and gives me a solemn thumbs-up. "You tried."

There's something about the way he says it, not even patronizing, just simply *disappointed*, that makes me squint at him, pick up another snowball, and try again, this time landing bang on target in the center of his chest. A false sense of achievement blossoms in my stomach.

Raising his arms into the air, he cries, "You're alive!"

I throw another snowball. Then he throws one at me and runs away. Before I even have time to realize what I'm doing, the whole thing erupts into a chase round the field. I fall over more than once, but I manage to stuff snow down the back of his shirt two times and he gets me right in the back of the head so my hair is now soaked, but I don't feel so cold because we're running around face-first into the swirling snow like there's nothing else in the world but the two of us and snow and more snow and more snow, no ground, no sky, no nothing. I begin to wonder how Michael can so easily make something wonderful out of something cold, and then I begin to wonder whether lots of people are like this, and I begin to wonder whether, if I weren't so busy thinking about other things, I would be like this.

Michael Holden is sprinting towards me. He's got a massive pile of snow in his arms and this giant grin, so I charge back across the field and into school. There's no one anywhere and the emptiness is somehow wonderful. I run into the sixth-form block and into the common room, which is entirely deserted, but I'm much too slow. Just as I open the common-room doors he lets the slush tumble onto the top of my head. I scream and laugh. Laugh? *Laugh.*

I lie faceup, panting, on a computer desk, moving the keyboard onto my stomach to make room. He collapses into a swivel chair, shaking his hair like a wet dog. The chair rolls backwards several centimeters and it sparks an idea in his head.

"Here's the next game," he says. "You have to get from here"—he gestures to the computer corner—"to there"—the door on the opposite side, past the maze of tables and chairs—"standing on a computer chair."

"I'd rather *not* break my neck."

"Stop being boring. You're banned from saying no."

"But that's my catchphrase."

"Make a new one."

With a long sigh, I step up onto a swivel chair. This is a lot more difficult than it looks because not only are swivel chairs very wobbly, but they also spin round, hence the name *swivel* chair. I get my balance, stand tall, and point at Michael, who has stood up on his own chair with his arms warily outstretched. "When I fall and die, I am coming back to haunt you."

He shrugs at me. "That wouldn't be so bad."

We race all the way round the tables, grasping at the plastic chairs to haul ourselves along. At one point, Michael's chair tips up, but he spectacularly manages to step forward over the back of the seat, landing before me in a sort of kneeling position. His face, wide-eyed, rests in a fairly stunned expression for several seconds before he beams up at me, throwing open his arms and crying, "Marry me, my darling!"

It's so funny I nearly die. He comes over to me and starts spinning round the chair I'm standing on, not fast, but fast enough, and then he lets go. I'm standing up, twirling round and round on this chair with my arms in the air, the windows of snow merging with the unlit room in a slushy vortex of white and yellow. I keep thinking as I'm spinning how everything looks so sad, but if this day were to go down in history, everyone would talk about what a beautiful day it was.

We've pushed all the spare desks together to form one enormous table, and we're laid out in the middle on our backs just under the skylight so that we can see the snow falling on top of us. Michael rests his hands on his stomach, locked together, and I lay mine out beside me. I have no idea what we're doing or why. I think he thinks that's the point. To be honest, this could all be imaginary and I wouldn't even know.

"Thought for the day," says Michael. He lifts one hand and touches the bandage on my arm, fiddling with the frayed edges at my wrist. "Do you think that, if we were happy for our entire lives, we would die feeling like we'd missed out on something?"

I don't say anything for some time.

Then:

"They were from you?" Those blog messages, those messages that I'd assumed . . . "You sent me those messages?"

He smiles, keeping his eyes on the ceiling. "What can I say? Your blog is more interesting than you think it is, *chronic-pessimist.*"

My blog URL. Normally, I'd feel like dying if someone found my blog. If Becky, or Lauren, or Evelyn, or Rita, or any of those people—if they found the place where I say stupid stuff about myself, pretending that I'm some unfortunate and tortured teenage soul, begging for sympathy from people who I've never even seen in the flesh . . .

I roll my head towards him.

He looks at me. "What?"

I almost say something then. I almost say something.

But I don't.

And then he says, "I wish I were more like you."

And the snow falls and I close my eyes and we fall asleep together.

I wake up and he's gone and I'm in the dark. Alone. No—not alone. There's someone here. Someone. Here?

As my senses come back to me, I begin to decipher hushed voices coming from the common-room door. If I had any energy, I would sit up and look. But I don't. I lie still and listen.

"No," says Michael. "You've been acting like a little shit. You can't fuck around with someone like that. Do you understand how she's feeling at the moment? Do you understand what you've done?"

"Yeah, but—"

"You give the full explanation or you say nothing. You be honest or you shut the fuck up. Dropping little hints and then hiding is literally the worst thing you could do."

"I haven't been dropping little hints."

"What have you said to her? Because she *knows*, Lucas. She *knows* there's something going on."

"I've tried to explain—"

"No, you haven't. So you're going to go and tell her everything you've just told me. You owe that to her. She's a real person, not some childhood dream. She has real feelings." There's a long pause. "Jesus fucking Christ. This is a fucking revelation."

I haven't heard Michael swear so much all in one conversation.

I haven't heard Michael and Lucas talk to each other since Pizza Express.

I don't think I want to know what they're talking about.

I sit up, still on the table, and swivel round to face the two boys.

They're standing in front of the door, Michael holding it by one hand. Lucas sees me first. Then Michael. Michael looks a little like he's going to be sick. He takes Lucas firmly by the shoulder and shoves him towards me.

"If you are going to do *anything* about *anything*," he says, addressing me, pointing viciously at Lucas, "you need to talk to *him*."

Lucas is terrified. I half expect him to scream.

Michael triumphantly raises his fist into the air in a Judd Nelson–like fashion.

"CLOSURE!" he bellows. And then he leaves the room.

It's just Lucas and me now. My former best friend, the boy who cried every day, and Tori Spring. Standing beside my table island, wrapped in a kind of parka over his uniform, he's wearing one of those hats with the really long plaits hanging down at the front and looks absolutely hysterical.

I cross my legs like you do in primary school.

There's no time for being awkward now. No time for being shy, or being scared what other people will say. It's time to start saying the things that are in our heads. Everything that would cause us to hold back—it's gone. And we are only people. And this is the truth.

"Your new bestie is crazy," says Lucas, with noticeable resentment.

I shrug. Michael at Truham. Michael with no friends. "Apparently, every-one already knew that." Michael the freak. "To be honest, I think it's just a defense mechanism."

This seems to surprise Lucas. I snort a little and lie back onto the tables.

"So you owe me an explanation?" I say in a dramatic voice, but it's too funny, and I start to laugh.

He chuckles, takes his hat off and puts it in his pocket, then folds his arms. "To be honest, Victoria, I can't believe you haven't guessed."

"Well then, I must be some kind of idiot."

"Yeah."

Silence. We're both totally still.

"You *do* know," he says, taking another step closer. "You need to think carefully. You need to think about all the things that have happened."

I get to my feet and step backwards. There's nothing inside my head except fog now.

Lucas clambers onto the table island and walks a little way across towards me, nervously, as if he's scared it's going to collapse under his weight. He tries to explain again.

"Do you . . . do you remember ever coming to my house when we were kids?"

I really want to laugh, but I can't anymore. He looks down a little and sees the bandage on my arm, and it almost seems to make him shudder.

"We were best friends, yeah?" he says, but that means nothing. Becky was my "best friend." Best friend. What does that indicate?

"What?" I shake my head. "What are you talking about?"

"You *do* remember," he says, his voice barely above a whisper. "If I remember, then you remember. Tell me about when you came round my house all those times. Tell me what you saw there."

He's right. I do remember. I wish I didn't. It was summer, we were eleven, and it was nearing the end of Year 6. I went round his house what felt like a hundred times. We played chess. We sat in the garden. We ate ice lollies. We ran all round his house—it was a big house. Three floors, with an abundance of hiding places. Everything was kind of beige. They had a lot of paintings.

A lot of paintings.

They had a lot of paintings.

And there is one that I remember.

I asked Lucas, when I was eleven, "Is that a painting of the high street?"

"Yep," he said. He was smaller than me back then, his hair white-blond. "The cobbled high street in the rain."

"I like the red umbrellas," I said. "I think it must be summer rain."

"I think so too."

The painting of the wet cobbled street with red umbrellas and warm café windows, the painting that *Doctor Who* girl was staring at so intensely at the Solitaire party; it's inside Lucas's house.

I begin to breathe very fast.

"That painting," I say.

He says nothing.

"But the Solitaire party . . . that wasn't your house. You don't live in this town."

"No," he says. "My parents are in property development. They own several empty houses. That house was one of them. They put those paintings in there to brighten it up for viewers."

Everything suddenly clicks into place.

"You're part of Solitaire," I say.

He nods slowly.

"I made it," says Lucas. "I made Solitaire."

I step back.

"No," I say. "No, you didn't."

"I made that blog. I organized the pranks."

Star Wars. Violins. Cats, Madonna. Ben Hope and Charlie. Fire. Bubbles. The fireworks at the Clay and the burning and the distorted voice? Surely I would have recognized his voice.

I step back.

"You're lying."

"I'm not."

I step back again, but there isn't any table to step back onto, and my foot falls onto air and I topple backwards into nothingness, only to be caught under my arms by Michael Holden who has been standing by us since God knows when. He lifts me a little and settles me on the ground. His hands feel strange on my arms.

"Can—" I can't speak. I'm choking, my throat is closing. "You—you're a sadistic—"

"I know, I'm sorry, it all got a bit out of hand."

"Got a bit *out of hand*?" I shriek with laughter. "People could have *died*."

Michael's arms are around me. I throw him off, climb back onto the tables, and march towards Lucas, who cowers a little as I face him.

"All the pranks were related to me, weren't they?" I say this more to myself than him. Michael had realized this right from the start. Because he's clever. He's so clever. And I, being me, didn't bother to listen to anyone except myself.

Lucas nods.

"Why did you make Solitaire?" I say.

He can't breathe. His mouth turns in and he swallows.

"I'm in love with you," he says.

$$\left(\cdots\right)$$

At that moment, I consider many options. One is to punch him in the face. Another is to jump out of the window. The option that I go with is to run. So now I'm running.

You don't pull pranks on a school because you're in love with someone. You don't get a whole party to attack a guy because you're *in love with someone*.

I'm running through our school, into and out of classrooms I've never entered, through dark and empty corridors I never pass through anymore. All the while, Lucas is in pursuit, crying out that he wants to explain properly, as if there's more to explain. There isn't more to explain. He doesn't care. Like everyone. He doesn't care that people get hurt. Like everyone.

I find myself at a dead end in the art department. It's the room that I stood on top of only two days ago, that I sat outside of earlier today—the art conservatory. I dart round the room, desperately looking for somewhere to go, as Lucas stands breathing heavily at the door. The windows are too small to jump out of.

"Sorry," he says, still panting, hands on his knees. "Sorry, that was kind of sudden. That didn't make any sense."

"Uh, you *think*?"

"Am I allowed to explain properly?"

I look at him. "Is this the final explanation?"

He stands up straight. "Yes, yes, it is."

I sit down on a stool. He sits on the stool next to mine. I edge away, but don't say anything. He begins his story.

$$\left(\cdots\right)$$

"I never forgot anything about you. Every time we drove down your road I would look at your house, pretty much praying that you'd step out of your door at just the right moment. I used to come up with all these scenarios where I would contact you and we would be friends again. Like, we'd find each other on Facebook and start chatting and decide to meet up. Or we'd meet randomly somewhere—in the high street, at a party, I don't know. When I grew older, you became, like, that one girl. You know? The one girl who I would end up having that great romance with. We start as childhood friends. We'd meet again, older, and that would be it. Happily ever after. Like a film.

"But you're not the Victoria I had in my head. I don't know. You're some-one else. Someone I don't know, I guess. I don't know what I was thinking. Look, I'm not a stalker or anything. I came for a tour of Higgs last term to see if I liked it, you know. The guide took me all over the school and the last place I visited was . . . the common room. And, er, that's where I saw you. Sitting literally right in front of me.

"I thought I was going to have a heart attack. You were on a computer, but you had your back to me. You were sitting there at the computer, playing solitaire.

"And you looked so—you had one hand on your head and the other just clicking and clicking the mouse, and you looked so *dead*. You looked tired and dead. And under your breath you kept saying over and over, 'I hate myself, I hate myself, I hate myself.' Not loud enough for anyone to hear except me."

I don't remember this happening. I don't remember this day at all.

"It seems dumb now. I bet you were just stressed about coursework or something. But I couldn't stop thinking about it. And then I started to get all these ideas. I thought that maybe you really did hate yourself. And I hated the school for doing that to you.

"I literally went into rages thinking about it. And that's when I came up with Solitaire. I talked to a guy I knew from Truham who'd joined Higgs, and we decided to start pulling pranks. I had this crazy, *crazy* idea that just a few small acts of hilarity might bring something bright into your life. And into everyone's lives.

"So, yeah, I organized the Ben Hope thing. I was so angry about what had happened to Charlie. Ben deserved that. But then . . . then the thing at the Clay happened. People got injured. *You* got injured. It got out of control. So after that I quit. I haven't done *anything* since Sunday. But there's so many followers now. We made them all take it so seriously, thinking they were anarchists or something, with the posters and the fireworks and the stupid slogans. I don't know. I don't know.

"Michael found me about half an hour ago. I know you're going to hate me now. But . . . yeah. He's right. It's worse for you if you don't know."

Tears start to drift down his face and I don't know what to do. Like when we were little. Always silent tears.

"I am the worst type of human being," Lucas says, and he puts his elbows on the table and looks away from me.

"Well, you're not getting any sympathy from me," I say.

Because he gave up. Lucas gave up. He let these stupid, imaginary feelings control his life, and he made bad things happen. Very bad things. Which caused other bad things to happen. This is the way the world works. This is why you never let your feelings control your behavior.

I'm angry.

I'm angry that Lucas didn't fight against his feelings.

Lucas stands up and I flinch away.

"Stay away from me," I find myself saying, like he's a rabid animal.

I can't believe it took until now for me to realize the truth.

He's not Lucas Ryan to me anymore.

"Victoria, I saw you that day and thought that the person who I'd been in love with for six years was going to kill herself."

"Don't touch me. Stay away from me."

Nobody is honest, nobody is real. You can't trust anyone or anything. Emotions are humanity's fatal disease. And we're all dying.

"Look, I'm not part of Solitaire anymore—"

"You were so *innocent* and *awkward*." I'm talking in rushed, maniacal trains of thought. I don't know why I'm saying any of this. It's not really Lucas I'm angry at. "I suppose you thought you were romantic, with your books and your fucking hipster clothes. Why shouldn't I be in love with you? All this time you were plotting and faking."

Why am I surprised? This is what everyone does.

And then I know exactly what to do.

"What," I ask, "is Solitaire going to do tomorrow?"

I have the chance to do something. To finally, wonderfully, put an end to all of the pain.

He says nothing, so I shout.

"*Tell me!* Tell me what's happening tomorrow!"

"I don't know exactly," says Lucas, but I think he's lying. "All I know is that they're meeting inside at six a.m."

So that's where I'll be. Tomorrow at six. I'll undo everything.

"Why didn't you tell me that before?" I whisper. "Why didn't you tell anyone?"

There is no answer. He cannot answer.

The sadness is coming, like a storm.

And I start to laugh like a serial killer.

I laugh and run. Run out of the school. Run through this dead town. Run, and I think, maybe the pain will stop, but it keeps burning inside, burning down.

FOURTEEN

The fourth of February is a Friday. The UK experiences the heaviest snow-fall since 1963. Approximately 360,000 people are born and lightning strikes the earth 518,400 times. 154,080 people die.

I escape my house at 5:24 a.m. I did not watch any films during the night. None of them seemed very interesting. Also, my room was kind of freaking me out because I pulled down all the Solitaire posts so my carpet was now a meadow of paper and Blu Tack. I just kind of sat on my bed, not doing any-thing. Anyway, I'm wearing as many clothes as possible over my school uniform and I'm armed with my phone and a flashlight and an unopened diet lemonade can, which I don't think I'll drink. I'm feeling slightly deranged because I haven't slept for about a week, but it's a good sort of deranged, an ecstatic deranged, an invincible, infinite *deranged*.

The Solitaire blog post appeared at 8 p.m. last night.

20:00 February 3rd

Solitairians.

Tomorrow morning, Solitaire's greatest operation will take place at Harvey Greene Grammar School. You are most welcome to attend. Thank you for all your support this term.

We hope that we've added something to what might have been a very boring winter.

Patience Kills

I have a sudden urge to call Becky.

"... hello?"

Becky sleeps with her phone on vibrate next to her head. I know this because she used to tell me how people wake her up in the night by texting her.

"Becky. It's Tori."

"Oh my God. Tori." She does not sound very alive. "Why . . . are you calling me . . . at five a.m. . . . ?"

"It's twenty to six."

"Well, *that* changes *everything*."

"That's a forty-minute difference. You can do a lot in forty minutes."

"Just . . . why . . . are you calling . . . ?"

"To say I'm feeling a lot better."

Pause. "Well . . . that's good, but—"

"Yeah, I know. I feel really, really, really good."

"Then . . . shouldn't you be sleeping?"

"Yeah, yeah, I will, once I've sorted things out for good. It's happening this morning, Solitaire, you know."

Second pause. "Wait." She's awake now. "Wait. What—where are you?"

I look around. I'm nearly there actually. "Heading to school. Why?"

"Oh my *God!*" There's the scuffling sound of her sitting up in bed. "Jesus Christ, dude, what the fuck are you doing?!"

"I already told you—"

"TORI! JUST GO HOME!"

"*Go home.*" I laugh. "And do what? Cry some more?"

"ARE YOU LITERALLY INSANE? IT'S FIVE A.M.! WHAT ARE YOU EVEN TRYING TO—"

I stop laughing and press the red button because she's making me tear up.

My feet sink into the snow as I hurry through town. I'm pretty sure that at some point I'm going to take a step and my foot won't stop; it'll just keep sinking down through the snow until I've disappeared entirely. If it weren't

232

for the streetlights, it would be pitch-black, but the lights are painting the white with a dull yellowish glow. The snow looks sick. Diseased.

Fifteen minutes later, I push my way through a hedge to get into school because the main gates are locked. I get a big old scratch on my face and, upon inspection using my phone screen, I decide I quite like it.

The car park is deserted. I trudge through the snow towards the main entrance and, as I draw closer, I see that the door is ajar. I head inside, immediately noticing the white burglar-and-fire-alarm box on the wall—or what used to be a white box on the wall. It's been torn away and is hanging from the plaster by only a couple of wires. The rest have all been cut. I stare at it for a few seconds before moving on down a corridor.

They're here.

I drift for a while, a Ghost of Christmas Past. I'm reminded of the last time I was here at a stupid hour of the day—weeks ago, with the prefects and Zelda, and the violin video. That seems like a long time ago. Everything seems colder now.

As I draw closer to the end of the corridor, I begin to hear unintelligible whispers coming from the corner English classroom. Mr. Kent's classroom. I flatten myself like a spy against the wall by the door. There's a dim light glaring from its plastic window. Carefully and slowly, I peer into the room.

I expect to find a horde of Solitaire minions, but what I see instead are three figures huddled by a cluster of tables in the middle of the room, illuminated by an oversized flashlight shining upwards from the table. The first is the guy with the large quiff who I've seen Lucas with a hundred times, in a very Lucas-ish hipster getup—skinnies, boat shoes, bomber jacket, and Ben Sherman polo.

The second person is Evelyn Foley.

Quiff has his arm round her. Oh. Evelyn's secret boyfriend is Quiff. I think back to the Clay. Had the Solitaire voice been a girl's? It's too cold for me to remember anything, so I focus my attention on the third figure.

Lucas.

Quiff and Evelyn seem to be kind of ganging up on him. Lucas is whispering hurriedly at Quiff. He told me he wasn't a part of Solitaire anymore, didn't he? Maybe I should jump into the room and start shouting. Waving my phone. Threatening to call the police. Maybe—

"*Oh my God.*"

At the other end of the corridor, Becky Allen blinks into existence, and I almost collapse. She points at me with an accusatory finger and hisses, "I knew you wouldn't go home!"

My eyes, wild and unfocused, spin crazily as she storms down the corridor. Soon, Becky is beside me, in Superman pyjama bottoms tucked into at least three pairs of socks and furry boots, along with a hoodie and a coat and all other kinds of woolly clothing. She's here. Becky came here. For me. She looks very strange with her purplish hair all scraped into a greasy sort of bulb, and I don't know why or how this happens, but I am actually *relieved* that she's here.

"Oh my God, you're ridiculous," she whispers. "You. Are. Ridiculous." And then she hugs me, and I let her, and for several seconds I really feel like we're friends. She lets go, withdraws, and cringes. "Dude, what have you done to your *face?*" She lifts her sleeve and wipes it roughly against my cheek. When she draws it away, it's stained red. Then she smiles and shakes her head. I'm reminded of the Becky I knew three years ago, before boys, before sex, before alcohol, before she started to move on while I stayed exactly where I was.

I point towards the door to the English room. "Look inside."

She tiptoes past me and looks. And her face opens up in horror. "*Evelyn?* What th— And why is *Lucas—*" Her mouth hangs wide open as the sudden realization dawns. "Is this—is this *Solitaire?*" She turns back to me and shakes her head. "This is too much mind-fuckery for this time of day. I'm not even sure I'm actually awake."

"*Shh.*"

I'm trying to listen to what they're saying. Becky dives past the door and we stand, hidden in the dark, on either side of it. Vaguely, we begin to decipher a conversation. It's 6:04 a.m.

"Grow some balls, Lucas." Evelyn. She's wearing high-waisted denim shorts and tights and a Harrington jacket. "I'm not even joking. We're *terribly* sorry to tear you away from your electric blanket and Radio 4, but can't you just *grow some balls.*"

Lucas's face, dotted with shadows, grimaces. "Can I please remind you that *I* am the one who started Solitaire in the first place—therefore, my balls are in no position to be questioned, thanks."

"Yeah, you started it," says Quiff. It's the first time I get a proper look at him and, for someone with such a large head of hair, he really is tiny. By his side on the table is a Morrisons shopping bag. His voice is also far more sophisticated than I'd anticipated. "And you left just when we started to do stuff that's actually *worthwhile.* We're doing something great and yet here you are saying that everything *you* have worked for has been, and I quote, 'total and utter bullshit.'"

"This isn't what I worked for," Lucas snaps. "I thought that messing with this school would help people."

"Fucking up this school," says Quiff, "is the best thing that's ever happened to this town."

"But this isn't going to help anyone. It's not going to change anything. Changing an environment doesn't change a person."

"Cut the crap, Lucas." Evelyn shakes her head.

"You must be able to see what an idiotic idea this is," says Lucas.

"Just give me the lighter," says Quiff.

Becky, her palms flattened against the wall like Spider-Man, whips her head round. *"Lighter?"* she mouths.

I shrug back. I stare harder at Lucas and realize that behind his back he's holding what at first looks like a gun, but is actually just one of those novelty lighters.

There's only one thing you can do with a lighter.

"Er, no," says Lucas, but even this far away I can tell that he's nervous. Quiff lunges for Lucas's arm, but he steps backwards just in time. Quiff begins to laugh like some evil mastermind.

"Well, *shit*," says Quiff. "You went to all this trouble, and now you're just going to steal our stuff and run off with it. Like a little kid. Why did you even *come here*? Why didn't you just go and tell on us, like the baby you are?"

Lucas shifts on to his other leg, silent.

"Give me the lighter," says Quiff. "Last chance."

"Fuck you," says Lucas.

Quiff puts his hand to his face and rubs his forehead, sighing, "Christ." Then, like someone flicked a switch in his brain, he swings his fist at lightning speed and punches Lucas in the face.

Lucas, with surprising dignity, doesn't fall down; he lifts himself up to his full height and looks Quiff dead in the eye.

"*Fuck you*," says Lucas again.

Quiff smashes Lucas in the stomach, this time doubling him over. He grabs Lucas's arm with ease and wrenches away the lighter gun, then grabs Lucas by the collar, holds the barrel against his neck, and pushes him against the wall. I expect he thinks he looks like some kind of Mafia boss, but it doesn't help that he's got the face of a seven-year-old.

"You couldn't just *leave it*, could you, mate? You couldn't just leave it alone, could you?"

It's obvious that Quiff is not going to pull the trigger and burn Lucas's neck. It is obvious to Quiff that Quiff is not going to burn Lucas. It is obvious to all the people who have ever lived and all the people who will ever live that Quiff does not have the strength, will, or malice to seriously wound a fairly innocent guy like Lucas Ryan. But I guess, if someone is holding a lighter gun up to your throat, then things like that aren't quite as obvious as they should be.

Becky is no longer at my side.

She karate-kicks the door open.

"Okay, chaps. Just stop. Right now. Stop the madness."

With one hand in the air, she strides out from our hiding place. Evelyn makes some kind of squealing sound, Lucas lets out a triumphant laugh, and Quiff drops Lucas's collar and steps backwards as if afraid that Becky might arrest him right there on the spot.

I follow her in and immediately regret it. Lucas sees me and stops laughing.

Becky stomps up and places herself directly between Lucas and the lighter gun.

"Oh, darling." She sighs at Quiff and tilts her head, faux sympathetically. "You actually think you're intimidating, don't you? I mean, where in God's name did you *get* that piece of crap? Costcutter?"

Quiff tries to laugh it off, but fails. Becky's eyes turn to fire. She holds out her hands.

"Go for it, dude." Her eyebrows are all the way up her forehead. "Go on. Set fire to my hair or whatever. I am relatively intrigued to see if you can pull that trigger."

I can see Quiff desperately trying to think of something witty to say. After a few awkward moments, he stumbles backwards, grabs the Morrisons bag, puts the lighter into it, and pulls the trigger. The lighter flame glows orange for approximately two seconds, before Quiff pulls it away and casts the bag dramatically towards the classroom's bookshelf. Whatever is inside the bag begins to smoke and rustle.

Everyone in the room looks at the bag.

The smoke gradually thins. The plastic bag withers a little before flopping off the shelf and onto the floor, upside down.

There is a long silence.

Eventually, Becky throws her head back and roars with laughter.

"Oh my *God*! Oh my *God*!"

Quiff has nothing to say anymore. There's no way he can take back what just happened. I think this is just about the stupidest thing I have ever seen.

"*This* is Solitaire's grand finale!" Becky continues to laugh. "Oh my God, you really are the most deluded of all the hipsters I've met. You bring a whole new meaning to the word *deluded*."

Quiff lifts the lighter and sways a little towards the bag, as if he's going to try again, but Becky grabs him violently by the wrist and with her other hand wrenches the gun away. She waves it in the air and withdraws her phone from her coat pocket.

"Take one step towards that plastic bag, bitch, and I'm calling the po-po." She raises her eyebrows like a disappointed teacher. "Don't think I don't know your name, *Aaron Riley*."

Quiff, or Aaron Riley, or whoever, squares up to her. "You think they'd believe some slag?"

Becky throws her head back for the second time. "Oh, man. I've met *so many* bellends like you." She pats Quiff on the arm. "You do the whole tough-guy thing really well, mate. Well done."

I steal a quick glance at Lucas, but he's just staring at Becky, absently shaking his head.

"You're all the same," says Becky. "All you idiots who think that by play-ing the self-righteous intellectual, you rule the entire world. Why don't you go home and complain about it on your blog like *normal* people?" She takes a step towards him. "I mean, what are you trying to do here, dude? What's Solitaire trying to do? Do you all think that you're better than everyone else? Are you trying to say that school isn't important? Are you trying to teach us about morals and how to be a better person? Are you trying to say that if we just laugh about it all, if we just stir up some shit and put smiles on our faces, then life's going to be hunky-dory? Is *that* what Solitaire's try-ing to do?"

She lets out a monstrous cry of exasperation, actually making me jump. "Sadness is a natural human emotion, you giant *dick*."

Evelyn, who has been watching with her lips pursed the entire time, finally speaks up. "Why are you judging us? You don't even understand what we're doing."

"Oh, Evelyn. Really. Solitaire? You're with Solitaire?" Becky begins to flick the lighter on and off. Perhaps she's as deranged as I am. Evelyn cowers backwards. "And *this* prick has been your special secret boyfriend all along? He's wearing more hair product than I've used in the past *year*, Evelyn!" She shakes her head like a weary old person. "Solitaire. Bloody hell. I feel like I'm in Year 8 all over again."

"Why are you acting like such a special snowflake?" says Evelyn. "You think you're a better person than us?"

Becky screeches with laughter and tucks the lighter gun into her pyjama trousers. "A better person? Ha. I've done some shitty things to people. And now I'm admitting it. You know what, Evelyn? Maybe I want to be a special snowflake. Maybe, sometimes, I just want to express the emotions that I'm actually feeling instead of having to put on this happy, smiley facade that I put on every day just to come across to bitches like you as *not boring*."

She points at me again as if she's punching the air. "Apparently, Tori understands what you guys are trying to do. I have no idea why you're trying to destroy our crappy little school. But Tori thinks that, you know, on the whole, you're doing something bad, and *I fucking believe her*." Her arm drops. "Dear God, Evelyn. You severely piss me off. Jesus Christ. Creepers are the ugliest shoes I have ever seen. Go back to your blog or Glastonbury or wherever you came from and *stay there*."

Quiff and Evelyn give Becky one last horrified glare before giving up.

It's kind of remarkable, in a way.

Because people are very stubborn and they don't like to be proven wrong. I think that they both knew that what they had been about to do *was* wrong though, or perhaps they didn't have the guts to go through with it, deep down. Maybe, when it came down to it, they'd never been the real antagonists. But if they're not, then who is?

We follow the pair slowly out of the room and down the corridor. We watch as they wander away out through the double doors. If I were them, I would probably change schools immediately. They'll be gone in a minute. Gone forever. They will be gone.

We stay there for a while, not saying anything. After a few minutes, I begin to sweat. Maybe I feel angry. No. I don't feel anything.

Lucas is standing next to me and he turns. His eyes are big and blue and doglike. "Why did you come here, Victoria?"

"Those two would have hurt you," I point out, but we both know this isn't true.

"Why did you come?"

Everything's so blurry.

Lucas sighs. "Well, it's finally over. Becky kind of saved us all."

Becky seems to be having a kind of stunned breakdown, slumped on the floor against the corridor wall with her Superman-logoed legs sprawled out in front of her. She holds the lighter gun up to her face, flicking it on and off in front of her eyes, and I can just about hear her muttering, "This is the most pretentious novelty lighter I've ever seen . . . this is so *pretentious* . . ."

"Am I forgiven?" asks Lucas.

Maybe I'm going to pass out.

I shrug. "You're not actually in love with me, are you?"

He blinks and then he's not looking at me. "Er, no. It wasn't love really. It was . . . I just thought I needed you . . . for some reason . . ." He shakes his head. "I actually think that Becky's rather lovely."

I try not to throw up or stab myself with my house keys. I stretch my face into a grin like a toy clown. "Ha ha ha! You and the rest of the solar system!"

Lucas's expression changes, like he finally gets who I am.

"Could you not call me Victoria anymore?" I ask.

He steps away from me. "Yeah, sure. Tori."

I start to feel hot. "Were they going to do what I think they were going to do?"

Lucas's eyes keep moving around. Not looking at me.

"They were going to burn the school down," he says.

It seems almost funny. Another childhood dream. If we were ten, perhaps we'd rejoice in the idea of the school on fire, because that would mean no more school, wouldn't it? But it just seems violent and pointless now. As violent and pointless as all the other things that Solitaire has done.

And then I realize something.

I turn round.

"Where are you going?" asks Lucas.

I walk down the corridor, back to Kent's classroom, getting hotter and hotter the closer I get.

"What are you doing?"

I gaze into the classroom. And I wonder if I've lost it entirely.

"Tori?"

I turn to Lucas and look at him standing at the other end of the corridor. Really, properly look at him.

"Get out," I say, maybe too quietly.

"What?"

"Take Becky and get out."

"Wait, what are you—"

And then he sees the orange glow lighting up one side of my body.

The orange glow coming from the fire that is raging through Kent's classroom.

"Holy shit," says Lucas, and then I'm racing down the corridor towards the nearest fire extinguisher, tugging at it, but it won't come off the wall.

There's a horrific crack. The door to the classroom has split and is burning happily.

Lucas has joined me at the extinguisher, but, however hard we tug, we can't get it off the wall. The fire creeps out of the room and spreads to the wall displays, the ceiling filling steadily with smoke.

"We need to get out!" Lucas shouts over the roaring flames. "We can't do anything!"

"Yes, we *can*." We have to. We have to do something. I have to do something. I abandon the extinguisher and head farther into the school. There'll be another one in the next corridor. In the science corridor.

Becky has leapt up from the floor. She goes to run after me, as does Lucas, but a giant wall display suddenly flops off the wall in a fiery wreck of paper and pins, blocking the corridor. I can't see them. The carpet catches light and the flames begin to advance towards me—

"TORI!" someone screams. I don't know who. I don't care. I locate the fire extinguisher and this one easily detaches from the wall. It says *WATER* on it, but also *FOR USE ON FIRES INVOLVING WOOD, PAPER, FABRIC, NOT ELECTRICAL FIRES.* The fire edges down the corridor, on the walls, the ceiling, the floor, pushing me backwards. There's lights, plug sockets everywhere—

"TORI!" This time the voice comes from behind me. Two hands place themselves on my shoulders and I leap around as if it's Death itself.

But it's not.

It's him, in his T-shirt and jeans, glasses, hair, arms, legs, eyes, everything—

It's Michael Holden.

He wrenches the extinguisher from my arms—

And he hurls it out of the nearest window.

FIFTEEN

I am forced down the corridor and thrown out of the nearest fire exit. Alarms have started going off inside the school. How Michael knew we were here, I don't know. What he's doing, I don't know. But I need to stop that fire. I need to be in there. If I can't do anything, then it will have been for nothing. My whole life. Everything. Nothing.

He tries to grab me, but I'm practically a torpedo. I race back through the fire exit and down the next corridor, away from the oncoming flames, searching for another fire extinguisher. I'm sort of hyperventilating and I can't see anything and I'm running so fast that I have no idea where this corridor is in the school and I start tearing up again.

But Michael can run like he skates. He grabs me round the waist, just as I tug the fire extinguisher off the wall, just as the fire bypasses the fire exit and closes in on us—

"TORI! WE NEED TO GET OUT NOW."

The fire draws Michael's face out of the dark. I flail around in his grip and burst forward, but he closes his fist round my forearm and squeezes it and starts to drag me, and before I know what I'm doing I'm yanking my arm so hard that my skin starts to burn. I'm screaming at him and pushing and I swing my leg around and actually kick him in the stomach. I must kick him hard because he tumbles backwards and clutches his body. I instantly realize what I've done and freeze, looking at him in the orange light. We meet each other's eyes and he seems to *realize* something, and I want to laugh, because yeah, he's finally realized, just like Lucas did eventually, and I hold my arms out to him—

And then I see the fire.

The inferno in the science lab to our right. The science lab that's connected to that English classroom by one single doorway, which the flames must have stormed straight through.

I leap forward into Michael and push him away—

And the classroom explodes outwards: crumpled tables, chairs, flying fireballs of books. I'm on the ground, several meters away, miraculously alive, and I open my eyes, but can see nothing. Michael is lost somewhere around me in the smoke. I scramble backwards as a chair leg soars past my cheek, and scream his name, no way of knowing if he's alive or—

I get up and run.

Crying? Shouting things. A name? His name?

Solitaire's eternal idea. That childhood dream.

Is he dead? No. I see a shape rise vaguely from the smoke, flailing around before disappearing farther into the school. At one point, I think I hear him calling me, but I might just be imagining it.

I scream his name and I'm running again, out of the smoke cloud, away from the science corridor. Around the corner, flames have reached an art classroom and the artwork, hours and hours of it, is melting into globules of fried acrylic and dripping onto the floor. It's so sad that I want to cry, but the smoke has already started that. I start to panic too. Not because of the fire.

Not even because I'm losing and Solitaire is winning.

Because Michael is in here.

Another corridor. Another. Where am I? Nothing is the same in the dark and the burning. Lights flash around me like sirens, like I'm passing out. Diamonds sparkling. I'm screaming again. *Michael Holden.* The fire growls and a hurricane of hot air careers through the school's tunnels.

I call out for him. I'm calling him over and over again, I'm shaking so hard, the artwork and the handwritten essays on the walls are disintegrating around me and I cannot breathe.

"I failed." I say these words right as I'm thinking them. It's funny—this never happens. "I failed. I failed." It's not the school I've failed. It's not even myself. It's Michael. I've failed him. I failed to stop being sad. He tried so hard, he tried so hard to be nice, to be my friend, and I've failed him. I stop screaming. There is nothing now. Michael, dead, the school, dying, and me. There is nothing now.

And then a voice.

My name in the smoke.

I spin on the spot, but there are only flames that way. What building am I in? There must be a window, a fire exit, something, but everything is burning, the smoke slowly starting to suffocate the air and eventually me, so before I know what I'm doing I'm tearing up a flight of stairs onto the first floor, smoke and flames at my heels.

I turn left, left again, right, into a classroom. The door slams behind me. I grab a chair, not thinking about anything except fire and smoke and dying, and smash the thin window. I close my eyes as a sprinkling of glass dust showers over my hair.

I climb out into the morning and onto the top of what seems to be a concrete roof and finally, *finally*, I remember where I am.

The beautiful place.

The small concrete roof of the art conservatory. The field of snow and the river. The black morning sky. Cold air.

Infinite space.

A thousand thoughts at once. Michael Holden is nine hundred of them. The rest are self-hatred.

I failed to do anything.

I look at the smashed window. What does that lead to? Only pain. I look at the metal stairs to my right. What do they lead to? Only myself, failing, time and time again, to do anything right, or say anything right.

I'm at the edge and I look down. It's far. It's calling me.

A hope of something better. A third option.

It's so hot. I take my coat and gloves off.

It hits me then.

I haven't ever known what I wanted out of life. Until now.

I sort of want to be dead.

SIXTEEN

My feet drift absently closer to the edge. I think about Michael Holden. Mainly about how he's secretly angry all the time. I think that a lot of people are secretly angry all the time.

I think about Lucas Ryan and that makes me feel sadder. There is another tragedy in which I am not the rescuer.

I think about my ex–best friend, Becky Allen. I don't think I know who she is. I think I knew before—before we grew up—but after that, she changed and I didn't.

I think about my brother Charlie Spring, and Nick Nelson. Sometimes paradise isn't what people think it should be.

I think about Ben Hope.

Sometimes people hate themselves.

And, while I think, Harvey Greene Grammar School dissolves. My feet peep slightly over the concrete roof. If I fall accidentally, the universe will be there to catch me.

And then—

Then there he is.

Charlie Spring.

A lone dot in orange-tinted white.

He's waving and screaming up.

"DON'T!"

Don't, he says.

And there's another figure running along. Taller, stouter. He clutches Charlie's hand. Nick Nelson.

Then another. And another. Why? What's wrong with people? Why do they never give you any peace?

There's Lucas and Becky. Becky puts her hands to her mouth. Lucas puts his hands on his head. Charlie's screaming in a battle with the wind and flames. Screaming, whirling, burning.

"Stop!"

This voice is closer and comes from above. I decide that it's probably God, because I think that this is probably how God works. He waits until your final moments and *then* he'll step in and take you seriously. It's like when you're four years old and you tell your parents that you're going to run away. And they say: "Okay, go right ahead." Like they don't care. And they only start caring when you actually walk out the door and down the road with your teddy bear under your arm and a packet of biscuits in your rucksack.

"Tori!"

I turn round and look up.

At the top of the school building, above the window that I smashed, is Michael Holden, lying on his front over the roof so that only his head and shoulders are visible from below.

He holds out an arm to me. "Please!"

The mere sight of him makes me want to die even more. "The school's burning down," I say, turning back the other way. "You need to leave."

"Turn round, Tori. Turn round, you absolute twat."

Something wrenches me round. I take out my flashlight, wondering briefly why I haven't used it until now, and I shine it upwards. I see him then properly. Hair all messed up and dusty. Patches of soot smothering his face. A burn mark on his outstretched arm.

"Do you want to kill yourself?" he asks, and the question sounds unreal because you never hear anyone ever asking that question in real life.

"I don't want you to do that," he says. "I can't let you do that. You can't leave me here alone."

His voice breaks.

"You need to be here," he says.

And then he does that thing that I do. His mouth sort of sucks itself in and turns down and his eyes and nose crinkle up and one tear creeps out of the corner of his blue eye and he raises his hands to cover up his face.

"I'm sorry," I say, because his face, all scrunched up and melting, physically hurts me. I start to cry too. Against my will, I step away from the edge and closer to him and I hope that this makes him understand. "I'm sorry. I'm sorry I'm sorry I'm sorry."

"Shut *up!*" He's smiling while crying, madly, throwing his hands from his face and raising both arms up. Then he punches the ground. "God, I'm stupid. I can't believe I didn't realize this any sooner. I can't believe it."

I'm pretty much directly under his face. His glasses begin to slide off his nose and he swiftly pushes them back on.

"You know, the worst thing is that when I threw away that fire extinguisher you were holding, I wasn't just thinking about saving you." He chuckles sadly. "We all need saving really."

"Then why—" I pause. Suddenly understanding everything. This boy. This person. How has it taken me this long to understand? He needed me as much as I needed him, because he was *angry*, and he has always been angry.

"You wanted the school to burn."

He chuckles again and rubs his eyes. "You do know me."

And he's right. I do know him. Just because someone smiles doesn't mean that they're happy.

"I've never been good enough," he says. "I get so stressed out, I don't make friends—*God*, I can't make friends." His eyes glaze over. "Sometimes I just wish I were a normal human being. But I can't. I'm not. No matter how hard I try. And then the school was burning and I thought . . . something told me it might be a way out of all this. I thought it would make me feel better, and you feel better."

He swivels into a sitting position, legs dangling over the edge mere centimeters from my head.

"I was wrong," he says.

I look back out to the edge of the building. No one is happy. What is there in the future?

"Some people aren't meant for school," says Michael. "That doesn't mean they aren't meant for life."

"I can't," I say. The edge is so close. "I can't."

"Let me help you."

"Why would you do that?"

He jumps down to the roof I'm standing on and looks at me. Really looks. I'm reminded of the time I first saw myself in his oversized glasses.

The Tori looking back at me now seems different somehow.

"One person can change everything," he says. "And you have changed everything for me."

Behind him, a small fireball erupts out of a roof. It temporarily lights the tips of Michael's hair, but he doesn't even blink.

"You are my best friend," he says.

A flush of red passes over him and it makes me embarrassed to see him embarrassed. He awkwardly flattens his hair with one hand and wipes his eyes. "We're all going to die. One day. So I want to get it right first time, you know? I don't *want* to make any more mistakes. And I know that this is not a mistake." He smiles. "You are not a mistake."

He turns abruptly and gazes towards the burning school.

"Maybe we would have been able to stop it," he says. "Maybe . . . maybe if, if I hadn't—" His voice catches in his throat and he brings a hand up to his mouth, his eyes filling with tears again.

This is a new feeling. Or a very old one.

I do something that I don't expect. I reach out. My arm lifts up and moves forward through the air towards him. I just want to make sure he's there. To make sure I haven't made him up.

My hand touches his sleeve.

"You shouldn't hate yourself," I say, because I know that he doesn't just hate himself for letting the school burn. He hates himself for a whole lot of other reasons too. But he shouldn't hate himself. He *can't*. He makes me believe that there are good people in this world. I don't know how this has happened, but what I do know is that this feeling has been there from the very start. When I met Michael Holden, I knew, deep down, that he was the best person you could possibly hope to be—so perfect that he was unreal. And it made me sort of hate him. However, rather than slowly learning more and more good things about him, I have come across flaw after flaw after flaw. And you know what? That's what makes me like him now. That's why he is a *real* perfect person. Because he is a real person.

I tell him all of this.

"Anyway," I say, unsure how to end this, but knowing that I must make my conclusion, "I'll never hate you. Maybe I can help you to understand why I will never hate you."

A pause, the sound of burning, the smell of smoke. He looks at me like I've shot him.

And then we kiss.

Neither of us is really sure whether it's an appropriate moment, me having almost accidentally killed myself and all, and Michael hating himself so much, but it happens anyway, everything finally making sense, knowing that it would be apocalyptic for me *not* to be here with him, because right then—at that moment—it's like . . . it's like—actually—I really would die if I don't . . . if I don't *hold him*.

"I think I've loved you since I met you," he says as we draw apart. "I just mistook it for curiosity."

"Not only is that hideously untrue," I say, feeling like I'm about to pass out, "but that is also the *dumbest* rom-com line I've *ever* had to endure. And I've endured many. What with me being such a fabulous guy magnet."

He blinks. A grin creeps across his face and he laughs, throwing his head back.

"Oh my God, there you are, Tori," he says, laughing hard, pulling me into another hug and practically lifting me off the ground. "Oh my *God*."

I feel myself smile. I hold him and I smile.

Without warning, he retreats back and points outwards and says, "What in the name of Guy Fawkes is going on?"

I turn, puzzled, towards the field.

The white is mostly gone. There are no longer only four dots, but at least a hundred. Dozens and dozens of teenagers. We hadn't heard them, I guess because of the wind and the fire, but now that they've seen us turn round, they've begun to wave and shout. I cannot see the faces clearly, but each person is a whole person. A whole person with a whole life, who gets out of bed in the morning and goes to school and talks to friends and eats food and *lives*. They're chanting our names and I don't know most of them and most of them don't know me I don't even know why they're here, but still . . . still . . .

In the middle, I can see Charlie being given a piggyback by Nick and Becky by Lucas. They're waving and shouting.

"I don't," I say, my voice cracking, "understand . . ."

Michael retrieves his phone from his pocket and loads up the Solitaire blog. There's nothing new there. Then he loads up Facebook and scrolls down the feed.

"Well," he says, and I look over his shoulder at the phone.

Lucas Ryan

Solitaire is burning down Higgs

32 minutes ago via Mobile

94 like this   43 shares

View all 203 comments

"Maybe . . ." says Michael. "Maybe he thought . . . the school burning . . . it was too amazing to let it go to waste."

I look at him, and he looks at me.

"Don't you think it's kind of magnificent?" he says.

And in a way it is, I guess. The school is burning. This doesn't happen in real life.

"Lucas Ryan, you damn miraculous hipster," says Michael, gazing down at the crowd. "You really did accidentally start something beautiful."

Something inside my heart makes me smile. A real smile.

And then things go blurry again, and I sort of start to laugh and cry at the same time and I am unsure whether I'm happy or entirely deranged. Because I'm sort of curled into myself, Michael has to lean over my head to properly hold me while I'm shaking, but he does it anyway. Snow falls. Behind us, the school crumbles and I can hear the fire engines making their way through the town.

"So," he says, slyly raising his eyebrows with typical Michael suavity. "You hate yourself. I hate myself. Common interests. We should get together."

I don't know why, but I start to feel quite delirious. The sight of all those people down there. Some of them are jumping up and down and waving. Some of them are only there because they tagged along for an adventure, but for once I don't think that any of them are conceited, or faking it. They're all just being people.

I mean, I'm still not 100 percent sure that I really want to wake up tomorrow. I'm not fixed, just because Michael's here. I still want to get into bed and lie there all day because it's a very easy thing to do. But right now all I can see are all these kids prancing about in the snow and smiling and waving like they haven't got exams and parents and university choices and career options and all the other stressful things to worry about. There's a guy sitting next to me who noticed it all too. A guy that maybe I can help out, like he helped me out.

I can't say that I feel *happy*. I'm not even sure if I would know if I *was*. But all those people down there look so funny and it makes me want to laugh and cry and dance and sing and *not* take a flying, dramatic, spectacular leap off this building. Really. It's funny because it's true.

AFTER

KARL BENSON: I haven't seen you since,
like, junior year. I thought you killed yourself.

ANDREW LARGEMAN: What?

KARL BENSON: I thought you killed yourself. That wasn't you?

ANDREW LARGEMAN: No, no, tha-that wasn't me.

***GARDEN STATE* (2004)**

So I suppose, even after going through all this very carefully, I still don't really know how this happened. I'm not traumatized. It's not anything dramatic like that. Nothing has been tearing me apart. I can't focus any of it around one particular day, one particular event, one particular person. All I know is that once it started it became very easy to let it carry on. And I suppose that's how I ended up here.

Michael reckons he's going to get questioned by the police. Probably me too. And Lucas and Becky, I suppose. We were all there. I hope that we don't get arrested. I don't think Lucas would tell what really happened. Then again, I don't really know much about Lucas Ryan anymore.

Nick, with surprising practicality, said that the best thing to do was get my parents to meet us at the hospital, so all six of us are now crammed in his car. Me, Michael, Lucas, Becky, Nick, and Charlie. Becky's sitting on Lucas's lap because Nick's car is a tiny Fiat. I think Lucas is genuinely starting to like Becky, I really do. Because she stopped Quiff theoretically shooting him, or whatever. He keeps looking up at her with this hilarious expression on his face and it sort of makes me feel a little bit less sad. She doesn't notice of course.

I've said a lot of nasty stuff about Becky. Maybe sometimes it was accurate, but sometimes it wasn't. I think I say a lot of nasty stuff for no reason. Even to people I love.

I'm in the middle seat. I'm finding it very difficult to concentrate on anything as I think I'm half asleep. Snow is falling. All of the snowflakes are exactly the same. The music playing on the car stereo is some Radiohead song. Everything outside is dark blue.

Charlie calls our parents from the front passenger seat. I do not listen to their conversation. After a while, he hangs up and sits silently for a minute, gazing emptily at his phone. Then he raises his head and stares out into the morning sky.

"Victoria," he says, and I listen. He says many things—things that you would expect people to say in this sort of situation, about love and understanding, and support, and being there, things that are supposedly not said enough, things that usually do not need to be said. I don't listen very hard to any of that, because I knew all of it already. Nobody speaks while he speaks; we all just watch the shops drift past, listening to the hum of the car and the sound of his voice. When he's finished, he turns to face me and says something else.

"I noticed," he says. "But I didn't do anything. I didn't do anything."

I have begun to cry.

"I love you anyway," I say, my voice hardly my own. I can't remember if I've ever said those words before in my whole life, not even when I was a child. I start to wonder what I was really like then, and whether I've been imagining myself as someone different this entire time.

He smiles a beautiful, sad smile and says, "I love you too, Tori."

Michael decides to pick up my hand and cup it in his.

"Do you want to know what Dad said?" says Charlie, turning back to face the front. He's not saying it directly to me, but to the whole car. "He said that this is probably because he read *The Catcher in the Rye* too many times when he was our age, and that it got absorbed into his gene pool."

Becky sighs. "Jesus. Can't any teenager be sad and, like, *not* be compared to that book?"

Lucas smiles at her.

"I mean, has anyone here even *read* it?" asks Becky.

There is a unanimous chorus of "nope." Not even Lucas has read it. Funny that.

We listen to the Radiohead song.

I have this real urge to leap out of the car. I think Michael can tell that I want to do this. Maybe Lucas too. Charlie keeps glancing in the rearview mirror.

After a little while, Nick murmurs, "Where are you going to go to sixth form, Charlie?" I have never heard Nick speak so quietly.

Charlie answers him by holding Nick's hand, which is clutching the gear stick so hard that his knuckles are turning white, and saying, "Truham. I'll just stay at Truham. I'll be with you, yeah? And I guess . . . I guess lots of us will be going to Truham now." And Nick nods.

Becky sleepily leans her head on Lucas's shoulder.

"I don't want to go to the hospital," I whisper into Michael's ear. This is a half lie.

He looks at me and he's more than pained. "I know." He rests his head on the top of mine. "I know."

Lucas shifts in the seat next to me. He is looking out of the window, at the trees zipping past, the blur of dark and green.

"This is supposed to be the best time of our lives," he says.

Becky snorts into Lucas's shoulder. "If this is the best time of my life, I might as well end it immediately."

The car revs to get up the slope to the bridge and then we're sailing over the frozen river. The earth spins a few hundred meters and the sun creeps a little closer towards our horizon, preparing to spread its dull winter light over what's left of this wasteland. Behind us, a channel of smoke has leaked into the clear sky, blocking out the few remaining stars that had tried to make an impression.

Becky continues to mumble, as if speaking through a dream.

"I get it though. All they wanted was to make us feel like we belonged to something *important*. Making an impression in the world. Because, like, we're all waiting for something to change. Patience *can* kill you." Her voice quiets to a near-whisper. "Waiting . . . waiting for so long . . ."

She yawns.

"But one day it'll end. It always ends."

And there's sort of a moment where everyone's sitting and *thinking*, you know? Like that feeling when you finish watching a film. You turn off the TV, the screen is black, but the pictures are replaying in your head and you think: What if that's my life? What if that's going to happen to me? Why don't I get that happy ending? Why am *I* complaining about *my* problems?

I don't know what's going to happen to our school and I don't know what's going to happen to us. I don't know how long I'm going to be like this.

All I know is that I'm here. And I'm alive. And I'm not alone.

RESOURCES

If you feel you may be experiencing mental health problems or need support, please don't be afraid to reach out for help from a parent, guardian, friend, partner, or health professional. There are also many services and resources online:

In the US, the 988 Suicide & Crisis Lifeline is a suicide prevention network of over two hundred crisis centers that provides 24/7 service via a toll-free hotline with the number 9-8-8. It is available to anyone in suicidal crisis or emotional distress.

For LGBTQIA+ youth looking for help, The Trevor Project offers a hotline at 1-866-488-7386. You can also use instant messaging to contact them through their website, thetrevorproject.org.

Help and information can also be found at:

National Eating Disorders Association Helpline:
(800) 931-2237, nationaleatingdisorders.org

Beat Eating Diorders: beateatingdisorders.org.uk

YoungMinds: youngminds.org.uk

MindOut LGBTQ Mental Health Service: mindout.org.uk

Rethink Mental Illness: rethink.org

Time to Change: time-to-change.org.uk

The Mix: themix.org.uk

ACKNOWLEDGMENTS

It has been over ten years since I wrote *Solitaire* and I feel incredibly lucky that it is still finding new readers. Thanks to my agent, Claire Wilson, for all your support over the past decade. Thanks to the original editors of *Solitaire*, Lizzie Clifford and Erica Sussman, and to all at HarperCollins, HarperTeen, and RCW involved in the original publication in 2014. Thanks to David Levithan and Scholastic for giving it new life in 2023. And thanks to my readers, old and new, for all your support. It's thanks to you that this new edition is able to exist!

A *SOLITAIRE* CONVERSATION

To commemorate the US release of Solitaire, *Alice chatted in October 2022 with her US editor, David Levithan, to talk about the book's history, the evolution of Tori Spring, and how the novel became the springboard for so many other creative projects.*

Hello, Alice. It's lovely to have a moment to talk to you about *Solitaire*.

Hi! Very excited to be here. I have lots of thoughts about *Solitaire*, over ten years after I first wrote it, and this new edition is the perfect place to share them.

I know you've been answering this one for a number of years now, but it seems like the best place to start: Can you share the origin story of *Solitaire* with us? Which came first, the premise or Tori's character? What about the story made you plunge into it?

Tori came to me first. Before writing *Solitaire*, I wrote a short story about a girl traveling to school on the bus and monologuing internally about the dismal world around her. That girl soon became Tori Spring. She wasn't a self-insert character, but she was a voice I had in my head at the time that was so bored, frustrated, angry, and melancholy. Writing that voice was cathartic and, to be honest, incredibly entertaining.

When your friends first read Tori's voice, did they think, "Ah, this side of Alice is finally emerging!" or did they ask, "Where is this coming from?!" because it was so different from your own voice?

All my friends assumed Tori was me and very few people believed me when I said she wasn't, which was pretty annoying. She was most definitely a part of me, but she is so different to me in so many ways. But many friends, family members, and even people who interviewed me about the book assumed she was me due to the style of the novel—Tori's raw, unfiltered inner monologue *feels* so real, so it *had* to be real, right? I suppose I should take it as a compliment!

The last name Spring seems laced with very heavy irony, in both senses of the word *spring*. She seems to be caught in a sort of mental winter, and I'm not sure she has a bounce-back personality, either. Although perhaps she's waiting for something to spring her from the prison she's in? What do you think of her, vis-à-vis the last name you've given her?

The choice of Spring was intentionally ironic. The season of spring classically represents rebirth and renewal, the coming of warmth and new life. It's what we desperately want for Tori throughout *Solitaire*, but instead she is trapped in this icy cold winter, both psychological and physical. Her name, to me at least, signified that, despite it all, there is hope for healing. I hadn't considered the other meaning of *spring*, but I think that works symbolically in a similar way too—we want Tori to bounce back from the darkness. So with either meaning, her surname signifies her journey to come, even if she hasn't quite begun that journey before the book ends.

Was the title of the book always *Solitaire*?

It was! I remember coming up with it early on and thinking it would just be a placeholder. But I ended up loving it. The word—which translates to *lonely* in French—has strong thematic meaning to the story while also being obviously plot-relevant. And that's usually my strategy for choosing titles.

One of the reasons I love Tori in this book is how completely over-whelmed she is by life and by her traumatized concern for Charlie, because I think it's important to show readers her age that it's pos-sible to be paralyzed and spiraling at the same time, even though that might seem like a contradiction. Could you share some of the meaningful responses you've gotten to the character over the years, in terms of issues of mental health?

Many readers have appreciated the rawness of Tori's melancholy. She is likely dealing with undiagnosed depression, and this manifests in her complete apathy to almost every aspect of her life, except for her brother Charlie, whose situation is—though she'd never admit it—incredibly stress-ful and upsetting for Tori. The rawness of Tori's psyche has been polarizing to readers, but many have appreciated the honest portrayal of someone in such a dark mental place. I've heard from readers who've found it relatable and cathartic to read and who have felt understood in a way they haven't before. I felt a similar way when reading many books as a teen. Although *Solitaire* doesn't provide many helpful answers, there is power in simply see-ing your feelings written in a book and consequently knowing that you're not alone.

It is astonishing to me how young you were when *Solitaire* was pub-lished. How did it feel to switch so quickly from YA reader to YA author? And now that it's been a decade (!) since you first drafted it, when you look back at yourself as a young author, what observations do you make?

It was a very exciting but very strange time, and there were certainly pros and cons to being published so young. The big pro, obviously, is that it launched my career. The main con was that *Solitaire*, being the first book I had ever finished writing, had a lot of flaws. I was still developing as a writer and finding my style, and also developing as a human, learning big things about myself and the world.

Despite that, I truly mean it when I say I wouldn't change it for the world. *Solitaire* was the catalyst for so many other wonderful things that have happened in my life. And I look back on the story with fondness, despite its flaws. Seeing its flaws now is a marker of how much I've grown since then, as a writer and as a person.

When you first wrote *Solitaire*, did you have any sense of how long you would be spending in the world you were creating, with the characters you were creating?

Not at all. I only envisioned it as a standalone story—it was Tori's story, through and through, and as I was writing I didn't spare much thought to the supporting characters and their stories. It was only after I'd finished writing *Solitaire* that I became intrigued by the potential story of Nick and Charlie.

When you look at *Solitaire* after seeing Tori from so many more angles, what do you understand about her now that you might not have when you wrote the book?

Something I had absolutely no idea about at the time was that Tori is obviously asexual. As I was writing *Solitaire*, I had never even heard of asexuality. I remember having thoughts like, *I don't want Tori to be drooling over Michael's physical appearance* and *Tori and Michael's relationship shouldn't stem from being physically attracted to each other*. I'm unsure what justification I gave myself for writing their relationship that way. Perhaps I thought that I was just writing a romance that didn't hinge on physical attractiveness, but the lack of sexual attraction from Tori towards Michael, in retrospect, reads clearly as Tori being asexual. She cares deeply about him as a friend, she possibly even loves him romantically depending on your interpretation of the story, but at no point in the book does she feel hot and bothered by his presence. She instead goes out of her way to reiterate that she doesn't.

I am sure this element of Tori manifested from my own asexuality, which I was totally unaware of at the time. There are a bunch of lines I can pick out now that are *so* incredibly ace-coded. I wish I could go back to my seventeen-year-old self and point them out and say: *Maybe you want to think about why you wrote Tori like this.*

Do you think Michael is ace as well? I'm fascinated by how much he seems to want to meet Tori on her own terms rather than trying to impose his own terms onto her. (Not without friction, of course.)

As I was writing *Solitaire*, I imagined that Michael was attracted to people regardless of gender, which I later learned was what pansexuality is (though, again, I had never heard of that term at the time—Becky's "So you're pansexual?" query was an addition in my 2020 edits of the book). Many asexual people identify as bi or pan before identifying as ace because many aces assume that "feeling the same about all genders" must signify being bi or pan, even if that "feeling" is nothing at all. I do think Michael is pansexual, but Michael and Tori experience sexual attraction in a very similar way: They both have an apathy towards it, a lack of interest. It feels irrelevant to both of them and irrelevant to the power of their relationship. There are far bigger and more complicated feelings on the table between them.

One of the through lines I find in all your novels is the very intense, sometimes fraught, but also ultimately anchoring nature of best-friendship (in these cases, all involving best-friendship between two girls). What keeps drawing you back to this dynamic?

I love writing about the power of platonic love. Perhaps because it's not often the subject of a story. Romance usually takes priority. I'm not a romance-hater by any means—I wrote *Heartstopper*, after all. But there's a special kind of magic in a life-changing, soul-wrenching friendship, and all the drama and heartache that can occur around it. And there are so many kinds of friendships too. Tori and Becky in *Solitaire* is a friendship that is hanging by a thread, held together only by a shared history. While Aled and Frances in *Radio Silence* is a new and passionate friendship, ignited by shared obsessions and an emotional intimacy neither of them has ever felt before. Juliet and Angel of *I Was Born for This* is a friendship that felt so deep on the internet but doesn't quite feel the same in the real world. Just like a romance, these relationships can have meet-cutes and breakups and devastating let downs and heart-racing thrills. There's so much potential for emotional anguish in a friendship. And that's exactly the sort of thing I love to write.

Factoring out Tori and Michael . . . is there any character in the novel, however briefly they appear, who's a secret favorite of yours?

I must also factor out Nick and Charlie—I *have* ended up writing a six-year-strong webcomic about them! But aside from those four, I do have a soft spot for Becky. She's a girl influenced so heavily by the society she's trapped in, concerned with social status and popularity rather than maintaining friendships. I'm not sure I'd describe Becky as a secret fave, but I have a lot of sympathy for her. She has a lot to learn about herself and the world.

I'm fascinated by the chronological choice you made when moving from *Solitaire* to *Heartstopper*. What made you want to rewind Nick and Charlie to the start of their relationship? What was it like to write that start knowing what Charlie was going to have to face, as detailed in *Solitaire*?

What drew me so strongly to Nick and Charlie's story was not knowing what had happened before *Solitaire*. How had they become this couple who are *so* in love, *so* supportive and strong and uplifting of each other? And what had their relationship journey entailed, particularly as Charlie's mental health worsened? There simply *had* to be a story there. It completely ignited my imagination. As I began writing *Heartstopper*, I was excited by the knowledge of what was to come for Charlie, because it allowed me to explore the buildup to that point, and his continued recovery journey after the events of *Solitaire*. Nick and Charlie's love story, their relationship progressing, Charlie's mental health journey, the simple passing of time in their ordinary lives—it was all exactly what I loved about writing.

How has it felt to develop Tori further, but in the guise of a supporting character? Have you ever been tempted to pull her into the foreground again?

Having Tori as a supporting character provides me with many opportunities to lean into the comedy of her personality. Her apathy and unending boredom are also incredibly funny to me, and I love to use that in *Heartstopper* for quick cutaway moments and snarky comments. But it also allows me to show more of Tori and Charlie's sibling relationship from Charlie's perspective, and we come to understand something that is difficult to see in *Solitaire*, which is that Tori is a deeply caring and protective older sister who would do anything for her two brothers. While I don't feel the desire to pull her into the foreground again—I feel her story is told—I still enjoy getting to write her from these different perspectives.

I have to ask the classic craft question: Are you a plotter, knowing where the story is heading? Or does the story reveal itself to you as you write it? (For example, did you know who was behind the Solitaire

blog when you began writing the novel, or did you figure it out once you had your suspects?)

I'm always a plotter. I find it very difficult to write unless I have a plan and know where the story is going. I plan very carefully and in a lot of detail. But sometimes the plan changes! And that definitely was the case in *Solitaire*. I changed who was behind the Solitaire blog at least once while I was writing. Plotting is my greatest struggle when writing (hence the need for a lot of planning) and I remember finding it quite tough to plot *Solitaire* because, in many ways, it's a detective story.

As someone who is a dictionary-definition punster (i.e., non-plotter), I have to ask some follow-up here! (It always interests me how different writing minds are wired in different ways.) When you say you plan very carefully, what structure do you use? Outline? Long lists of notes? A murder board? Scene breakdown? Copious Post-its? And does the process change when plotting a novel vs. a graphic novel, or is it the same for whatever story you're telling?

I have so many different things! I usually end up with pages of notes about the themes of the story and ideas for scenes or elements of character journeys. I write out the plot in bullet points repeatedly, expanding it in detail each time. I do character summaries where I make sure I'm clear about where each character starts emotionally and where they end up.

The process does change when plotting a graphic novel. As these take much, much longer to create, I plan them in less detail, and only plan more carefully when I get closer to when I need to draw the scenes. I feel more comfortable improvising because the story is more episodic than a prose novel. Prose novels, particularly standalone novels, rely on a tight beginning-middle-end structure. But *Heartstopper* has been going for years, so I feel more able to relax and trust that I'll know where to go.

My all-time favorite question to ask other authors is whether or not you visualize the story as you write it. I am in the minority, in that I don't see a thing as I'm writing—I'm guided by the sound of the words rather than the sight of the scene. So I'll ask: What, if anything, did you visualize when you first wrote *Solitaire*? And, to complicate matters, since there have been so many (wonderful) visual representations of the characters since you wrote the novel, if you sat down to write it again, what do you think you'd see?

I am a very visual person and I absolutely visualize the story as I'm writing! While I was writing *Solitaire*, I used to spend time at school and on the bus daydreaming about certain scenes from the book. The scene where Tori watches Michael in a speed-skate race is the one I daydreamed about the most. I could picture every moment of that scene!

If I sat down to write it again I'm sure I would visualize it differently, especially as I have spent so many years drawing some of the characters for *Heartstopper*. But if I sat down to write it again, everything about it would change. I don't think I could ever write a book like *Solitaire* again; I've changed too much since then.

I'd love for you to elaborate on this—what do you think has changed about your writing?

I think the thing that has changed the most is my empathy for supporting characters. *Solitaire* is extremely insular in its point of view. We see everything through Tori's perspective, and we learn little about most other characters. But in my later novels, I find myself drawn to supporting characters and wanting their stories to shine through too. As a result, my writing style has changed quite dramatically. I think my books feel bigger in their view of the world—there are more voices at work than just the narrator's. I'm not sure that's a good or bad thing, but it is different.

One of the things I love about your novels, as a fellow music geek, is the way you deploy musical references to underscore states of mind—i.e., Radiohead isn't just a band, it is a mood signal of the highest degree. So if you were creating a *Solitaire* playlist, what five songs would have to be on it?

I happen to have a very carefully curated *Solitaire* playlist from 2013! Here are the five songs that remind me the most of *Solitaire*:
"Everything in Its Right Place"—Radiohead
"It's Not"—Aimee Mann
"Our Window"—Noah and the Whale
"Up in Flames"—Coldplay
"Bloodflood"—alt-J

Does "a carefully curated playlist" mean that you create the playlist before the book (or for certain scenes) so you can listen to it as you write, or do you round up the sounds that feel like the flavor of that novel afterwards? (Sidenote #1: I love that Aimee Mann is in here, because I feel in many ways I aspire to write a novel that feels like an Aimee Mann song.) (Sidenote #2: I was going to say something about how I recently rediscovered Noah and the Whale . . . and then I realized the reason I rediscovered them was because "Our Window" was in *Heartstopper* and suddenly my sentiment felt very circular.)

I collate songs as I'm writing and after I've finished. I usually don't listen to the playlists while I'm in the act of writing as I can't listen to any music with lyrics while writing—I find it so distracting! I can only listen to instrumental music. My playlists usually take months, if not years to compile as I often come across songs that make me think of one of my stories long after I've finished writing.

This is a hard question to ask about a book you've been talking about for a decade, but is there anything readers might not know about *Solitaire* or its creation that you can share with us now? Any strange or random memories from when you were writing it?

Lucas did not originate in *Solitaire*. He was a character in my first attempt at writing a novel, which was an unfinished YA fantasy about teenagers who are sporadically possessed by the ancient Greek gods. *Very* different vibe to my current work. Lucas was one of the two leads, a kind of tragic hero, always getting hurt in his plight to save the world. I think I wrote him into *Solitaire* because I was somewhat embarrassed by him. As I got older, growing less attached to this fantasy novel, the concept of him started to feel overly dramatic and juvenile (I did write him when I was twelve, so, let's be fair). I tried to play on that in *Solitaire*. Lucas in *Solitaire* thinks he is a tragic hero, but his plight ends up being vapid and meaningless. Perhaps that was how I felt about that fantasy book as I started working on *Solitaire*. In retrospect, writing about teens with godly powers was a whole lot of fun.

I definitely want to read that book. (I feel I'm seeing Lucas in a completely different light now.) Since you set me up for this, I have to ask: If you could give Tori, Michael, Nick, Charlie, and Becky each a superpower (or godly power—whatever suits), what would it be?

Tori: Invisibility. I think that's what she craves . . . and she'd probably use it to take down some bullies.

Michael: Flight. As a speed skater, I bet he'd want nothing more than to be able to fly!

Nick: Super strength. It suits his gentle giant personality!

Charlie: Telepathy. Charlie is very empathetic so I think he would be good at telepathic communication!

Becky: Shape-shifting. I think Becky has a tendency to act differently around different people, so perhaps that part of her personality would translate to being a shape-shifter.

Now, a more serious question. Despite your affinity for planning, I am going to guess that there was no ten-year-plan at the start, and that Alice of ten years ago would be a bit agog at (and supremely proud of) all you've created in the past decade. It took me about ten years to think, *Oh, wow, I'm not just writing books . . . I'm creating a body of work.* You most definitely, in a decade, have created a body of work. When you look at it, what would you say your great themes are? What's the unifying spirit of everything you've created so far?

Young Alice's mind would definitely have been blown! I think the one thing that unifies my work is the power and beauty of finding that one person who just gets you. Whether that's a platonic or romantic or familial relationship. Humans need other people, and having the support, love, and understanding of someone else is a magical, special thing. I'll never get tired of writing about that.

If I were to ask you an added goal for ten years from now, what would it be? (Hopefully you have more than one, and most of them are

nobody else's business. But perhaps there's one you'd like to use as a marker for the horizon.)

I've had a longtime dream of writing a choice-based/dialogue-heavy video game, similar to something like *Life Is Strange*. I'm sure it would be incredibly difficult, but I would have SO much fun with it.

Finally . . . I know it is an easy trap to mistake a character's opinions for the author's. So I must use this as an opportunity to ask: How do you, Alice Oseman, feel about Jane Austen's work?

I like it! Lots of people assume that, like Tori, I am a Jane Austen hater. I wouldn't describe myself as a super fan, but I love *Pride and Prejudice*, and I usually enjoy adaptations of her other works. They're just a bit of fun and Tori should lighten up sometimes.